SCARLET'S CONFESSION

SCARLET'S CONFESSION

TALES OF A BRITISH PSYCHIC

JOANNA GARZILLI

Published by Joanna Garzilli

ISBN-13: 9781796240764 (paperback)

First edition

CONTENTS

CHAPTER 1

SCARLET EXPOSED

1st January

If I'm such a wonderful psychic, then why is my life a bloody mess? Something I've discovered is spiritual people can be very un-spiritual and that includes myself. I fear what goes on inside my dysfunctional thirty-year-old head. If anyone ever found this journal, would I be judged? Oh, if only they knew the shameful truth of Scarlet Ray.

As I write this, I'm in Notting Hill, in the basement of Nancy's flat on Kensington Park Road, sitting on a single bed, wearing large pink Juicy pyjamas, with £20 to my name and a mountain of lovely glorious debt. Yes debt, which I wonder how I will clear in time for my wedding to Bill, on 1st May. I have a dress to buy and a ring, which I assume I must pay for myself. Will my parents come to the wedding? Will Bill and I stay together? I have faith in the divine, lying in this single bed. Yet I don't know how the miracles will happen. Why will God look upon me? How will I turn my life around? Why is my arm aching so much as I write? A dull pain, deep like a knife. What will I do this year that changes my life for the better? I see the light above me, gold and aqua marine. There are smooth roads ahead and it is time. The right train has arrived and I pray I may be a passenger to step aboard and journey into paradise.

2nd January

I carry a heavy sickness in my stomach that is not mine. As I slept last night, Nancy's mother appeared twice. It was more that I heard her. A hacking cough, her presence scared me, made me feel uneasy because she was of the other world. It is a cold day, hints of blue sky are fast filling with clouds. We are clearing Nancy's space today and Bill is in Manchester now.

I am hungry for success and luxury living. I have an element of guilt as millions around the globe starve and die of illness at an alarming rate. An old part of me clings to the "Sloane Ranger" lifestyle. Shopping in Harrods and Harvey Nichols, the lure of Prada and Gucci on Sloane Street but the shoppers are sleepwalkers. I am conscious now and cannot deny that these people are dead as they buy. Their physical selves trundle along marble polished floors and spray perfume, try make-up, grab at the latest Hermes belt. It is sad. I see the people as cattle, part of a herd, terrified not to partake in the Harrods sale, the Last Supper. Will Christ be present to break bread and share wine, to drink cappuccino and champagne, croissant and smoked salmon platters? I am lost in a blur, a haze of nothingness. I fear and grieve the fact that I was a cow for many years and in someway still am as I try to merge into the crowd. My stomach turns as Nancy coughs hard, the hacking reverberates through me. Will I conform to society's wishes, the wishes of my mother, or aspire to the dreams of my fiancé? What is to become of me?

3rd January
Peter's House, Manchester

Bill has just proposed I write "I Can Be Successful" a non-fiction self help book. Yet I feel I am at the precipice and unable to take the next step, let alone jump. Help God help! If I could just get over my fear and write.

4th January
Peter's House, Manchester

Sex has a negative impact on my life because I feel unable to express who I truly am. There is a wild woman inside. She is untamed and shut down, so she blocks my creative talent. I think about it but hold myself back because a part of me feels dirty and gross, misunderstood. Sex needs to be a rollercoaster for me, so I create dramas in my day-to-day life because I do not have a sex life. I don't know who I am and I fear who I am. I fear my sexual power and prowess. I am over sex.

Money is my biggest burden because it takes up chunks of my time worrying about how I am going to pay my bills. I think of boring ways to make it rather than be creative. Money is my Achilles heel, I want it and I am a prisoner to it. It is my ball and chain. I love it and hate it all at the same time.

I carry wounds where I have been wild, vulnerable and open. I try to be someone else. "I'll be whatever you want me to be". The archetype and energy of the prostitute. I have areas of disgust and underlying this disgust is uptight clenched anger like a fist ready to punch. As I open my hand, deep great grief like Niagara Falls lies inside.

Drugs dull my mind and open me to demons. They have made me throw up. They have led me to spending time with men who are addicted to cocaine. I am the rescuer, the martyr who thinks, it is my duty to save everyone.

Yes Sex again! I want to write about it because I'm not having it. It's made me feel dirty and worthless and that turns me on. I feel I have to look perfect and beautiful to be able to let myself go and enjoy sex. So I let myself go and eat chocolate instead.

My magic moments are cappuccino and warm croissant with strawberry jam and melted butter. My silk smelling cushion with butterfly wings from Bill. Santa Monica sand; like velvet beneath my feet. Steaming hot chocolate. 300 percent thread count sheets and my moonstone engagement ring. Swimming and gliding in the ocean, melted cheese with gooseberry sauce. A rare burger with lots of ketchup and peas minted with butter. Oh, the smell of a fresh wood fire.

Monday 5th January

Bill and I arose at 10.30am. We both blamed each other. Do I go to London? Do I stay in Manchester and complete the first three chapters and synopsis of "I Can Be Successful?" Am I copping out? Am I in cloud Cuckoo Land? Help me God what do I do? Have I wasted time this morning? Am I aiming too high, too low or am I just potty? What is my highest good now? Is it to complete my creative projects or go and temp? What will I gain? What will I loose? Am I a fuck-up? No, that's Dad's old perception. That's not how it is? Is it?

10pm

Little bugger, Bill pisses me off!!! Maybe I should have gone to London. I hate being told what to do. I hate it, hate it, hate it!!! I want to do what I want to do, when I want to do it and at the same time I love Bill, but I'm so tired and fearful inside. I'm an ostrich with my head in the sand. Just want strength to finish some work and be proud rather than put on lots of weight. I keep asking for Bill's approval every five seconds when I'm writing "I Can Be Successful," instead of trusting myself. Why didn't I go to London? Because I didn't want to be in a depressing, poky London flat. I wish I could be more grateful but I'm not. Shame on me for such a lack of gratitude. I am wallowing in my self-inflicted shit.

8th January
9pm: Peter's House Manchester

I must write "I Can Be Successful." I am scared to do it. It's like walking through thick gooey sludge and fudge. I can't quite bring myself to be a success. I want to suffer still. Elicit sympathy and lots of it. Oh the struggles and drama, poor Scarlet wallowing in debt. Do I stop myself finishing so I can't be rejected by an agent? As long as I don't write, I'll never know. I've managed to sabotage myself for thirty minutes so far by deleting files and creating a photo slide show. Congratulations Scarlet, you managed to sabotage yourself for a total of one hour and forty-five minutes, clearing the computer of memory!

9th January
1.45am: Peter's House Manchester

I sang and danced to MTV videos before finally settling down to write six pages of "I Can Be Successful". When I read it over, I thought what a load of crap.

10th January

The high of yesterday evaporated when I spoke with my mother after five weeks, since she said "I'd have more respect for Bill if he worked in McDonalds," and she topped it with "he's an absolute berk!" Lovely, my mother who tests me so dearly.

13th January
2.30pm: Manchester

I feel a bit sluggish in my body after lots of chocolate and biscuits. My thighs feel big. I dreamt I was homeless and a tree sheltered and protected me. Someone wanted to cut it down. I must preserve the trees.

After doing a Creating Money meditation last night, I met with Gary Williams, a psychic healer for coffee at The Patisserie today in Manchester. It was a wet cold rainy day. We sat in the room at the back. It had been six months since I saw him last. He drank tea, I, hot chocolate. We decided to manifest a workshop in London. We will teach together. The weekend will be called "I Can Be Successful." I am very excited and then a fear creeps into my consciousness. I will be fat when we teach the course. People will scrutinize my weight and this will pressure me. Then I'll put on weight to fulfil people's perceptions. So I'm eating a lot of chocolate and biscuits to sabotage myself now.

16th January
12am: Peter's Home Manchester

Bill, do not tell me how I should keep in shape! I do not appreciate you snapping my g-string and telling me to get in shape before I lead the "I Can Be Successful Weekend." It doesn't help me. It makes me very fucking angry!!! It hurts. Who do you think you are? Look at your own life before you start criticising and taunting me. No one is telling me to fuck off or shut the fuck up. I will scream and scream at the top of my lungs until it hurts you too, like it hurts me. I'm tired of not being free. I hate being hurt by you and your body language to make me feel insecure about my weight and how I look. After such a lovely night why do you pick on me? When you know how sensitive I am. Do you want me insecure so I put the weight back on and then you feel safe? Is that what you want? Affirmation: "I am the perfect weight and I eat the perfect amount of food and it's none of your fucking business. No! No! No! Fuck you!"

11.20am

I dreamt of old friends from the past who I haven't seen for years, George Weiner and Hiron Keller. They both got in a lift with me. I told them I needed to talk with them as we ascended. We arrived at the thirteenth floor but then they got out and disappeared. I wish I had the opportunity to speak with Hiron, I know it's important. I haven't seen him for over ten years and don't know how to get in contact with him.

19th January
9am: Bill's Mum's Flat, London

Locked out of Bill's mum's place last night as, her key wasn't working. Thank goodness Clive was with me, one of my dearest friends.

I'm not hungry this morning. I think its anxiety that I have under £30 in my pocket and have to survive this week, which I will. I'm waiting for the phone to ring from all the secretarial agencies. There's an expectancy and fear that I will have to sell myself, prove myself. I feel the urge to sink my teeth into work and earn, succeed, create and most important focus on clearing my debts! Yes I will do it. So the phone is yet to ring but perhaps the agencies will email?

Both Kate and her flatmate June have gone off to work and I'm sitting here alone drinking orange juice and fresh coffee but don't feel like German rye bread and what the employment agencies may wonder is if you're so fucking great, why do you need a job? Uh duh? I have no money, I'm bankrupt all but in Law! So there you have it, this is where I am.

3pm

I feel so sick, like the life-force has been drained out of me. Desperation because I don't know how to get a job, make it through the week. I am scared, I feel like shit. My talents are unrecognised. I can't even get a temp job. I am nauseated, crippling pains in my chest. I have no energy to go on. Help me God, I don't know what to do. I'm trying and it all feels wrong. No one is signing up for my workshop. I'm putting on a veneer of confidence, I feel like shit under someone's shoe. I have hit rock bottom. Just spoke with Dawn, my spiritual mentor. Her words helped.

"Surrender to it," she said.

"It's so painful for me," I replied. "My throat is dry and parched, scratchy. How do I create change? How do I get up from rock bottom?"

"You will," she said. Her voice sounded so reassuring.

As I put the phone down, I heard a voice cry faintly from deep inside me, it sounded so distant, yet it was loud and clear "Please don't take me any lower!"

22nd January

I feel blank and listless after walking from the West End, back to Queen's Park. Got up 7.15am after setting my alarm at 6.45am and did thirty minutes chi gung. Put posters up in Regents College and Zen Studios but still just three people signed up, two of them at half price. I went into The Park College thinking maybe we should cancel it but the energy of the room felt perfect and I thought wow this is a great space, I could actually see the workshop happening here.

I didn't have enough money to take the tube back to Queen's Park. I walked all the way from the West End. It challenged me. All doors seem to be closed and yet I feel the light at the end of the tunnel but how do I let it shine on me? How do I change this huge ebb into a positive flow?

25th January

I dreamt Great Grandma Ruby sang "I've got the whole world in my hands! I got the whole world in my hands."

31st January
12.15am: London

Night before workshop, right side of my neck went red and I burnt my left wrist. The same spot I had fractured it in the playground when my parents divorced.

5th February
London

I spent £100 today on Bill and I joining Zen gym with the money I made from my workshop. I've always wanted to be a member there. It is so peaceful and decadent. I love the pool and statues. It feels like I'm in Greece and the steam room with eucalyptus is like being in a luxury spa in France.

6th February

It's grey, raining and cold. Have a strong intuition to move back to London. Release the Manchester flat. Take Nancy's place when she goes abroad in April.

15th February

I woke up thinking this morning "What do I need to let go of now to allow financial abundance and prosperity into my life?" Is it Bill who I love so dearly?

16th February

Wow most amazing dream! I'm in a dimly lit bathroom and as I look in the mirror I somehow see my back reflected and light emerges out of the dark and I am in awe as I see my wings, the left one is particularly iridescent and growing beautifully, snow white. And the right wing is forming and then they shape shift and another set of wings appears, those of a shaman and it is like I have eagle feathers on my back, textured, and powerful, brown and speckled black, markings of power and fearlessness, courage. There are colours of gold, magenta, violet pink and blue on my body and I am in deep awe.

23rd February
11.55pm

Amazing synchronicity today. I was thinking of people for my workshop and spontaneously I called Veronica Lewis who I'd given a psychic reading to in a London pub over a year ago.

"Hi, it's Scarlet," I said.

"Scarlet, the tarot reader?" she said.

"Yes," I said.

"Oh my God, you really are psychic," she said.

It turns out the day before she had been talking with her executive producer about a new show featuring clairvoyants and how they needed someone who looked good for TV and could read tarot cards. She had suggested me and was going to call me today but I had beaten her to it. That was major confirmation for Veronica because we hadn't spoken for almost two months.

I'm scared my ego may get in the way. That I'll freeze on camera, get the reading wrong or get no insight at all. Please God, let this meeting be divine loving energy beyond any expectations I may have. If it is for my highest good, which I believe it is, please let me receive this TV show.

25th February

Wow what a great day today. Bill suggested I wear Emily's magical silk coat, which I did and I arrived to the meeting three on the dot at Mega TV's office on Oxford Street. I heard the receptionist Mary say, "She's tall in a multi-coloured coat, brown hair."

I knew she was talking about me. Brown hair, oh it really was greasy. As I'm given directions to find Barry Peck, the Executive Producer, he appears in the street with his technical director, Mac from Aussie-land. We trot off to the pub and while they drink vodka and Redbull, I succumb to lime cordial and tonic. A coffee would have been better. We connect immediately. I see Barry is relieved, that I am down to earth. I want to say normal but I'm far from that and I do a very accurate psychic drawing and reading for him. I explain I'm also a producer and he says, "Fantastic, you can present and produce the show."

Bill later said, "It's like out of "Bridget Jones Diary." When she got "'Sit Up Britain."

I wished that I could have my own show and now it might just happen?

CHAPTER 2

PSYCHIC GURU, BEWARE!

2nd March
12.22am: Manchester

I got the job! Psychic presenter on my own TV show! Now fear is setting in about how it'll unfold. I was honest with Clive about my fears of him taking over my show after I'd brought him in to co-present with me.

"Let's call it The Healing Guru," Clive said.

"It's not about gurus, but finding your own sense of self and keeping it real," I said.

Clive said he was impressed by my professionalism. I felt dishonest, because I said others were trying to take over the show without naming Clive and yet he knew I was suggesting him. So, I will allow myself the perfect amount of time to make decisions from the highest part of my soul. Om.

12.07pm

Dear Bill, I really hashed up his hair. I forgot to put the grade two blade on and ended up shaving it all off! I became very emotional and cried. Then Gay Brown phoned from Stonehenge and offered the sacred site for Sunrise on 1st May, 5.30am to get married. Am I ready?

3rd March
Nancy's Flat, Notting Hill, London

I'm yawning in the basement. It's warm with soft sheets and I've created an abundance altar for myself. I'm in a lovely neighbourhood with communal gardens abound. Lucky me!

4th March
8.55am: Nancy's Flat, Notting Hill

I need coffee to align. Don't quite know what I'm meant to be teaching, presenting, producing. What a testing day at Mega TV. I had no idea, the agendas I would be subjected to. My supposed assistant, Carina Layton is trying to take over my job. It upsets me. No, it makes me feel uneasy in my gut, this competitive bitchiness. I want directness and truth. Power struggles are at hand big-time. I will not lower my vibration. This must be why I am clogged up in my sinuses and coughing. Carina has a good heart but she is tainted and misunderstood. I mustn't engage in her game. Best not to respond to her, rise above and release any negative thoughts. I'm bringing in my own team of people when the time is appropriate. Get the job done. Focus on my strengths. Keep my personal life to myself. Listen to people. See no evil, hear no evil, speak no evil, remember it's year of the Monkey that little trickster.

8th March
11.47pm

Dreamt I was on a motorbike with Sir Ian McKellen who plays Gandalf the Grey & White in "Lord of the Rings." He was protecting me and I supporting him, very symbiotic. He was taking me to an awards event with hundreds of people. Someone was still trying to take over my job as TV presenter. I had to be very firm and say "I am the producer."

On waking, it draws my mind to Cinderella and how the ugly sisters and all these people are trying to claim Cinderella's glass slipper but the handsome prince still managed to find her. I have to set my boundaries as ugly sisters abound. I shall go to the ball no matter how many obstacles are put in my path.

9th March
3.30pm: Baguette Café

I am so fucking pissed off right now! Why am I creating this polarity/reality? Do I walk away? This is the shittiest management in the history of…! How am I'm meant to produce a spiritual show in a mafia-run porn studio? Then there's so much bloody red tape I can't do my fucking job. This situation is a mess. Barry never replies to my texts. How do I get him to respond and respect me? What am I allergic to? Tits and bad behaviour? Something has to shift. I am definitely having a negative physical reaction to the situation I'm in. I am so fed up. I can't even think about the show now because everything is so undefined, like warm bullshit. The psychic workshop ended up being so amazing and this situation is so shit. I don't like the energies. There is too much dishonesty in this job and I really want integrity. Do I let it go? Surrender? Aaaghhh. I so want to do a TV show but it's got to be in truth, magical and loving. How do I create a bridge to achieve this? Do I overcome this hurdle? Is it an obstacle to block me or challenge me?

10th March

Letter to Nancy:

"Oh my God Nancy! I don't even know where to begin or explain what happened last night. I am so sorry for not keeping to our original meeting time. Please forgive me. I had a major spiritual healing/love/past life/future connection arise. I have never had this many synchronicities in my life with one person. I met this guy called Matt at the gym and had this intuitive urge to give him psychic guidance because of a vision I received from his tattoo. Anyway, we talked and there were lots of confirmations between us and then it gets wild. I have never met him before and somehow we end up talking about past friends and I don't know why I mention Ralph Weiner, an old friend of mine whom I hoped to contact because he was in my dream doing business with another guy I knew called Hiron Keller who I haven't seen for ten years. Matt was silent and then said "You know I said I don't have synchronicities anymore."

"Yes," I said.

"Well, I live in Ralph's flat, he's my landlord," Matt said.

"You're joking," I said.

"No. Even more crazy, Hiron Keller and my father were business partners for many years," he said.

I show him my dream journal that happens to be in my gym bag. His mouth drops open.

"What?" I said.

"The next day, it was my brother's birthday. We had dinner to celebrate. Ralph Weiner sat at one end of the table and Hiron Keller sat directly opposite him and Hiron's also best friends with my brother," Matt said.

"Do you have Hiron's number?" I said.

"Yes, I can get it from my brother," he said.

I have never experienced a connection like this in my life with anyone. We also discovered we both ate Chinese on Valentine's Day. He runs a DVD distribution company with his brother next door to the gym. I have a major past life connection with him, I know he is a spiritual teacher to me and he's only twenty-five-years-old. I am so blown away. There really is divinity at work and he is also helping my heart to heal. So again I apologize. Thanks for your understanding. I promise to make it up to you tomorrow. Love & light, Scarlet."

Nancy replied "Silly, silly girl, nothing to apologize for, you must get out of that habit. I was a little concerned because so out of charter for you that I wondered if something happened to you and I could sense something major, will explain later. Mediation tonight? Lots of love & hugs, Nancy."

15th March

Matt, I would like to do healing with you. I feel you connected to my heart and soul and it is hurting me and giving me pleasure and joy to feel a greater connection to myself. I fear you do not understand me. My love for you is deeply spiritual, beyond the physical and this is why I feel overwhelmed and I'm trying to comprehend what my connection with you truly is and why I met you now at this time in my life. Why did I meet you? I so want to speak with you and I am scared you will reject me. I want an affair with you and yet I don't. I am a faithful and loving girlfriend who is confused about her identity and soul that is blossoming. I wish to release these overwhelming feelings that are too deep to understand.

16th March
8am: Emily's House

I feel very sad. Spirit is showing me all signs my split with Bill is imminent. It's hurting me so much and I'm terrified to hurt him, especially when he said, "The ball is in your court, it's out of my control."

17th March

I'm going to Manchester this weekend for my seven-year anniversary. I feel detached.

Matt hasn't called. I suppose that's a good thing. It gives me space to contemplate my soul journey. I slept with my fairy wishing stone on my heart. I'm feeling more confident about the TV show now. I know it's going to work. It's quite surreal for me that I will be on TV every day.

7.20pm: Tube

Feel tired but satisfied. Still no word from Matt. I've booked my train to Manchester on Saturday. Everything is shaping up well for the show. I must phone and email the psychics, get Petra in for a test reading on Monday. I feel more grounded, at ease with everyone at work now. Positive breakthrough. I need to rest. I feel dehydrated, must drink more water during the day. I am a little nervous about presenting. I know Veronica tried to manipulate the presenting situation. That's ok, I'm grateful to her for my job.

Thursday 18th March
11.05am

I'm on the tube. Time seems to be running away. Am I organized enough? Do I need to prepare myself more? Something that says, "Today we will be talking about love and relationships, let us know if you require guidance?" I definitely do!

Kevin has suggested an executive producer role for me, perfect. I'm looking forward to spending time with Bill this weekend.

9.05pm

Feeling odd right now. Guilty emotions for shopping. I know I deserve it but I feel bad and good at the same time. After meeting Oscar and psychically reading from his portrait depiction of Adolph Hitler, it finished me off and I had to shop the rest of the day to wind down.

I feel guilty as hell for thinking about Matt more than Bill. I feel overwhelmed, frustrated, confused and pissed off when Clive Gray said he thought I wasn't ready to do the TV show. Bloody fucking hell, I am seriously pissed off! Triple pissed. Am I diverting myself from dealing with the TV format? Got to create, structure the show now!

19th March
8.30pm: Oxford Street Tube

I'm so exhausted! Truly drained. When I saw Barry, I got blasted. Felt like he was on a major coke comedown. Feel the knives from Veronica. Team is key. I have to be very authorative and assertive. Bring on my leadership qualities now. I am concerned people won't respect me. A big old fear. Secretly I want to kill Barry. Secretly I'd love to tell Barry to go fuck himself. Secretly I'd love to tell Tracy who looks like Muffin the Mule to get off her high horse. Secretly I'd like to stab Carina, Kevin's corporate pet in her own back, give her back her own venom and see how she digests it. Secretly I'd love an easy effortless ride. Secretly I'd love to say you're all a bunch of wankers. Secretly I'd love to sip Pina Colada on a tropical beach and make love to Matt in the ocean.

I'm in the office and Barry is being a total wanker of the highest degree. I guess that's why he's perfectly suited for Pleasure Zone TV. Big judgement. Barry wake up and smell the roses instead of the stinky dirty pussies you don't respect. I see vile black widow spider energy around you. You're caught in a web of deceit and despair. How sad, I feel so sorry for you, such pity. Guides why are you putting all these assholes around me spewing shit and then making me eat it? And Clive, how dare you tell Bill I'm not prepared for the TV show. Go fuck yourself! Egotistical guru bastard!

20th March
8.10am: Train to Manchester

The Innovator within me says "I feel held back in my relationship with Bill, everything stuck, me having to support us and burden the debt."

The Conserver inside me says, "Yes, but you have a wonderful friendship and gifts of love to share."

"I want passion, sex and romanticism," the Innovator says.

"Create it, make your dreams a reality," the Conserver says.

"I've got a TV show to launch and I feel how will I have enough time to write the show, overcome the back stabbing and make it profitable without losing my creative integrity?" the Innovator says.

"Little by little, take baby steps. Look at what is possible in the day. Get up earlier and have quiet time to contemplate and meditate upon what you need to do," the Conserver says.

"But all the obstacles, how do I overcome them?" the Innovator says.

"See them as fences to jump and lift you higher to new states of awareness, invoking the qualities of ease and grace," the Conserver says.

My emotions have been playing me like a trombone and piano in one, synthesized. I feel like a young child, teenager and adult all rolled into one. What surprises me is my wishing for an affair and my desire to end my relationship with Bill. I have lost my passion. I feel I've been in an abusive relationship and put myself second. My dreams and goals washed away like those beautiful chalk drawings in Mary Poppins. I gave up my own torch. I picked up Bill's. Funny he's called Bill and I have all these bills to settle. I took his every blow. Where's my bodyguard?

21st March
6.35pm: Manchester

Bill and I had our anniversary dinner at a little French restaurant in Manchester. We ate snails and onion soup. In the back of my head, I was thinking, "This is our last supper."

22nd March
8.40am: Baguette Café

Treating myself to a lovely breakfast of fresh orange juice, egg muffin royale, a latte and cinnamon roll to perk myself up because Sophia, Emily's daughter kept me awake all night. I hope I have plenty to say on TV. Every time I try and write the script, I freeze up. I feel excited about the potential and scared about the potential failure. Profit vs. loss and integrity vs. money. I am concerned and confused about people's expectations that are not in alignment with mine.

23rd March
8.25am: Queen's Park

I moved into Kate's flat and finally got a full night's sleep. I feel ugly this morning and I can't get my make-up right. I get paid £1,200 today!

24th March
9.15am

Going Live on The Psychic Show today. It has been rather intense getting it off the ground but I feel really positive and excited about it. The rehearsal was disastrous, yet somehow I know it's all going to work out. Larry, my LA producer friend and I spoke on the phone and it upset me that he said I would scare guys away, as much as they may like me because I'm dominant. Maybe this is why Matt can't cope with me or rather he doesn't want to. Bill is a pillar of strength to me. I am very fortunate to have such strong support and love.

27th March
3.45pm: Ciao Café

Waiting for Bill, he's fifteen minutes late. That's ok. I had a great time at the Equinox concert last night. The music was like a meditation unlocking nostalgic memories for me. My left eye is a little blurry. I think it's to do with Bill. Thankfully I am arriving at all my meetings on time now. Felt like one of 'The Sex and the City' girls, as I drank rose champagne back at Liberty's flat with Nancy and Gloria. I did a self-love and receiving clear inner guidance meditation. I am more relaxed and calm now.

29th March
10am: Baguette Café

I feel sick to my stomach because I know the magic is gone with Bill. It is so hard for me. I'm really sad. I feel the energy has strongly been removed from my path with Bill. He held my hand on the tube this morning, so reassuring and loving and yet I felt like he wasn't with me. His energy is ungrounded. I feel like I'm going through the motions of being with Bill. It's not if it's over, it's just when? He looked so handsome and huggable, but it's not enough for me anymore. This is a tough realization. We didn't have coffee together. We kissed each other goodbye at Piccadilly Circus. Heartbreaking.

4pm

Speaking with Barry Peck, my executive producer was interesting. I felt like I had to protect my baby from being transformed into a child I don't recognize. I felt uneasy that Barry suggested a regular TV presenter rather than a real psychic on "The Psychic Show." We need to convey we have the knowledge and can give answers. I want to establish myself in front of the camera. Heart is pounding. I feel overwhelmed, in limbo, fear of losing my job, everything, my identity. I can't feel. Why? What is my future?

30th March

I felt dizzy this morning as I took off my engagement ring. I asked for illumination in my dreams and dreamt I was kissing someone else, I don't know who. When I had dinner last night with Mum at The District Club, the restaurant was practically empty. This guy sat down on the table next to us and it gave me so much joy because it was Charlie Silver, someone I really respect. He's great fun, sexy and a Scorpio. He also challenges me in a good way. If I'm going to kiss anyone first after seven years, he is a great start because I know him already and we have chemistry together. Charlie looked anxious. I sensed something was up.

"You look tired, what's going on?" I said.

"Nothing, I'm good," Charlie said.

"No you're not, I know you Charlie, tell me?" I said.

"I've just broken off my engagement," he said.

My jaw dropped.

"That's surreal. I was discussing with my Mum whether I should call off my wedding. You've given me confirmation, it's a sign I'm not meant to go through with it," I said.

I looked down at my engagement ring, this was the last time I would be seen in public wearing it. I felt a mixture of sadness and relief at my imminent decision to let Bill go. I know my angels and guides are working overtime for me, talk about synchronicity. I hadn't seen Charlie for eight years. When he looked deeply into my eyes, I could see his pain and sadness and I wanted to tell him everything would be ok. Instead he wrapped his arms around me and nuzzled his face into the curve in my neck. As I took in his scent, memories of when we'd been together came flooding back to me. I suddenly longed for him, now that he was within my grasp. I pulled away and blocked this thought out of my head. I felt guilty for the magnetic attraction between us.

31st March

Bill arrived in London without asking me in advance if it was ok to borrow money from me. He stated almost proudly to me, "I've got nineteen pence left." What an odd number, less than a pound, more than a ten pence piece and less than a twenty pence coin. My fears are that I need to earn money right now to survive and yet without Bill, I'll have more for me. Why can't I get my head around that?

So weird me not wearing my engagement ring today, I feel vulnerable. When wearing it, I felt secure and trapped. Wow I can do what I want when I want. Oh God, I feel so worthless right now. I feel like the ground is cracking, splitting beneath me. It's been so arid. I sense water gushing below. Matt was definitely sent to me as a catalyst for change.

6pm

My heart, head and stomach are whirring. I finally spoke with Matt. Called him, he called me back. I was so honest with him, shaking as I tried to extract my words. Told him he was the catalyst for me not marrying Bill. He was very sympathetic and now we are about to meet in the gym. It's 6.05pm and I'm at Oxford Street tube, waiting for a Central line train. I'm shaking like a leaf because I know I want to kiss him and cut my physical connection with Bill. Oh God help me! He said, "Let's meet in the usual place."

I know that place well because I've thought about the vision I had the night I met him. I feel so connected to him and yet unattached and free. Life is turning. I'm on a new wave. I just want peace and passion in my heart. Lots of it. I need to calm down. I need to relax. I need to get over it. I'm sorry Bill but my soul is crying for change. I'm a new woman. I really am. My dreams are finally coming true. Have to surrender to the animal magnetic attraction. I don't know how to control it. Perhaps I'm not meant to. Can Matt handle me? I know I look different since I saw him last. More groomed, sexual, sensual and scared. I feel like a teenager, I'm fourteen years old all over again. His voice is so reassuring on the phone. I feel I know him so well and yet we don't know each other at all. I'm needing sexual healing and passion but I want to let go of the guilt and accept my feelings, my power. It's almost 6.15pm, in thirty minutes I'll be in Matt's arms, because I know it's meant to be and I'll read this back later and cry because the shift will have occurred, my fate with Bill as a lover will be sealed.

CHAPTER 3

SCARLET THE HARLOT

1st April
11.40am

It is officially over with Bill. I will not marry him. I am a little frightened of being so free. I'm dressed in grey trousers, jumper and trainers with a grey bag and pink scarf. My hair is wet with a bit of gel and it's scruffed up in a bun, tendrils flowing down. Even a guy in a BMW stopped to let me cross the road because I have that fresh love glow.

Matt and I did a heart meditation last night. We symbolically unlocked each other's hearts with a key, visualised them filling with gold. Then sealed our hearts together and surrounded ourselves in a golden glow of ethereal light, it felt like a wedding ring, a spiritual marriage. Then he leant forward and kissed me tenderly. He was so gentle. God I love his voice and confidence, the way he looks at me and touches me. Makes me feel totally alive. He has a beautiful smile and divine, almost jet black hair. He's slimmer in build than Bill. When he touches my breasts I get so turned on, I open up like a flower coming into bloom. I'm buzzing inside. I feel like a container that's going to explode sparkling light, a spiritual bombshell of delight.

1.40pm

Had a very good meeting with Clive Gray just now. Charlie Silver didn't call me, that's ok.

6.45pm

"The Psychic Show," is a good title for the TV show. I did some research on the web to find out about Medusa and Benjamin Franklin as Matt would not have given me these symbols for no reason, even though he didn't understand why these images came to him clairvoyantly. The first website I found on Medusa honoured her true nature beyond current misperceptions. It tied in so strongly with my dream the night before of a white and gold snake forcing me to embrace my shadow. It unsettled me that Medusa is historically perceived as negative. Then I found information on Benjamin Franklin signing "The Declaration of Independence," and that he invented the lightning rod, equals enlightenment, equals my vision from Matt's tattoo of a Stag being struck by lighting on the Native American Plains. Our connection blows me away. I know my buttons are being pushed to awaken me to the next level of self-awareness.

2nd April
3.03am: Kate's House

I'm now in bed drinking tea, just ate steak and béarnaise and I'm longing for Matt and sort of grieving that Bill and I are over. After seeing so many unattractive guys out tonight, I realize even more that Matt is totally fucking gorgeous and sexy. Oh my God, I want him so badly. His eyes are divine, they see me fearlessly and his smile melts me. I love my connection with him. I also know it is transitory.

"The Psychic Show," official start date is 24th April, yes! I have three weeks now to get it all up and running brilliantly. Prove to the board members of Mega TV that there is a demand and an audience for psychics on television and not just tits, so I'm right where I am meant to be.

7.25pm: Oxford Street

Today was a good test show. My dear friend Paula and I presented. People loved the colour essences. We got a lot of texts and I did a spot on psychic reading for a woman called Doreen. I suggested she move into child care and social services and she said she had the application form right there! It's so nice to get the confirmation. Am I wrong for feeling angry with Clive? No, I would say I am reasserting my boundaries. When I say "I feel great." And he goes "Oohh," and I say, "No, I feel good," and he still says "oh." Psyching me out like he's the great psychic. Fucking asshole, it just pisses me off. Gary White pointed out he's trying to lower my vibration by the sound of the tone in his voice. I don't like it. Please God let me hold a positive intention towards Clive, I don't want to be a bitch. I do not want to be negative in any way. I want to be in truth and love. I know it's a tough line to take but I don't know another more effective way for him to listen because I'm dealing with a nine-year-old in a fifty-seven-year-old body.

"Anything to help," Clive said.

Clive I don't need your help because you are being manipulative and calculating. I see the energy. You are not my teacher. I am not yours. We are all equals and mirrors so how am I being condescending, because that's how I find you? How do I shift this sickening energy I feel when you sit next to me on the Psychic Sofa. You feel like a leech trying to suck me dry. I don't need that Clive. Why do you need to blow your own trumpet? Are you that insecure you do not trust yourself and your ability?

I feel loud inside and positively rebellious. I'm finding my voice. I need psychics for the show. How do I create more phone calls and texts? How do I urge people to text and phone in? Need to prepare questions for tomorrow's show. Martha, who organizes the phone lines was a bit offish. I think she's jealous, I'll keep holding love and light. Please protect me Great Spirit. I hope I'm doing more than my best.

3rd April

I went to sleep doing a self-love meditation. I now have the physical sensation of heartburn confirming my separation from Bill. I dreamt I was at a table having dinner with Charlie Silver. We were holding hands. It was very romantic and respectful. Unlike with Matt, who is exposing my shadow. I guess I'm in depression now because I have space to think and I feel my wounds. I feel alone, heavy, and weary tightness in my body. I get butterflies of fear with Matt because I know I can't stay who I am out of this experience and I'm scared who I'll transform into.

Why mend a deflated soufflé, it can't ever be exactly as it was. Now that I'm single and free, feels like I'm the other woman with Matt. Not quite sure how this sits with me yet. Uncomfortable because he was having problems with his girlfriend when we met and now they seem to be getting on better. I'm scared of being hurt.

Bill's brother Peter phoned. He thought Bill was with me as his Dad hadn't heard from him. I feel sad, the grief is kicking in now and I'm trying to dull the pain of our separation. It hasn't really struck me that my relationship with Bill is over. I feel alone. Thankfully my friend Liberty Cloud just phoned from Portugal to check if I was ok. I want to run from my emotions. If only I could drop into them.

I watched the movie "In the Cut," with Meg Ryan. The love, passion and murder made me feel very vulnerable. The realisation, that I have a deep desire to live the depths of my soul. I'm looking for people to fill the gaps and holes in me. I need to repair, become whole again in a new way. It's now 1.55pm and I'm tempted to phone Charlie out of need but instead I sit with myself, rather than bury the pain. I'm so grateful to be moving home tomorrow. My angel card today is "Freedom," a woman standing naked on a beach, that's me.

Steven Kruger, the sexy Oscar winning filmmaker popped into my head this morning, I wonder how he is?

4th April
9.30am

I'm angry with Matt because I'm not setting healthy boundaries. He asked me to leave the gym separately from him. He still hasn't given me Hiron's telephone number. He says he has to ignore me in the street. He says he's not doing anything with me, equals denial and infidelity. How can he can kiss me in his car and know his girlfriend is at home? He's not dealing with his relationship honestly. He says he wants it to be spiritual but he's not acknowledging the physical bond between us. I have such a special bond with Hiron, why won't Matt let me connect with him? Is he jealous? It really fucking hurts, annoys me, makes me feel like a clandestine woman, some bit on the side, more than that, worthless, belittled, enraged, frustrated, loss of respect for Matt and me, no self esteem, denial, living a lie by not acknowledging our friendship. I know we've just kissed and he's touched my breasts but he's being unfaithful in my eyes. I think he's creating huge guilt. If he really loved his girlfriend, he wouldn't kiss me, if he respected her. So he's thinking, "She doesn't have to know, it won't hurt her." But you know Matt and you live with it happily! I can't bear denial in a relationship. It doesn't sit well with me. Matt if you want a true spiritual connection with me, these patterns between us need to transform into love because it's our responsibility karmically! I think Nancy is right when she said, "This is an initiation." I'm the poisonous snake and he's the dangerous tiger to be tamed. Do I still meet him on Tuesday?

12.50pm

I dreamt that Bill's mum was pleased we'd split. Then Bill appeared and we stood by an icy lake. I laid my head on his shoulder and we watched the sunset.

I fear ending up alone. I think people don't love me, that there is something wrong with me. I'm unworthy, unlovable and a leper. I feel rejected by Matt and Charlie. Felt guilty for taking condiments from Kate's fridge and not asking! I've been trying to swim the channel with a large anchor around my ankle and now that I'm free and lighter, I don't know what to do with myself.

I nearly cancelled meeting Matt on Tuesday. I'm fucking angry with his treatment of me, my treatment of myself. I want my boundaries and self respect and yet I feel so weak, like I'll let myself give into him and allow myself to be hurt again. I'm torn about Bill. This separation is so scary and painful. I'm confused. However, my psychic gifts are increasing. I'm getting stronger, even though I feel I'm a china doll breaking into pieces.

I'm so happy to know Charlie. He's so lovely and makes me laugh. He's witty and intelligent with a sharp powerful mind. Charlie is giving me a sense of beauty, success, play and passion for life.

What gift is Bill giving me? Bill is making me take care of myself and learn forgiveness so I may have self esteem.

5th April

I dreamt Bill and I were about to get married and I said, "I can't, I haven't got my wedding dress!" Bill wanted to go ahead with the wedding anyway.

Nancy's travelling to Argentina today and I'm in her beautiful flat with Black Cat, lucky me! This is the year I'm going to build myself up and create lots of success!

7th April

I'm seeing Charlie tomorrow for dinner. Know we could go out but felt it would be more chilled to eat at home. Drink wine, listen to music and talk about life. I don't want to feel like I'm on a date with him. Am I too eager? Thank God Charlie is coming over because it's something for me to look forward to, it'll give me more willpower with Matt.

9pm

I'm freaking out because there is so much anger, hurt and pain in me and I feel like I'm going to direct it all at Matt! I want to be in my highest state, to wear no masks and reveal myself entirely. I feel like I'm the tower about to be destroyed. So a garden may be created and filled with roses. Yet I'm so fucking angry and scared and feel worthless, as if I'm being treated like a piece of shit!!! I'm frustrated sexually, I'm a pressure cooker on a spiritual flame that's about to explode. How do I temper my fire? How do I stop my shadows kicking in and sabotaging me? I want to cry and cry and cry but the pain is too deep. Please don't let me fall apart and cry in front of Matt. Now I'm furious, it's 9.30pm and no word from Matt. Disrespect. I am so pissed off and yet I want to fuck Matt's brains out, not a good combination really. I'm putting myself through self-abuse, big time. Don't know how to control my emotions when he does arrive.

8th April

Last night finally made love with Matt and it was fantastic, amazing. When he touched me inside, I had a full on orgasm. Today my body feels so relaxed, like a weight has been drained. We talked till 5am in bed. It was lovely. I thought he'd go but he stayed.

"I need a hug," I said.

He wrapped his arms around me and we curled up together and sleep ensued. I am so grateful for my connection with Matt. I feel more connected to myself and I'm trusting how and when we meet again. I feel sexy and alive. I love Matt, if that makes sense. Life is good.

Part of me feels like I should be in the office, another part says, "Take rest and healing now because you need it before the rush of activity when you go back on Air."

I feel like I'm in a game with Matt. If I open too much, he may lash out and I am vulnerable.

"Guilt here, you spent £120 after a psychic, warned you not to buy those new expensive shoes and that you would never wear them."

"How did you feel when you put them on?" Wealth said.

"Fantastic, a million dollars!" Guilt said.

"That's "£999,880 more than the £120," Wealth said.

"Yes but I don't have it," Guilt said.

"I've got a real fear I'll loose my job and won't be able to pay off the money I'm spending and create more debt," Lack said.

"Why?" Wealth said.

"Because that's always how it's been before," Lack said.

I made a collage representing my inner demons. I put lots of scary things on it I can't bear to look at. As I placed all my fears, judgements and disgust in one pot of delightfully huge anger, I can now look it in the eye and say, "You are not me and you will not touch me and I offer you the gift of love, so you may transform into your highest form of love. I chose an eerie line from a Rwanda AIDS rapist. He said, "I knew I was raping which is bad. But my body was tempted and I was excited. I can't say I felt no pleasure."

This is terrifying for me because there is a demon part of me that feels what this inmate feels. I empathize with his actions and thoughts that feel so wrong and awful and guilty to me. It's the abuse we as women put ourselves through. The self-punishment of, "I'm not good enough, I don't deserve, so I'll just take the punch on the chin, the blow to my stomach, the knife in my back, allow a hand to grip, strangle and choke my slender elegant, swan-like neck. Trapped and at the mercy of self-inflicted imprisonment."

The death, destruction and pain. The rape of woman, so fragile disgusts me and scares me and yet as we are all separate and all one, I feel both points of view and experience. Acceptance of my shadow is now flowing through me.

I met Liberty, Christiana, Tracey and Liz at Dante's restaurant. Glass after glass of wine, emotions flying due to differing points of view. I felt very detached, calm and disconnected. Want to be in Matt's arms. Feeling sad that Bill thinks we may get back together. My spleen hurts, I've had too many cups of coffee today.

10.30pm

Oh my God, Universe what are you trying to tell me? At 6.30pm I decided to walk to the gym. As I walk along the cobbled stones, I see Matt's brother Paul on the phone, who I haven't seen for years. Moments later his Mum arrives and then Matt pulls up alongside us in his car. It felt awkward between us. I think Matt is freaked out after being so intimate. I get a tea to take to the steam room and as I climb the spiral staircase, I see a wallet on one of the steps. I pick it up and check out one of the credit cards, it's Matt's. I text him and he meets me in the pool area but he is distant. It hurts so much because I feel close to him, like everything has been accelerated between us and I have no physical control over the vehicle. Why do I feel so deeply this fast?

It was weird eating dinner alone. I didn't feel hungry. All I wanted to do was share my meal with someone, except I did have Black Cat nagging, demanding my chicken. I've gone from a major high to an intense low. I feel like shit.

9th April

I want to see Matt and I don't want to because I have all these judgements about what love and attraction should be. Just cried as I ate my lunch. A part of me misses Bill but I know I need this time to become whole again.

10th April

Oh Matt, now I remember who you are. I took a shamanic journey to the Underworld. A snake wrapped herself around me and travelled and propelled me. I was in a forest with a lake, very Arthurian. I saw a regal stag. I sensed wolves close by but followed the stag with beautiful antlers and white body. I wore a chiffon type gown. I was naked beneath. I knew Matt was the stag. He guided me and I followed him until I arrived at a cave dwelling entrance. A small fire was lit, made of twigs and there were furs. I laid down on them and the stag shape shifted into Matt but he looked different, slightly older, in his thirties and like a king. A man who had led people into battle. I knew I was his queen. He lifted the dress and ran his hands over my naked skin and he placed his gold chain around my neck. I then felt myself journey much deeper, further back in time, to see a past life together. I asked him not to go into battle again for I knew he would not return and we made love and then he disappeared out of his body and I cried tears into the lake and I filled a gold chalice with those tears and drank them and then as I grieved, the stag returned again and I was now ethereal, made of light, human and yet not in the physical world and the stag who I knew was Matt carried me as I lay face down on his back. As he did, he said to me, "I will return in your current life and you will know who I am."

"How?" I said. But I then found myself on a sailing ship, travelling dark oceans and stormy weathers to the Promised Land and Matt gave me his coat of arms, which I wore around my neck and over my heart for protection and this guided me safely across America to California, where I buried this gold coat of arms in the sand and it grew into a golden apple tree and a palm rose above it in another dimension and we both ate from the golden apple and then I was struck by lightening which took me into the depths of the ocean. Matt appeared before me and we had our wrists cut, my right and his left and then joined together in spiritual marriage. I was frightened to lose my own identity but we merged into light, out into the universe, we were two cosmic flames, entwined, dancing and then my power totem, the snake led me back down the tunnel and I returned to this world.

11th April
3.30pm

Bastard, I can't believe Matt blew me out, but at the same time I can. Now I know I have to step right back and move on. Except I hate the idea of being a "One night stand."

12th April

Why cling onto what I can't have? Why want someone who doesn't want me? The other end of the spectrum is Bill, always there – gorgeous and handsome. A part of me misses Bill but I know I now need to stand on my own two feet. So I sent a text to Matt.

"Dear Matt, I am sorry I have pushed you. It is my own insecurity and vulnerability because of the transformation I am currently experiencing. I am loving you conditionally and this is not a good thing. I have put pressure on you, created expectations and I am trying to control you and how you see me and connect, rather than allowing the purity of our journey. I don't know how to behave now. To step forward by stepping back? One thing I do know is I am not a game player, I am not your teacher, I am your equal. I believe you have a lot to resolve with Louisa and my connection with you is not allowing you to address your relationship with her in it's full light because I have clouded your path with uncertainty. Go and find your truth and love. I am sorry for my emotional response and guilt inducement. Forgive me please if you can. Love & light, Scarlet x x x"

CHAPTER 4

WELCOME TO THE PLEASURE ZONE

13th April
12.55pm

What a night! Had a lovely meal at Giorgio's restaurant with Veronica and Barry. Then had three vodka ices at The Cock & Bull Pub and really bonded with the production team but encountered slight hostility from the techhie team, who Barry made apologize to me for calling me a "posh snob" because I grew up in north west London and labelled me a "hippie" because I produce and host "The Psychic Show." Then went back to the studio for Pleasure Zone and met all the girls with their tits out, parading around in tacky jewelled polyester g-strings.

"Quick we need a close up on Rosa," Barry said.

Suddenly I find myself behind the camera zooming in and out of the porn star's ass, as she moans into the phone. The phone lines were inundated which can only mean that a lot of men were wanking off and a serious amount of orgasms created a healthy profit for Mega TV. Now Barry wants me to recreate this sex format, psychic style. I suppose we're all searching for the same thing except from different chakra levels. I like how everyone bonded as a family on set. I think and hope the psychics are more reliable. It seems that the viewers prefer the girl next door look, softer and prettier. They're not so into the "fuck me hard," porn vibe. Cherie's term of endearment to lure in the callers is, "I like you, I want you to lick my cunt." She squats down, her pink lips exposed, perfectly groomed only wearing white sneakers and the phone rings once again.

15th April
1am: Bed

Just had a lovely dinner with Bill's mum. I felt almost tearful hearing that Bill thinks are separation is temporary. I so don't want to hurt him. Darling Bill, I was suffering, drowning, as we were. In time you will meet a good woman and me a great man and we shall be happy apart but friends, always connected on the soul plane in love and light, eternally Scarlet.

16th April

Matt never replied to my text. I've analyzed my situation with Matt till the cows come home. I think he's not really bothered about me. In the same way I feel I can let go of Bill. So exhausted. Tried to get up earlier but my body and soul really need to heal before going back into the office. I dreamt I saw Bill and told him that it was fully over between us. I think that's why I cried so much. My heart hurts because I feel Bill doesn't truly understand why I've left him.

I totally freaked out dear Charlie. He made me laugh so much because he said, "I don't need to tell you anything because you already know! I was thinking about you the very moment I received your text."

I think it's great he had the courage to reconnect with his ex-fiancé but I also have this strong feeling it will not work out for them. He loves her intellectually, not with his heart, although he believes he does. In time this will be revealed to him. I think she really loves him but her heart is different from his. It may be broken and Charlie can't fix it, she has to do that for herself. Sending them lots of love.

Question for spirit guides "Is there any new romance coming into my life?"

"Yes, a lot of it. Different experiences, with different people. You will be inundated and this will help take your mind off Bill and wanting to get back together with him. It is important you continue to let go of each other very gently."

17th April
8.08am

Hiron Keller appeared in my dream. He pulled up in a sports car and was dressed in a suit. I hadn't expected to see him so soon.

12.12pm

I dreamt Charlie took me for dinner and at the bar he offers me his neck to kiss. I did but it felt intellectual. Then we left the bar and suddenly his hand is up my dress and he's feeling deep inside me and I'm quite shocked and uncomfortable but I don't stop him. Charlie why are you now showing up in my dreams? I feel Charlie is thinking about me a lot and that it's just a matter of time before we make love again but it's too soon.

The flat is so lovely and peaceful right now. The cat is sleeping on the multi-coloured woven cushion. The rain is pattering, soothing my cells. My feet are elevated. I am relaxed after going to bed at 7am! It's such fun to be out and about, socially active again.

20th April
11.54pm: Mega TV Office

I see how I am looking for answers outside of myself instead of trusting my own heart that sings like a Tibetan bell, loud and clear, if I just vibrate and open to its tone. I sense people's fear as I bring in more love and yet those souls in my office, they are wide open and resonating beautifully. This is interesting and enlightening to me.

28th April

Feel so angry with Bill in my kidneys equals fear when I see all the debt legal proceedings. I am fucking angry!!!

Spirit guides said, "Scarlet, stop handing your power away. Claim your sword and reset your boundaries with all whom you know. Please ensure this please! The structure will break down if you do not take control tomorrow. Stand firm and get behind that camera to ensure you claim your charge with haste. You need to change the format of the show and add new energy, make it more lively and fun. If you do not set your boundaries with Clive, you will both lose your jobs. Get behind the camera and take heed for when you step in front again, you will truly shine as a butterfly. Add Big Breakfast style, include the producers of the show, off camera "on.""

I so need to buy myself a vibrator…tension release.

29th April
9.30am

On the tube, feel much clearer now. Big shift for my dear psychic friend, Gary White. Just spoke to him and he's separating from his pretty blonde girlfriend, Orly. He thought it would be a month before it happened. Instead it was two hours. He said he cried and cried for the loss of Adam, Orly's son but the silver lining is he will be Godfather. Exactly what he wished for.

I am so pleased to have Mum's support. I'm happy Stuart my step dad is impressed that I'm doing the TV show. That's a big compliment from a successful entrepreneur.

Today's show is about clairsentience, receiving intuition through feelings. I will talk about the movies "The Gift" and "Ghost," that have inspired me.

CHAPTER 5

MR. WESTBOURNE & THE BIG-O!

1st May
9am: Bed

I had a very strong dream with Bill in it. I was going down a pathway with Bill. He was showing me steps to climb. I stopped and then headed in the opposite direction. Today would have been our wedding day.

3rd May

Felt like taking the bus this morning. I dreamt something to do with falling, definitely know I went through a surrender in my sleep. Other stuff also, I wish I could remember. Last few days have been a beautifully intense experience. I feel like I'm living in a movie. The Clive situation has been pretty horrible. I'm observing and learning how I need certain people's love and approval. Why did I feel the need for Matt's love? More and more I am letting go. If someone wants me and loves me and I them, it will come together of its own natural volition. There is no rush. I have a strong desire to experience a romantic intimacy and it's like spirit is saying "Scarlet take your time. Experience life and love will follow. Let yourself ride the wave and in its turn, the power will rush to you."

I like Mr Westbourne who I named after the Westbourne pub

because I met him there and am yet to discover his name. He is very earthed and powerful in a lot of ways that sound different from how he appears on the surface. Saw the actor Buck Bentley yesterday outside Fresh & Wild while I was having coffee with Sandra. A few weeks before I saw his brother Charles Bentley in Hampstead while I was with Emily and Tina. I knew instinctively I would see Buck again. Then after he drove off in his Jaguar convertible with a beautiful brunette, I was glad I hadn't approached him.

4th May
10.30am

Why can't I get to work earlier? Because I don't have to, yet I feel guilty. More organization and time management is necessary. It's the constant scheduling and planning. I need to do a whole load at least one month in advance. That way I'll be more on the ball. Publicity is also very crucial, creating awareness about the show. A.S.A.P. want the success to come in now! Trust today will be a good show. I really rushed breakfast and I'm ungrounded.

7.55pm

Thank you for the protection. Wow, did Clive have a freak out or what! Rick Jenkins, my powerhouse TV executive friend watched Friday's show when I had Harry Morrison on presenting with me. He said he liked it. Anyway Clive turned up 11.20am and had an absolute fit. I feel the colour essences have really pressed his buttons in a big way. I was arranging the colours on the table and then he walked in and said, "I knew it. I knew you'd do this to me!"

I stayed very calm, got up and approached him. He pointed his umbrella in my face, I felt his anger, and I wondered if he was going to hit me. Well energetically he tried but I felt angels block his punches. I remember Bill telling me, "Never make a scene in public, talk to the person privately."

"Where's my money? You haven't got it have you," Clive said, spitting venom in front of the crew.

"Actually, I've got a cheque for you in the office," I said.

"Oh," he said, no wind filling his already billowing sails.

We went into the office and he was viscous. Thankfully I felt transparent to his attack.

"You're not in your angelic nature, you're ugly like a human, and you're horrible!" Clive said.

"Thanks Clive," I said, really appreciate it.

Then he threw the letter he'd written in my face. I put it in the bin but decided to take it out and read it later on.

"I told my daughter I don't want to be friends with you anymore," he said.

That's great, what are you trying to prove Clive? Please enlighten me! I feel pity for Clive, the little nine-year-old boy snatching his toys. The realization he has no one to play with and then wondering why and feeling very hurt.

Just did a Divine Will meditation to receive clear inner guidance. I cried. A part of me was scared to let go. Let go of what? I must get life in perspective, it is important to feel at a heart level without judgement. Please God let me be safe in love and send healing to Clive so he may understand his actions and I mine. Clarity, truth and true love shining through! I move into my highest power. Yes I feel a little fear, I may do it anyway.

6.30pm

So Clive phoned up and slagged me off to Kevin. Nice Clive. Thanks. Just as I was feeling empathy for you.

Matt just came into my head. Feel he's going through it. Do I text him? No, let him reconnect, it's too soon. Send positive energy and there will be a right timing. But I feel he really needs my support.

Spirit guide said: "Scarlet, he has to support himself and come to you from a place of strength, not need. Remember "need" energy is pretty icky."

Would be great if I can get David Doggart on the show with me, author of "Talk with Heaven." I think I'm doing very good things with the show, especially from the psychic perspective. Shall I wear my blue top, floral skirt and green shoes tonight or my black dress to the party? Blue and green could be fun. Black is more sexy and ravishing. We'll see.

5th May
10.10am

Went to bed 4.20am. Drank three vodkas and a glass of champagne. Definitely have a hangover now. Show starts in an hour and twenty minutes. Aaahhh! Please angels get me through the day effortlessly, gracefully and gratefully.

Rick Jenkins picked me up in his BMW and we went to The Palace Club for the "Live Pleasure Zone" launch party which was totally under-rated. Rick took lots of photos of me, embarrassing. He didn't want to socialize with the others. As I arrived, saw Oscar Pitt. He introduced me to Stefano who I thought was good looking but I didn't think much else about it, as I had to look after Rick. We sat and talked about marriage, sex and business. I also had an interesting spiritual/sexual chat with one of the porn stars, Heather. Then I finally connected with Stefano who I concluded was gorgeous, very sexy, handsome and Italian. Whoa! Where do I start? He grew on me the more I listened to him. He had this childlike quality and joie de vivre.

"I find you really handsome," I said.

He said no one had ever told him this directly or unconditionally. He told me about his one-year affair while married. This didn't phase me, I was hypnotized.

"I don't need you, I desire you and I really want you to kiss me," I said, as we sat on a corner table in East West night club with a bottle of champagne.

"My wife would get very jealous," Stefano said.

"I still want you to kiss me," I said, rather intoxicated.

He grabbed hold of me and kissed me passionately, in true Italian style. Blew me away. He suggested we go party back at his friend's house but it was already 3.30am and I knew I had to do the show in the morning. So I got a cab home on my own from Regent's Street while Veronica went back with Oscar and Stefano. She phoned me as I got into bed. I lay in the dark talking with her wishing Stefano was in bed with me. I could hear Stefano talking in the background about me with Oscar.

"Scarlet's amazing and she kissed me so that makes me amazing." He didn't know I could hear him.

His kiss was passionate but I would have liked a deeper connection, to feel it in my whole body. Every cell tingling and energized. Nothing quite like kissing Matt.

Had a great psychic reading from Pearl Watkins. I feel great things are going to happen in my career. It's such a positive turnaround. I'm so tired now. Just need to collapse into a lovely sleep. So amazing to have all the fan mail, really like the positive feedback. I feel Martha Blackwell's jealousy. Must send her more light. It's like she wants or is waiting for me to fall and that's not going to happen.

7th May
7.50pm: Oxford Street Tube

Nothing from Matt. No word. Got Paula, the psychic healer's birthday party tomorrow night. I love my job. I feel so blessed.

8th May
9.10am

I dreamt of horrible harassment from Clive Gray. I was in a room and he was trying to corner me, trap me. Think it was a dining room. Clive grabs me and throws me down on a table. I'm screaming for him to let me go. He physically abuses me by putting his fingers inside me. I'm horrified.

"See how you like that, Scarlet," he said, laughing.

There are people around and it is shocking. He is abusing his power and me sexually. This is rape, very sly and devious without full penetration. Clive you make me sick because you are an abuser and a bully.

6.30pm

I've been having the most amazing flirtation with Stefano. He's married, unhappy and soul searching. I'm being daring and in the moment. Thought about Matt a lot while swimming. Want to text him badly. Is he thinking of me at all? It feels like it. But if I text, he may back off and retreat into his shell again. I hope not. Matt call me! Text me! See me! Kiss me! Make love to me! I miss you.

**9th May
10.55pm**

Wow! Talk about manifestation. I wrote all my desires for animal passion and then it happened last night. I met Heather, one of the Pleasure Zone porn stars at Dulwich station. She didn't know I'd fantasized about her on the train. We went to Paula's party and drank red wine, fiery ginger beer and Jamaican rum. Felt rather tipsy. Then we went to The District Club and up to The Chill Room first. I was wearing a pink "Sex Goddess" t-shirt, jeans and white fluffy hat. We headed downstairs and as we walked through the bar, everyone's eyes were upon Heather's enormous cleavage and very high heeled black PVC boots. Neither one of us had enough money for a drink. This made me feel insecure so we went back up to The Chill Room and saw some space on one of the sofas.

"I think we should leave, my hair's greasy, I'm feeling insecure," I said to Heather, but she's already sitting. I reluctantly join her. Suddenly this guy sits down and almost head-butts me in the process. I notice he is very cute, sexy. I feel like I know him and yet I struggle to look in his eyes. He's wearing a Hell's Angel t-shirt, a skull with wings extends from either side. I should know I'm playing with the dark side of my soul. Delicious. He directs pop promos and he's called Wayne. He knows my cousin Natalie. This bonds us in an already incestuous London.

"She's not your cousin," Wayne said.

"Yes she is," I said.

"I don't believe you," he said.

"Why would I make this up?" I said

"It's too much of a coincidence," he said.

"Synchronicity," I said, correcting him.

"Text her," Wayne said.

"It's one in the morning," I said.

"So?" he said.

"I don't have her number on me," I said.

Wayne leans over to his mate Clay, then returns to me.

"Here's her number, you can text her now," he said.

So I do.

"Hi cousin, Scarlet here, I'm at The District Club with Wayne, catch up soon."

"Happy now," I said to Wayne.

"What do you want to drink?" he said, smiling.

I'm embarrassed. Don't feel like I can accept a drink. Heather chimed in and said, "I'll have a G&T."

"Well?" Wayne said, his eyes looking into me.

"You decide," I said.

I'm feeling coy. I look down and bite my lip as Wayne heads off to the bar.

"See I told you we'd get drinks," Heather said, in her cockney accent.

"He's really cute. Amazing that he works with my cousin," I said.

"I'm going to the loo, powder my nose," she said, smiling "Let you two get to know each other a bit better."

"Heather?" I said, but she was already gone and Wayne was walking back from the bar. He hands me a mojito. "That's my favourite drink," I said "You're very tuned in."

Wayne sits down close to me and looks into my eyes.

"I feel vulnerable," I said.

"Why?" Wayne said.

"I don't know what to say," I said.

Wayne leans into me and whispers in my ear.

"Kiss me."

"I can't," I said, but I wanted to.

"Scarlet, kiss me," he said, and my body overrides my mind. I lean forward and my lips brush against his. The kiss is beautiful, tender and sensual. Heather comes back and we stop. I want more. Instead we all talk together with Wayne's friends until 2am when the lights go up.

"Come back to mine," Wayne said.

"Where do you live?" I said.

"Queen's Park," he said.

"I live round the corner," I said.

"Ok, we'll come to you," he said.

So Wayne and his two friends walk around to my place with Heather teetering in her high heels. We enter through the communal gardens. It's very dark. We get to the back door but I've double locked it.

"Shit, we can only get in through the front. Wait here and I'll walk round," I said.

"I'll go with you," Wayne said. Perfect. This time we stroll through the garden hand in hand, alone, while Heather flirts with the boys.

"I want you to kiss me on that bench," I said.

I sit down and he straddles me. Wayne lifts my t-shirt and touches my breasts for the first time. I feel I'm only connecting with him physically, it's shallow.

"Come on, the others are waiting," I said, pulling my t-shirt down.

I drink herbal tea, Wayne drinks beer with the boys and Heather drinks wine. Wayne leans over.

"So am I going to stay?" he said.

"No," I said "But I'd like to see you tomorrow, alone."

I take his hand and invite him into my bedroom. My intention is purely to kiss him goodnight. Wayne pulls me down on the bed and kisses me but I'm resistant. He pins down my left arm with his hand and my right arm by his head. He runs his hand over my breasts. Sublime.

"I just want to turn you on," Wayne said. He brushes his hand over my pubic bone.

"No," I said, feeling self-conscious.

"I'm just teasing you," he said and then he's kissing my stomach and stroking inside my thighs and suddenly I'm turned on and he manages to slip his fingers inside me. I'm wet. I gasp and sit up.

"You have to leave," I said.

He gently but firmly pushes me back down onto the bed and whispers "Let me give you one orgasm before I go."

I'm conflicted. I want it but I know if I surrender, I'll want more and he may not come back. He kisses, licks, caresses me and I have the most intense, pleasurable cunnilingus of my life, my legs are shaking. We lie together on the bed. Then we're kissing again and then his penis is in my mouth and he comes, I gag a little but he doesn't notice. I realize I still have a feeling of repression and fear towards fully receiving men.

"That was amazing," he said.

We lay there a while longer. Wayne takes my number. We go next door and everyone is asleep on the sofas. Heather and I get into bed and then I get a text from Wayne, "Hey sexy. C u tomorrow."

Except on Sunday he blows me out. I'm gutted, depressed, hurt and vulnerable.

His text, "Hey Scarlet, good 2 meet u last nite. Gonna take a rain check today, lots 2 do! C u soon. Xx"

"Rain check?" That doesn't make me feel great after full on intimacy. We both had interesting synchronicity of having come out of almost seven-year relationships two months ago. He was also engaged to be married and didn't go through with it. So I'm pulling in semi-available men. I am reminded I have to find the love inside. It's the only way. I really wanted to have sex with Wayne tonight. I think he likes me and wants to keep the door open but without any strings. I sense he wants to play the field, which I know he will and I will too but I'd also like us to play together. We'll see, my psychic ability doesn't show me the outcome.

So this afternoon, I needed to distract myself, stop thinking about the rejection. I went swimming. As I come out of the gym with soaking wet hair, I see Matt get out of his car with his friend Steven. We walk towards each other and Matt smiles at me knowingly. Matt invites me into his office. Today I'm wearing my brown Sex Goddess t-shirt.

"You look like you got up to something last night," Steven said.

I happily confess in front of Matt that I kissed Wayne. I want to make Matt jealous, show him I don't need him. I omit the details of cunnilingus, blowjob and that he'd just blown out our date for tonight. Matt suddenly relaxes, it's like a safe emotional distance has been created between us. Matt finally admits my suspicions that he's really been going through a tough time but he won't give me the details. I guide him through a golden heart meditation, allowing him to receive clarity. After the meditation he confides that he doesn't want to be with Louisa but he doesn't want anyone else to have her either. I repress my judgement. Matt walks me outside to say "good bye" away from Steven. I don't want to tell him the truth but I can't help myself.

"It hurt me because you know you're the first person I've slept with since Bill. You haven't come to see me since."

Matt wraps his arms around me but I feel guarded.

"I'll come and see you soon."

I don't believe him and pull away. He senses my distance and kisses my lips.

"Every day I think about what you said to me when we first met in the jacuzzi but I need time to work everything out. I'm really confused," Matt said.

Nancy had warned me Matt would back away from me.

"It's fine, call me when you're ready," I said.

I'm casual on the surface and feel the knife pierce through my heart as I walk away.

10th May
9.55am

Pretty sure Wayne will reconnect with me, if I can just hold out.

6.50pm

Thought about Wayne a few times this afternoon because I felt rejected. Scarlet, get over your insecurity. What is wrong with you? I have butterflies in my solar plexus thinking about it.

I feel Barry is trying to stab me in the back. He's got Eric, one of the Pleasure Zone producers working on the show with me now.

Why does Barry put down what I say? He's not giving me enough opportunity to create a successful show that is already beginning to see positive results. I must trust. Despite all the shit, I feel very protected and that the angels are looking after me.

So Andy, will be filming me interviewing David Doggart. Must check out "Talk with Heaven". When I emailed Andy about the shoot he replied "Is this a date?"

I said, "This is a spiritual interaction. I promise not to put a spell on you."

A part of me would like it to be, there is something quite sexy about him, because I'm attracted to the bad boy in him. I would like to snog him but I know this would be dangerous.

So I never heard from Mr Westbourne, oh well.. Wow, the power sex has over my emotional body. Can send me into an unbalanced frenzy of euphoria and depression all at the same time. Oh come on Wayne, text me so I can shag you!

CHAPTER 6

SCARLET'S DELIGHT

11th May
10.02am: Baguette Café

Wow! What an amazingly positive turnaround! All my debt cleared now is a miracle in action. Thank you Mum for helping me!!! Thank you God!!! I am so grateful to have a clean slate and I will do my best to maintain abundance, be wise and balanced in my spending and never have any shopping binges.

Now I have to go and address my work situation. Ask for a hard copy of a contract because I am giving away too many good ideas in creating a successful show which I know will be huge, only for me to be pushed out if I'm not careful and don't set my boundaries now. I've already had people who've seen the show ask if I'd like to collaborate on projects. Barry's away for two weeks from today, time to learn and practise "Warrior Assertiveness."

7.45pm: Oxford Street Tube

Figures are going up on the show now. We hit 690 minutes of phone calls yesterday. Text messages increased today. I spoke with Kevin and asked for a three-month contract, which he agreed to give me on Friday after he's seen Claude who's coming over from France.

12th May
9.40am: Westbourne Park Tube

Thanks to Sandra, I had a lovely texting session with Wayne. I asked no questions, just shared and I got a question back at 12.10am. The texting session went like this:

"Hello you. Harry Morrison the astrologer said Sagittarians shouldn't work so hard…interesting. I'm seeing cousin Natalie on Saturday. Happy Moving Friday x." I texted at 10.45pm.

He texted at 12.10am, "Why did he say saggies shouldn't work so hard?"

I said, "…all work and no play…"

He obviously needed some time to think of a good response. Fifteen minutes later he said, "I'm definitely up 4 play no work…"

I was now in a frenzy, as I concocted the next text response with Sandra supporting me on the landline. Ten minutes later I came up with "I know some gr8 games."

I knew this was a good text and that he wouldn't want to be caught out. For the next eight minutes, I speculated his response with Sandra and then he replied, "Oh yeah, like what?"

Oh my gosh, now he is getting totally sexy. I've got him. I'm finally learning how to play the game and have some fun instead of be so fucking needy. I'm in a panic. I will not let Sandra get off the phone. I write my text and decide to wait. I know because he asked the question. He's enticed and I'm going to reel him in gently.

I texted him at 1am, "I'll show u in the playground…sweet dreams x"

So for the next twenty minutes I hope he's wondering, perhaps now fantasizing about kissing me and remembering the intimacy and chemistry between us but he didn't respond. I went to sleep optimistic on the surface but inside my voice screamed, "Rejection."

8.30pm

Spoke with Natalie this afternoon and discovered that she'd had lunch with Wayne on Monday. She said, "I told Wayne keep your hands off my cousin or else."

"What did he say?" I said.

"He seemed a bit miffed, he asked why?" Natalie said.

I decided not to mention we'd kissed, I wanted to extract more information.

"So is he dating anyone?" I said.

"He's seeing a couple of girls, think one of them is a waitress," she said.

Shit I need a couple of extra guys, to stop myself thinking about him, one for Wednesday, another for Saturday. He probably blew me out on Sunday for another girl?

13th May
12.38am: Home

Wayne hasn't texted me. He plays the game better than me and he's got his fingers in more than one pie. Am I past my sell by date?

Matt is Mr Non-Fucking Communicative. Stefano is crazily weird and fucked up. Andy at the office is a total asshole. I'm gagging for it. Is there no one gorgeous who will fuck me?

Tina lent me her book, "Zen and the Art of Falling in Love," by Charlotte Kasl. Let's see what gifts I may learn. She also invited me to a hippy party in Chelsea on Saturday night. One thing is certain. My sex-drive is back.

8.40am: Bed

I am obsessed with the feelings I have for Wayne. As I pushed Black Cat away last night, I realized all the kitty wants is love. Maybe I am being pushed away by Wayne and kept at a distance because I am keeping Black Cat at a distance?

It's Thursday today and Dad's coming on the show as a sceptic guest with Paula co-presenting. That'll be fun. Please let it be a good show.

I feel I'm at an impasse. It's as if I'm taking a rest stop on the mountain and yet I want the exhilaration of new scenery and adventure. If I look where I am, I have so much, it's quite incredible from where I started at the beginning of the year. I'm going to The District Club tonight in the hope of bumping into Wayne, how sad Scarlet, get over it.

Matt is totally unavailable as a friend. Why do I feel drawn to these types of men?

Charlie Silver phoned me yesterday. He told me he's really happy, selling his house and moving in with his ex-fiancée, Ashley so perhaps things will turn around and they may get married after all. I told him about my snog with Wayne and he said, "Ah, so I could have put my lips on you at breakfast, that's what I should have done."

So he did want to kiss me!

I think Andy at the office is very immature, can't be dealing with that and Jen who he's seeing is so sweet. I'm not interested. Going to steer well clear of him. Time to get ready for work and, allow miracles and new people into my life.

10.45pm: Bed

The trickster inside my head says, "Ha! Gotcha! You didn't really think he fancied you? Liked you? Would want to spend real quality time with you and then want to see you again?"

I think Wayne decided I was a mistake, purely a shag because he perceives me as too weirdly New Age. So I try and loose myself, except there's no escape from my tugging solar plexus.

My belly says, "Scarlet you hand away your power when it comes to matters of the heart. You're not valuing yourself. Instead you piss champagne down a sinkhole. What a waste."

What will help me is breathing, being present with the hurt

feelings, not stuffing them down but letting them flow and transform. Next time I fear sending a text, send it. Next time I feel affronted, say it. Next time I have an opinion, honestly express it. Stop hiding. Be present. Own my feelings by being true to myself and see how Wayne and Matt respond.

I was texting Wayne and then Oscar called and put me on the phone with his friend Bob who's Sagittarius like Wayne. Bob is a triple fire sign so wouldn't want to get on the wrong side of him. He just invited me over to his flat in Chelsea but I declined. Do I still send the text to Wayne? No.

11.11pm

I've got this twang in my stomach, it's flipping out. I can feel the energy pushing out my edges, testing my boundaries. It doesn't feel good. I want to text Wayne but I stop myself. If he wanted to contact me, he would, wouldn't he? It's Friday night, maybe I can see him, fuck it, I'm texting.

"Congratulations on new home. Remember not to absorb negative energies," I said. Shit, I'm shaking like a leaf now.

"Thanx. What u up 2?" he replied.

"Would like to play. R u up 4 it?" I said.

No response for forty-five minutes. Why's he taking so long to reply?

"Totally," he said.

Why am I doing all the chasing? So I hand my power away a little more and text, "prove it…if u dare…I like truth. Truth or dare?"

Nothing! It's been an hour! Yes I dare you to come over and give me the orgasm of my life. Wayne you're such an insecure game player. Why can't you just respond to my text? I'm tired now. So I spiral downwards and text, "Do u want to play or not?"

I'm going to sleep if you don't text me soon. It's too much effort. I am a woman possessed, I texted again, "I guess you don't want to play. Shame, I think we would've had fun. Ok truth pls r u a) lost for words b) don't want to play or c) scared of the result…my philosophy is win-win."

Now, I'm fucking gutted. Wayne blew me out again, but I still stayed open hearted. Going to sleep now. I feel alone now. Want to cry but can't. Now I feel really depressed.

16th May
5.25pm: The Garden at Home

The birds are chirping. It is warm outside. The sunlight is lovely. Cars hum in the distance. Kids kicking ball. Breeze fluffing my hair. I am peaceful in the garden. Mr Westbourne just texted. He's another Sagittarian. What is it with me drawing in the Saggies? Anyway, he's spiritually aware and I like that his favourite movie is, "The Big Blue." I was shy when we met for a drink. He evoked my femininity, as he leaned against the street sign of Westbourne Park Road but I liked it.

I had a vile dream that Heather had psoriasis all over her belly. A spirit guide spoke to me and said, "Heather has been a great mirror to you."

I realized that when I met Wayne, I had been attracted to Heather's energy and now I was repulsed by it. It felt sleazy and needy. My vibration probably felt pretty disgusting, low and sexually desperate towards Wayne. I cannot change the past with him but I'd like our interaction to be different in the future. I had a severe moment of darkness as I opened my body to him physically. Skeleton woman appeared. I think she scared the shit out of him.

17th May
8.15am: Bed

I keep hoping I'll bump into Wayne at The District Club because I met him there. Why can't you let go Scarlet?

19th May
10pm

Wayne presses all my buttons. I'm struggling to be present. He hasn't said if he'd watched my show yet. I want what I can't have. I'm driven by sexual desire. I need the intense connection and then rejection. I am a sad little girl who doesn't know any better. I am an angry bitch, ready for a tantrum, an outburst, will slap you before you slap me because I've laid myself open to abuse too many times before. I don't know how to let go. So I've concluded I'm a very needy, powerless and extremely sad woman who wants an emotionally unavailable man who's going to charm me, fuck me beautifully, dump me the next day and make me feel like shit so I may reaffirm the truth of all my thought forms.

20th May
8.36am

I stopped myself calling Wayne, not as a game but to dance with my own energy. It feels uncomfortable. My challenge is believing I truly deserve love. Wayne is an unrealistic obsession for me. I'm raw inside. I have everything I desire materially right now and I'm still not happy.

CHAPTER 7

HE LOOKS JUST LIKE
COLIN FARRELL

21ˢᵗ May

Last night I was walking home with wet hair, no make-up in the pouring rain feeling very tired from work. As I arrived three steps from my front door, a gorgeous sexy guy came out of a building a few doors down and said ,"Do you want to go for a drink?"

I paused and then allowed spontaneity, "Yes," I said.

He was very chivalrous, gave me his velvet jacket, as we walked to a bar around the corner. His name, Max. He drank whisky and smoked a lot of cigarettes. I drank a fruit juice cocktail topped with grapes. We talked and he suddenly leaned forward to kiss me and I gasped. He looks like Colin Farrell and definitely has a bad boy quality. He talks six languages and speaks really fast, I couldn't understand half of what he said. Max invited me back to his flat but I felt so exhausted I suggested he come back to mine. He did and invited himself to stay. He promised not to make any moves on me in bed but before I could blink, we were naked and he was inside me. I burst into tears. He stopped immediately and wrapped me in his arms. We went to sleep except I couldn't because of his incessant snoring. I woke up in the morning feeling horny and we slept together. It felt very natural. I came on top of him and he came on top of me.

22nd May
9.30am: My bed

I have very swollen glands and aching body. I had a lovely time with Max on Friday and Saturday night. I can't remember the last time I had sex that many times in twenty-four hours. It's so intense, so quickly and we've both just come out of long-term relationships and I'm questioning whether I want this, him? Too much attention and I shut down.

I had a dream that Clive tried to trick and trap me. It was a very uncomfortable feeling. He was trying to hurt me and I escaped.

"You'll never get anywhere without me," Clive said.

I walked away and found myself upon a forest path. I sense something new is beginning. The leaves on the trees were sapphire, emerald and gold in the sunlight and the banks, mossy. The ground was damp and moist so I knew I would need strong footing but I had a feeling of abundance.

24th May
10am: Tube

I have tonsillitis and a fever. I slept for hours and hours and still need more. I read "Zen and The Art of Falling in Love," last night, as I could feel myself clamming up as Max pulled away. In truth, I was pushing him away because it's too much intimacy too quickly for me. I texted him at 10.26pm "wish you had come back 2 say 'bye'…hope it wasn't something I said…praying I'm better 4 tmrw, got major fever! Sleep well beauty…really enjoyed my time with u x".

Then I turned my phone off to release any attachment to him and get some sleep. I awoke to a lovely message at 10.50pm and bless him he'd called again at 9am and then again, as I got out of the shower. He said he'd had a business thing to sort out. At night?

I think Max has a fear of getting hurt, especially having lost his mother five years ago to cancer. I can see he's so used to looking after himself and yet he craves nurturing.

I've now been at Mega TV almost three months. I'm enjoying my job, apart from the politics. How do I get the financial figures to increase for the show? Saw Barry, Kevin and Dick, one of the Mega TV owners this morning. Barry was friendly. Kevin and Dick weren't. They're such chauvinists. Think my temperature has gone but the tonsillitis is still very present. What am I not expressing?

4.35pm

I just emailed Kevin regarding my contract and claimed my power, spoke with him in a positive way. It was good. I don't know the outcome except my right tonsil is totally inflamed and that doesn't bode well. A lot of unspoken issues on my part because I'm feeling powerless. I sense my work path at Mega TV is ending but a new higher pathway is coming in. I'm struggling to receive gracefully because I'm scared to let go.

25th May
4.38am: My Bed

Just woke up from an awful dream. I'm by the ocean in a house, it is beautiful out because the new moon shines brightly onto the beach. The waves are lapping at the shore. I begin collecting my things from inside a house and Bill follows me wherever I go, like a leech. I attack him with words, "If you weren't so fucking boring and actually allowed yourself to get out…"

"Who says I'm boring?" he said.

"Everyone," I said.

I can see he doesn't feel good. I leave the room and go to the bathroom. He follows me. It's dark in there and the toilet is backed up. He grabs hold of me and kisses me. I don't kiss back, just pull away. I see his skin is covered in psoriasis. It's all flaky and he scratches avidly in front of me. I am repulsed.

"Oh my God, how long have you had this?" I said.

"Months," Bill said.

"Is it getting worse?" I said.

"Yes," he said.

"Have you gone to a doctor?" I said.

"No," he said.

Again, he lunges to kiss me. I scream and then shout at him to, "Back off."

Bill gets angry at me. I throw open the door to the bedroom. I see his mother basked outside in moonlight.

"You have to help Bill now," I said.

Bill looks angry and yet helpless, he is like a leper. I feel I cannot be near him, the man I was with for seven years.

Please let my voice be good for the show tomorrow. I can barely speak and my throat is getting worse. I pushed myself too hard last week, burn out from an excess of work, sex and lack of sleep. My body has rebelled and said, "Enough!"

Everything is so good with Max, it seems too good to be true.

10.35am: Tube

Although I've only known Max a few days, I feel he is so supportive and I love that. Please throat, get better so I can see Max and have a lovely time.

2.35pm

Just left the studio. Somehow managed to do a good show and had fantastically positive feedback from the viewers. Nice and encouraging. Would be good if I could get that support from within Mega TV. I do feel the TV show will continue and I'll move through this rocky patch with them.

Mum is like a spiritual warrior urging me on. Tiffany, my meant to be sceptic co-presenter, who totally believes is great on the show. I really like working with her. She's fab. It's turned into a really lovely team. I'm tired now, an hour's rest would be good before tidying up all this mess. Might need to get Petra, the witch for tomorrow's show.

11pm

Max came to see me. That was so sweet, he said he didn't care how I looked. He led me to the bedroom within ten minutes and a voice inside of me said, "What's the rush? Just let the desire build."

Which manifested as him getting pissed off, leaving to see a friend and we didn't sleep together so now I want him even more coz he's so fucking sexy. He said he'd call tomorrow and I said, "I'm out."

"I'll call anyway," Max said.

Wish he didn't drink and smoke so much.

26th May

So my intuition was spot on. Just spoke with Kevin after the show and from Monday he wants Eric to take over my role of producing and for me to focus on presenting.

27th May

It's been a turbulent twenty-four hours for me. Even though I intuited Kevin wanted to stop me producing the show, it was still a shock to me.

Miss being with Max, can't believe I only met him a week ago. I'm not going to tell Max about my full on sexual experience with Karen last night. We were talking about vibrators and I said, "Yes, I've got a rabbit."

"Could I use it?" Karen asked.

"Sure," I said.

"Could you use it on me?" she said.

And I did. Max doesn't need to know.

28th May

Absolutely exhausted and enlivened by last night. The most

incredible sex I've had in years and Max said he feels the same. It's going to be super hot outside today. I love that Max's confident and can say he's, "a good fuck." Yes he most definitely is. Bill and I never had that chemistry. The fact that I can lie in bed feel so turned on, even though he's a smoker! That's a miracle. Today Max confessed that he lied about his age to me. Turns out he's twenty-nine and not thirty-two.

"Why did you lie?" I said.

"Thought I'd never see you again, a one-night stand," Max said.

I think Max is suppressing his emotions by smoking three packs of Marlboro Lights a day and drinking a quarter bottle of Jack Daniels each night.

30th May
2pm

Max's cigarettes and drinking scares me. I'm doing my best not to judge but it scares me. So I wonder what addictive patterns and behaviours do I have in me?

11.42pm

As Max opens his heart to me, I feel myself withdraw in panic. I felt suffocated and claustrophobic when I awoke with Max in the morning. It's only nine days that we've been seeing each other, yet it feels like a full blown relationship.

31st May
10.35am: Ladbroke Grove Tube

Beautifully sunny, fluffy cotton littering the skyline. The melodic hum of cars whizzing along The Westway. I'll soon be Live on Air. I felt very emotional last night. I cried again while making love with Max. It was one deep thrust that hurt me while I was very open. I then held a part of myself back and this made me sad. I have a fear I'll be knocked down because that's what it felt like when Max was inside me. It feels like Max and I have dived into some kind of inexplicable love. It's too soon to say the word, "love" but that is what it is in my heart and soul.

This morning got a text from Stefano. He said, "Hi there. How are you? I have been thinking of you very much. Why?X"

Good question Stefano, why have you been thinking of me so much? I'm interested in how men think. What makes them emotionally available, then unavailable, available?

Max isn't letting me get any sleep. Solution: Create a time to spend quality moments together and discipline myself by writing a list of goals and fulfilling them one by one.

Barry Peck, he's a user wanker who steals my ideas. Solution: leave the company and set up ideas with people who will respect, value and acknowledge all my good work.

Kevin Block, triple fucker wanker user. Stole my ideas and is ripping me off and using me like a c-u-n-t. Solution: leave the company and take my ideas and agree a deal upfront where I'll be truly appreciated.

Clive Gray, egotistical mother fucking c-u-n-t backstabbing self-important guru shit fucker. Solution: send Clive love and light so he may heal his own heart.

Matt, he used me for sex and I'm still wounded, in a halfway house of a friendship. Solution: set the record straight and change the dimensions. Ask for support in the friendship.

Wayne, bastard wanker user, he holds me back from trusting myself. Solution: be friendly and loving. Ask how the decorating is going.

11pm

My first memory is when I was three-years-old. Being wheeled to an operating theatre, all the while, screaming, feeling lied to, deserted and tricked and throwing up when I awoke.

When I was eight, Rhonda Pew whipped me with a towel and

stole my chewing gum in Florida. She also chewed off one of my fingernails.

At ten, I got into trouble at school for running around the playground naked.

My parents divorced when I was eleven and I thought it was my fault.

I remember my gay music teacher with odd socks slamming down the lid to the piano and scaring the shit out of me. It killed my dreams of being a great piano player.

At thirteen, got myself into lots of trouble. I let two boys kiss my breasts at the same time and threw a glass of red wine over a rude French guy at dinner, slapped him round the face for criticising me about my three way antics.

At fourteen I lost my virginity to rape, loaded with Bacardi and Coke. I threw up in the morning.

At fifteen Marcus Gold burst into the bathroom and caught me naked in the shower.

Jackie Collins novels really turned me on.

1st June
8.45am: Bed

It's raining outside. I ate steak and chips and a hamburger yesterday. Also had fantastic sex with Max on the sofa but I didn't have an orgasm. Nancy gets back in just over a month so soon will be time to manifest a new home. I'm about to go and do the show. Think I'll go get a muffin with smoked salmon, scrambled eggs and hollandaise sauce for breakfast. My throat feels like it's getting better as I'm releasing all that excess anger and frustration. I think Max likes drama, his life is a big budget movie and he is the A-list star but he'd never admit it. That's ok, I like drama to, I guess that's why I picked him.

10.08am: Memories

At four years old, I learnt not to rely on boys or girls. It was a dog eat dog playground. Rhonda was definitely my nemesis, she was viscous and evil, a troubled soul who attacked, attacked and attacked me. She was angry at the world. I think she still is. I remember her eating her pooh in front of me, now that is truly fucked. I loved her white dress with flowers and the long shawl that I didn't have.

At five, I remember no one wanting me to sit on their table in class. Ironically, I ended up being put on the cool bitchy table. Technically, I had it all but I was a loner, trying to fit in.

Being put on a diet at six years old was horrible. I wondered what I did wrong. That really hurt me. Why did I put on so much weight? Because Mum gave me everything I wanted from the supermarket but the food didn't fill that huge emotional well inside me. At this time, I was a spiritual soul. I will always remember vividly the dream of being bitten by an Egyptian snake that killed me.

From eight years old, I had a desperate need to arrive first at school. It gave me a real thrill because it was peaceful before anyone else arrived. I have this poignant memory of lying on a sun lounger with Dad under the apple tree, listening to Pink Floyd feeling melancholic and loved.

At fourteen, I dreamt of floating in a Cadillac over graves in Highgate cemetery.

2nd June
4.30pm

Slept all day, tried to get up. Max pissed me off to high Heaven. I slammed the door and threw my phone on the bed. He said he was "sorry," and so did I. I explained that I was rude because he was and that isn't right for me to react that way, I'm also angry at myself for not getting anything done today. I'm angry because I'm not allowing myself to feel special with Max. I'm out of one relationship and straight into another without the courting, chase, dating, wooing, appreciation and adoration. I feel his desire waning.

I dreamt I tried on a wedding dress on in LA. It makes me feel I will eventually marry an American.

My first visit to America was when I was six years old. We flew Pan Am to Disney World. On the trip back from New York, I had sweet and sour chicken on the flight, this was one of the highlights of my adventure. I befriended two Hare Krishna's dressed in robes, a big Hill Billy oh and a wonderful Native American Chief, I think Sioux Clan. I told them all the story of how Dad got up on stage in front of the audience when there was a bomb scare at the theatre. I was really proud of him.

My first game of kiss chase was at eight years old in Mallorca. I was into a blonde haired, blue-eyed boy named David but his friend held me and my other friend down and spat in our eyes, so this was the polarity of my sweet tender kiss. Interesting to experience abuse and pleasure, all in a fleeting moment.

My favourite TV shows were "Dallas", "Dynasty", "Martians Chronicle", "V", "Space 1999" and "The Outer Limits". I also loved "Wonder Woman", "The Bionic Man", "Starsky & Hutch" and "Dr Who". I loved creating stories and dramas. A magic TV moment was when the band "Bucks Fizz" won "The Eurovision Song Contest", "yes!"

8pm

Not yet made it to the gym. Just ate a smoked salmon, pickled cucumber sandwich followed by Lindt chocolate bunny.

Max just texted, "Sorry 4 my mood."

I replied, "sorry for my reaction, how u going 2 make it up 2 me?"

10.45pm

Had a lovely time at the gym and ate a nice hamburger and salad. Now watching "Sex and the City." I so relate to the subject matter of needing an orgasm. Where's mine? I don't want Max to get lazy and take me for granted.

I remember sitting at Emma Green's house for Passover dinner, as Elijah was invited into drink a glass of Palwin's no. seven wine. A fifty-year-old man named Mervin rubbed his hand up and down my eleven-year-old thigh. I felt sick to my stomach.

"Stop," I said.

"I'm just being friendly," Mervin said.

I felt helpless as his wife and daughter sat across from him at the table. I saw the bulge in his pants. I tried to get up, help in the kitchen but Emma's mum insisted I stay at the table.

"Keep Mervin company," she said.

I wanted to throw up, as he rubbed his hand between my legs. I grabbed hold of his hand to stop him. He leaned over, whispered in my ear, "It's meant to feel nice, you'll see."

I prayed someone would see, notice what was happening but everyone was oblivious. I couldn't understand how this was possible. My innocence was shattered and then I was saved but the damage was already done.

"Scarlet, you're the youngest one at the table, will you open the front door, let Elijah in for the glass of wine?" Emma's mum said.

I couldn't get up from the table fast enough, as Mervin was forced to release his hand from my crotch. I rushed flustered, out of the room and opened the door to the house.

"Elijah, why did you let this happen to me?" I whispered as I felt a cool breeze brush across my cheeks.

At the end of dinner, while washing up in the kitchen I approached Emma's mum.

"He touched me?" I said.

"Touched?" Mrs Green said.

"Between my legs," I said.

"What do you mean?" Mrs Green, a look of confusion on her face.

I lowered my face in shame.

"Sexually," I said.

"Oh Scarlet. You really mustn't make up stories," Mrs Green said.

I was shocked by her response, how couldn't she believe me?

"That's impossible, with his wife and daughter at the table? I'm ashamed of you. Let's forget this was ever mentioned," she said.

As Emma and I climbed the stairs to her bedroom, I struggled to assimilate, that I'd been accused of being a liar. As we closed the door to her room, I sat on the bed.

"You believe me. Don't you?" I said.

"Of course," Emma said.

"So why didn't you say something?" I said.

Emma shrugged her shoulders.

"I wish he was dead," I said.

Three weeks later Mervin died of a heart attack. I thought I'd killed him.

3rd June

Max stopped by at 2am, looking very gorgeous and sexy in a suit, smelling of alcohol, cigarettes and French aftershave. Max undressed, removed his tattered black strap of his Cartier watch that he said his dad gave him, put his dark rimmed glasses on the bedside table and slid alongside me in bed.

"So did you play with yourself?" he said, the breath of his words entering my mouth.

I didn't answer.

"Did you?" he said

"Do I have to be honest?" I said.

"Tell me?" he said.

"Yes," I said.

"Did you use your vibro?" he said.

"Yes," I said.

"Did you have an orgasm?" he said

"Yes," I said.

"Do you want another, do you want more?" he said.

"Yes," I said.

Max slipped his thigh firmly between my legs, pulled me closer by wrapping my arm around his lower back and placing my hand on his hardness. Then pulled me on top of him and put himself inside me but I felt myself holding back. Just as I was about to come he stopped.

"I have to give some money to my neighbour," Max said.

"But it's 3.30am, can't it wait?" I said.

"No, I promised," he said and walked out onto the patio for a cigarette.

Fuck him. Then he put his head around the door.

"Do you want me to leave?" he said.

"Just come to bed," I said, exasperated.

Max turned around and shut the bedroom door behind him and then I heard the front door slam shut. I cried, more out of frustration.

I texted him at 4.05am, "That hurt me, I just wanted 2 curl up w u + go to sleep in your arms."

I got a text back at 5.30pm "It's me not you."

What can I say to that?

4th June

Max invited me to South of France with him next weekend.

"I may regret saying this," Max said.

"Then don't," I said. I sensed what he was about to say and I wasn't ready to hear it.

"I'm falling in love with you. Are you falling in love with me?" he said.

"Yes," I said.

"So you're crazy as I am," he said.

I remained silent.

"Move in with me?" he said.

But I felt an alarm bell go off in my head ringing, "It's too soon!"

9.10pm: Home

Got back from the studio and found Max still in bed at 3.45pm, lazy git. That made me really angry. From such a lovey dovey night to such a blow out.

"I'll live my live how I want. No one tells me what to do," Max said.

"Fine, go and lie in your own bed!" I said.

He left. I felt relieved. Suddenly I could breath. I took a blanket out to the garden and lay down to rest and then the phone went. It was Wayne. What an absolute surprise.

"Hey?" Wayne said.

Fuck his voice is so sexy.

"Hi?" I said, curiosity enveloping me.

"I need to ask you a favour," he said.

"Yeah sure," I said.

"I need to get one of my clients into The District Club as all the members I know are out of the country," he said.

"You mean you're not a member?" I said, rubbing it in.

"No," he said sheepishly.

"Sure, no problem," I said.

What a lame excuse he used to phone me. I suspected he'd heard from my cousin that I was dating a French hunk who looked like Colin Farrell and now he wanted to get in there.

"So what about that offer for tantric sex?" Wayne said.

"Oh, you missed the boat," I said, playing the dumb fox.

"Is there some else?" he said.

Bingo, he wanted what he couldn't have.

"Yes," I said, taking great satisfaction in this moment. It was delicious, karmic gratification.

"Shame, I think we'd have great sex," he said.

"Well it's never going to happen," I said.

Oh shit, his voice was turning me on so much. I wanted him and I think he knew it.

"I'm playing with myself," he said.

"Stop," I said.

I couldn't let him take control, but I wanted him to.

"I can't," he said.

"I've got to go, call me when you get to The District Club," I said.

But he didn't. Instead he texted at 11.11pm "U know its gonna happen."

Bastard, he was in the driving seat and Max was about to be thrown out of the car.

5th June

I got up at 1pm. Slept twelve hours solid, much needed rest, after having Max wake me up every hour on the hour. If there's any hope of our relationship continuing, I need a decent night's sleep. I love the sex but this is a high price to pay.

Found out that "The Psychic Show" hours will be extended from 14th June. That's very exciting, means the show is doing well. Yet I've got this fear of getting out there and launching my own projects. The only thing holding me back is fear of rejection.

I'm about to go and see Bill's mum. I feel the need to gather my energy so I have strength when I see her. I'm going to bury my engagement ring in The Rose Gardens of Regents Park.

Must get all my belongings from storage. Where am I going to move to in July? Who knows except I want to get these DKNY or Gola trainers, just can't decide.

12.20am

I remember falling in the playground at school and fracturing my wrist. I feel the fracture was an omen for the imminent split between my parents. I thought it was my fault they divorced. If I hadn't had the accident, Mum wouldn't have threatened Dad with the ultimatum. During their separation, I used to suffer excruciating heartburn which I now know was me connected into their energy clairsentiently. The pain stopped once their divorce was complete.

1.15am

I'm exhausted and my throat is sore from the frustration that I'm having to address the debt Bill owes me and the horror at myself that I bought into that pattern for so long. His mum has a book full of "I owe yous."

"How much is it now Victoria, £500, £600?" I said.

Victoria looked uncomfortable. She nodded in acknowledgement. I felt sick to my stomach.

"Yes it has to stop. I took him to the cinema on Friday and it cost £20," Victoria said.

"£20?" I said.

"Well he insisted on having ice-cream and earl grey tea," she said.

"Of course," I said.

Then she began to defend him.

"But he said he'd go without popcorn," Victoria said.

"That was generous of him," I said.

Victoria looked at me sheepishly and then continued, "I paid £60 for a locksmith yesterday, he locked himself out of the flat."

"Why did you pay? He's rent free!" I said.

"But he's working so hard at night," Victoria said.

"Yes and sleeping all day," I said.

Suddenly I could see the connection between Bill and Max. Oh no, I was recreating a pattern. Soon enough Max would be reliant on me, no wonder I was picking emotionally unavailable men because then they're be no risk of having to support them because they'd never stick around long enough for me to find out. Perfect safety mechanism, Scarlet.

Max was right, it was a mistake to tell me he was falling in love with me. It scared the shit out of me. I want to be in love from a place of strength and desire, not need and despair.

6th June
9am: Communal Gardens, Home

Max turned up at 7.15am after texting at 5am, "Love."

He stank of alcohol and cigarettes and was coughing and spluttering. It's too much for me. I can't go to the South of France with him. I don't want to owe him anything. I can't be trapped. I'm sad because I want to want Max but I've lost respect for him. He's not respecting me and my bedroom now stinks of stale smoke. The anger in my belly clairvoyantly looks like a nuclear fallout. It's so peaceful in the garden. Max I don't want to hurt you but I also need to protect me. The energy has to shift now. I'm claiming back my power, the old parts I've forgotten to love. The ragged frayed ends of my soul. The bruises on my heart. The stitches that hold me together piece by piece. I don't understand the pain, can only feel the emotions.

Spirit guide said to me, "Slow down! Feel! You can't run away from the pain because it's inside you and it'll never go until you confront it, accept it."

I remember the words, "Scarlet is a slut whore," written in blue pen on the walls of the girls toilets at school. They had no idea how much that hurt but then I did it to myself.

11.30am

I'm having breakfast at Beau Cafe. Max is fast asleep in my bed. I wish he wasn't. He'll probably be there till four this afternoon. I have to get him out of my home. I shouldn't go to France with him.

At 11.45am spoke with Sedrick and he confirmed to me that I have to finish this relationship with Max. Why were the psychics so right and then so wrong with Max. I think I made a dramatic internal shift and no matter how good the sex is, it's not worth it. I feel edgy now because I have to go back home and end my relationship with Max. I'm avoiding dealing with Max. I've eaten so much the last couple of days to stuff down my denial. Wow, just saw a newspaper headline, "Ronald Regan dies at 93," end of an era.

At 2.40pm, Max was still in my bed, on his back, body splayed, my favourite blanket and cuddly toys banished to the floor and he's snoring like a banshee.

"I need to talk to you now," I said.

Max jolts up, disorientated then lets his head fall back onto the pillow. He pats the mattress.

"Come here," he said.

The room smelt stale, I could sense his dead parents scent, lurking around him, attached and in my space. I remained by the doorway, unable to step over the threshold into my own bedroom.

"Shall we get some breakfast?" he said.

"No Max, it's 2.45pm and I've already had two coffees and a

work meeting. I've been up since 9am," I said.

"So come back to bed," Max said.

"Let's talk in the garden," I said and hurried outside. I was scared there would be an explosive confrontation. I heard Max coughing and spluttering in the bathroom. He came out to the garden ten minutes later, blurry eyed.

"I need space," I said.

Max didn't say anything. He sat down on the chair across from me and lit up a cigarette.

"I have an issue with you staying in bed all day, smoking and drinking a bottle of Jack Daniels each night," I said. I didn't know how he'd react but I knew that I could make a run for it if he got angry and I had my cell phone in my hand.

"I agree. So?" Max said.

"I don't like you turning up in the middle of the night. I find it disrespectful," I said.

"Ah, putain!" he said.

"That's rude, I know it means bitch," I said.

"No, it means Jesus Christ," he said.

"It's over," I said.

"So let's see each other less," Max said.

"I don't feel good about that," I said.

"Do you want to go for coffee?" he said.

"No," I said.

"An orange juice?" he said. Wow he was tenacious.

"No," I said, feeling my power returning.

Max got up, kissed my head and then put his hand on top, like some type of Catholic blessing which I didn't ask for and didn't need.

"Ok sweetie," he said.

Five minutes later I got a text from Max, "Left my glasses."

I just couldn't get rid of him. I also found his cashmere sweater in my bedroom. I walked down the garden path with his belongings. I'd scoured the flat to make sure no Max items were remaining. He was waiting for me outside the gate, bars separating us. I felt as if I was in The Garden of Eden and he was wishing for the Gates of Paradise to be opened. Go to someone else you dangerous man. I danced with the devil, now I'm free, that was potential ruin for me.

7th June
9.50am: Tube

I had a full night's sleep! But I felt bad about Max, had I been too harsh?

I texted at 9.52pm, "I'm sorry babe. Really not my intention 2 hurt u. I'm happy I met u. Had some gr8 fun. Take care beauty x."

He replied at 9.59pm, "You did not."

I nearly responded, "Ok good," but decided best to leave it.

3.40pm

My tarot foretold the separation from Max because I had the three of swords, that's where Wayne comes in, and the future card was the queen of swords, me reclaiming my power. So what lies ahead with Wayne?

I feel very relaxed about men right now. No need, not even desire, just complacency. Off to the bank now to put in a £4,000 pay cheque!

CHAPTER 8

THE PENALTY SHOOT OUT

8th June
10.15am: Beau Cafe

Wow, it's going to be so hot today. I'm in Lacoste flip flops, Hennes turquoise shorts and a white "Be The Change," t-shirt kicking ass! The sky is aqua and the temperature is rising. Car alarms are sounding in the distance a warm wind like the Santa Ana is blowing. Last night I had a fantastic time with Petra, the psychic witch. We sat in the garden on the rug. She witnessed me begin a texting frenzy with Wayne. I raised my the stakes at 5.12pm with, "So, did yesterday meet or exceed your expectations?! I know I'm curious + naughty 4 asking…I had v eventful wknd and it's not wot u think…I've opted 4 celibacy!"

"Why the celibacy?" he texted at 5.20pm.

"Because then I don't have to be answerable 2 anyone! U still haven't answered my Q," I texted at 5.40pm.

"Well we didn't have sex coz of women's things! Nice day tho, lazy Sunday afternoon kinda stuff…its not going anywhere tho," he texted at 5.50pm.

Is he hitting on me?

"U mean you didn't get a BJ?!" I texted at 5.55pm and then did an immediate follow up "sry, v unlady like + out of character 4 me 2 ask…feeling rebellious!"

"Well I guess she should've at least offered eh! So come on wots happened?" Wayne replied at 6.18pm.

"I decided 2 let him go even though the sex was gr8…not worth loosing my freedom. Now I feel so much better!" I texted at 6.28pm.

"That means we can shag then?" Wayne said at 6.50pm.

"I told you already, I'm opting 4 celibacy. However would b gr8 2 hang w u and hear all your exciting news," I said at 10.05pm

"Would rather just have sex," Wayne said at 10.13pm, music to my ears.

"Shame…I like talking/texting w u," I said at 10.18pm.

"Well I didn't say we couldn't talk afterwards," he texted at 10.27pm.

"You mean you don't just roll over afterwards and go 2 sleep?" I said at 10.32pm.

"I suppose it depends how much u wear me out," he said at 10.43pm.

This is like virtual sex.

"Hypothetically speaking…if u were inside me…I'd b riding u so full on…well…I suppose the answer is you'd b lost 4 words. Remember I said hypothetical," I said at 11.34pm.

"Sounds good 2 me…hypothetically of course," he said at 11.49pm.

All these texts while having a lovely roast dinner in the garden followed by a shamanic healing initiation that I gave to Petra.

9th June
10.15am: Beau Cafe

I woke up to the phone ringing at 9am. Then lay there for another forty minutes. Just contemplating. Being, wondering, judging myself. Feeling incapable of achieving anything. On another level, I feel fantastic, strong happy and clear. There's this dualistic nature in me. Being good and bad. Feeling beautiful, fat and ugly all at the same time. I'm changing so fast, I don't know who I am. Friends are arriving and leaving my life very quickly. Some of my friendships feel plastic, sugar coated with worms and bugs in the middle. I'm in the void right now. I feel no spiritual being can help me in this moment. I feel like I've been let loose in the candy store a second time and God is saying: "Scarlet, don't binge because you know what will happen!"

Yes, I know. I'm feeling this personality arising in me "The Addict" and oh another, "The Shopaholic" who always needs another drink from the department store. £10 here, £20 there, oh it's only £100,000, so easily done.

As a teenager, I considered myself arrogant, cool, vulnerable, alone, hateful and spoilt.

In my early twenties, I fucking loved myself on the surface and thought I was very important. I was so pretentious. During this time, my relationship with my mother was terrible. But then I let go of the material world and dived into spirituality and that created even more denial. In my mid-twenties I felt liberated, rebellious and misunderstood. I started to believe I had all the answers to life, that I was the wisest of them all. Then I had this dawning realization years later that I was fucking up my life but it was too late. Now I feel the more I learn, the less I know. I am a human being. I am fallible. "What am I meant to be doing with my life?"

10th June
2.50pm: Tube

Energy feels so barbed on "The Psychic Show." It's lost its heart and soul because it has been flagellated. It's so sad. All the life force and nurturing that I put in has been squeezed out, suffocated. The river runs dry because it has been damned. I must move on gracefully. The budget is being severely cut. "Pleasure Zone," has won the day.

11th June
9.24am: Beau Cafe

I dreamt I was in a department store and saw a child, sitting on a ledge, playing. It started dropping toys down below. They fell many storeys. The child had nothing else to throw away, so it let itself descend from the ledge. The father ran to get his child but it was too late. I felt the extremity of his pain. I rushed behind him and placed my hands on his lower back for support. He cried. Those who loved him surrounded, consoled. It was devastating. How did such loss occur?

Last night I was at The District Club with Gary. As we arrived, who should be standing on the stairs but the actor Buck Bentley. We looked at each other. Then I signed in and went upstairs. I got lots of compliments about looking twenty-one. I wish! Drank three mojitos and then at 11.13pm succumbed and texted Wayne, "R u building that tantric energy…" worked my self into a drunken frenzy and followed up at 11.29pm "…or have u wasted it already…"

The lady sharing our table said not to send the second part of the text but it felt right to me. Wayne didn't text back! Maybe he was out on the pull. Wayne is a cheeky fucker.

So what now? It's time to get my ass in gear, manifest and stop messing around. Black Cat threw up this morning. I'm about to go and do the show now. I'm a bit hung over. It'll be fine, fuck it, life is good. Want to have sex again soon.

4.10pm

Fantastic show today with Petra. Didn't expect that at all. Great fun. Sang "Pretty Woman," and said, "Hollywood, come to Hollywood, where all your dreams may come true…" Also sang the theme to "Star Wars," and gave a blindingly brilliant response to a mega sceptic Scottish man. Was hysterical. Tired now. Think I need a snooze, maybe in the garden would be good. Lots to do. Bought Dolphin and Mermaid cards and my first card was "Blessed Change."

12th June
10.20am: Home

Feet up on sofa. Listening to Outkaste. Hangover of four mojitos and smoky hair. Waiting for Oscar to show up. Oh my God, dreamt I saw my ex-love Drew Connor. We really connected and kissed so tenderly, it was lovely, like we were in love again.

13th June
2.22am: Home

Feel very vulnerable. Night turned out different to how I expected. Went onto District Club, bumped into Shane Bentley who said he snogged me in a nightclub in front of my friends when I was seventeen and that I was really embarrassed. I don't remember. We talked and talked and I didn't contact Wayne. So now Wayne's playing hard to get. When Shane insisted he drop me back home in his black jeep, I felt guilty. Especially when he lent over and kissed me passionately with Scissor Sister's "Comfortably Numb" playing in the background. Felt nice but I was thinking of how I was meant to be kissing Wayne.

14th June
12.25am: Bed

I bumped into Giorgio talking to two women outside the Westbourne earlier. Carla thought he was gorgeous.

"Why haven't you called? I want to have you over for dinner. I'll cook. Just give me twenty-four hours notice," Giorgio said.

Italian men are seriously good cooks. Very tempting.

"Do you still have my number?" Giorgio said.

I played it cool and said, "I think so."

"I'm sure you'll find it," he said.

Not calling Giorgio this weekend was a good move. He says he travels a lot to Spain, Switzerland and France. Carla thinks he's a playboy. Maybe. I am a playful girl. Speaking of play, I don't like the game Wayne is playing with me now. I feel we're going into a penalty shoot out and that's not my style. I'm guilty of playing too hard and wearing myself out. Time to recuperate and step back. I think my moon-time (period), is anytime soon.

Why didn't Wayne want the Sunday shag?

Wayne texted me during football and I got cocky. He said at 8.05pm, "Hey babe, u watchin the footie? Enjoyed last nite, u r v naughty, thanx."

I replied at 9.39pm at end of game final score: England 1, France 2. "Yes watched it...on a positive note, I think we played better together than England xx."

Wayne said at 11.31pm, "Well, that was a win win situation!"

I texted at 11.32pm, "so u coming 2 get your watch?"

He texted at 11.42pm, "Oh yeah, guess I'll have 2. Don't know when I'll be able 2 tho…"

I texted at midnight "yellow card 4 your play...I thought u liked taking a shot at goal…guess you're more of a mid-fielder."

Jade, Bella and Juan, a very handsome half American Brazilian, ex-super model stood on the street outside The District Club doing a post-game mortem, rather disappointed by the outcome of this text session. Juan offered to come back and have sex with me instead. I was close to considering it a "yes."

It's now 12.45am and forty-five minutes has passed since I sent Wayne the text. Next time it's a red card and he'll be sent off and won't be able to play again…shame.

11.09am

After last night's dolphin & mermaid card reading, healing set in. The cards mirrored I was to spend some time alone, albeit one night. The past was to "Wait," the present "Contemplation Time," and the future, "Healing Heart."

In my dream this morning, it was Bill's heart I needed to heal. He came to me. I was lying in bed and he crept up behind me and he tried to slip inside me. I sensed him. I must watch my back and let go of the past to move forward positively. When I said "no," to making love with him, he was devastated and began to cry. I placed my hands on his heart. I feel the pain in my spleen now. All these men who need healing, and the women to. We play so many games and something that sets out as fun results in someone getting hurt in the end. It always seems to end.

There is a pretty squirrel sitting up in a tree eating. I think it's a she, on her haunches, leaning against the bark, nibbling nuts while I eat peanut butter and jam on toast in the garden. She's watching me and I'm observing her. A breeze blows, it's divine. I've made myself latte and have to get ready soon to go do the show. Arrive by 11.45am, go Live at 12.30pm. Hello squirrel. I worked with the self-healing bottle and Native American stone that Karen gave me as a gift. I put Wayne's watch on my healing altar and the fairy wishing stone on top so all his dreams may come true as well as mine and he may open to allowing more love into his life. Wayne is very cute, definitely doesn't look thirty-three, more like twenty-seven. So angels, I'm putting a request for Wayne to receive love and healing now because he deserves it and has a beautiful heart. Also for Bill, lovely Juan, the Calvin Klein model who I met last night, Gary, Jason, Giorgio, Shane Bentley, Max who needs a lot and Stefano as well. And lovely Tom Spiegel who invited me over for coffee. He's very cute but the ex-heroine addiction thing totally puts me off. Scary or I might go there. Sex would be pretty full on with him, probably too much.

My friend, Jade was in my dream singing this hip hop song and she'd dyed her hair peroxide blonde. I was so excited because she'd finally had a big success with her music and a producer out of the U.S. called Chad helped her. She was dancing on stage and I was so happy she'd made it into the pop charts.

It's 11.30am now and I have to get ready although I'm feeling lazy, tired and contemplative, needing to recharge my energy. Spent £500 in Yates & Buchanan on beautiful moccasin boots from a Canadian reservation and an amazing necklace by Antonia de Venetto. Quick shower, make-up and I'm off to do the show!

12.05pm: Westbourne Park Road Tube

First time I'm almost late for a show. Usually I have time to spare. Is this a subconscious "fuck you?!"

I'm thinking about Wayne but I'm feeling more relaxed inside now. Weights are being lifted from me. I'm wearing my beautiful new necklace, which I've had a lot of compliments on already. It's so stunning, makes me feel like a million dollars. I felt guilty for spending money on myself. Yes it's money I earned but I wanted to delude myself and put it on my credit card. Want to get more responsible and focused. I am having the best summer ever.

3.55pm: Ciao Café

Buying a Barbie Mermaid doll in John Lewis triggered off a lot of sensations in my belly. I feel very awkward and funny, off centre, scared and let down. Will people find me childish? Am I irresponsible? I have PMS. I'm trying to think of it as pre-moon-synchronicity. I feel tetchiness, irritability and frustration rising in my body. Bumped into Giorgio's friend Giuseppe as Carla and I were leaving the Circle Club. I have out of control angry feelings. After empowerment, I feel powerless, like Wayne is trying to steal my energy. Well I'm claiming my power. I am power! That's mirror work for me to do when I get home. Had no lunch, didn't feel hungry. I feel angry and resentful about my position on "The Psychic Show." I don't like being used. I must protect myself. I feel vulnerable and my womb is aching a lot. When I get my moon-time, all of Max and Wayne's energy will be released from me.

15th June

Dreamt at 7am that Shane Bentley had a charm bracelet for me, with all these beautiful gifts on it. He told me his dream is to have a lot of money so he can have a home and land. His dad's a film producer. He lives round the corner on Ladbroke Grove. I decided to text him from Jade's restaurant at 9.39pm, "Hey u…enjoyed re-connecting at District Club + that u played my fav scissor sisters song x"

He texted me straight back, "me 2 – Great 2 see u again. Spk soon. Xx"

Decided to text Giorgio at 10.14pm, "Well I hope your cooking is better than how you played football tonite…let's c if u live up 2 the standards you've set…ciao Scarlet x"

Italy 0, Denmark 0 and he still hasn't replied. Probably because he doesn't know what to say and he's too cool to rise to the bait.

Funny, how I magnetise in particular people. I don't bump into Matt now because we're vibrating on a different frequency. I wonder if Matt will get through his shit?

Thankfully I haven't bumped into Bill. Candy, my chirpy Texan friend phoned last night from LA, so lovely to speak with her. We're in very different headspace because she is now married and I'm single but we had a meeting of minds.

Yesterday I felt like a stranger on my own show, that I'd been ousted and my power had been taken away. Eric felt distanced from me but I held my poise and grace.

I'd love to tell Barry to fuck off and get a taste of his own medicine. In the most delightful way!

Secretly I'd love Wayne to appreciate me. His watch has stopped ticking. Time is standing still. The next move is his. Off to the show now and then got to stop obsessing about men!

7.45pm: The Circle Club

Shit! Just missed a call from Max. He texted this afternoon at 4pm saying, "Back from France, how are u?"

I didn't reply. He left a phone message, "Hi Scarlet, it's Max, got a new job, starting in September, just phoning to see how you are, like to meet up…"

16th June
1.57am: Bed

Max phoned again at 11pm but I'd missed the call. I only noticed when I got in the cab. He must have tuned into the manifestation circle of juicy sex, love, passion and calling in angels and Cupid that Oscar, Carla, Mary and I were doing in the corner of the hallway at Circle Club. A guy that fancied Carla came up to her just as we finished and asked for her phone number. She was so embarrassed. She was also on the hunt for Giuseppe, Giorgio's Italian sidekick. Must set them up! So as I went home in a minicab a withheld number showed up on my caller display and I automatically assumed it was Dad.

"Hi Scarlet, it's Max, why didn't you return my call?"

Hello, I broke up with you.

"I was in the Circle Club, you can't speak on the phone in there," I said.

I felt very defensive. A text and now three calls, Max was determined.

"Yeah, I got a new job at Mann," Max said.

"Great," I said.

"You know who they are?" he said.

"No," I said. He expects me to know?

"Uh they're only a multi-million dollar turnover company, very prestigious," he said.

"Great," I said again really not impressed or interested, just uncomfortable and wanting to get off the phone. My throat is hurting at the thought of Max smoking fifty cigarettes. It's truly passive. I see "the Ashtray," in my bed and it horrifies me. I smell his dead mother and father in my bedroom, it scares, repulses and horrifies me.

"So how are you?" Max said.

"Good," I said, not wanting to engage any further. Now home, I hear a noise outside and pray it isn't him. Thank God I didn't go to France. He's not interested in how I am, he's invested in me being interested in him and getting laid. No woman turns him down, there has to be some mistake.

"I was rude to you," Max said.

"Yes you were," I said.

"Listen, I'm with my lawyer, call me when you get home," he said.

"Ok," I say and am horrified by my response as I get off the phone. Who's with their lawyer doing business at midnight?

After texting and calling four times he said so casually, "Call me when you get in," trying to regain some sort of control over me? It's just not going to happen. Max held out for almost nine days and then succumbed. I later discovered how he's treated past women, a hairdryer up some girl's ass and then switching it on! Fuck that's disgusting. His violent snoring and I can't imagine having good sex with him now. So I called Oscar for help.

"Leave it," he said, but I knew Max would call again or worse still, turn up.

"I've got to text, get closure. What do I say?" I said.

Oscar is so on the ball. "Need time to myself right now, catch up soon," he suggested.

I added to the front of the text, "congratulations on job," to soften it. I don't want to reject him badly. I feel guilty. I feel his vulnerability and I don't want him to feel bad. If he'd respected my boundaries, maybe it all would have been different.

17th June

I wish I had Nancy's flat to myself for the summer, my own glorious space. I'm so gutted that I'm moving to the basement but grateful to receive at the same time. Perhaps I must set my sights higher. Currently sorting out my financial stuff. It's taking a lot of time. Was tempted to use my credit card the other day, but didn't. Internet is working again, only didn't when Max was here. Confirmation I can't have him in my life.

18th June

Feel like absolute shit! Started to feel unwell at Jason Briar's while watching football. Just too full on and then that disgusting food from the local Chinese restaurant finished me off. Terrible flu. Shaking, shivers, dizziness, aching bones, almost felt like going to throw up earlier. Too much alcohol the night before, four glasses of champagne and three District Club shots and then vodka cranberry. I caned it and now I'm paying the price. Had fashion launch party earlier in the night with Sedrick, Kitty and Jade. We went to this Moroccan restaurant down in a basement with very loud music. Nice but boring. Met some of the Saudi Arabian royal family. Then just us girls went back to Notting Hill. Stopped at The Cock & Bull, virtually empty so of course we were destined for The District Club and that's where it all kicked off, and we're not talking football! It was busy inside. Saw Tom Spiegel and met Jade's friend Dean. Bored and ready to leave, I turned around and Charlie Silver was standing there.

"Charlie Silver!" I said.

"Scarlet Ray," Charlie said.

Neither one of us had planned to meet but the night felt fated and now I'm suffering from going to be at 4.30am and a connection of romance and passion while wearing my Native American boots. Wow I feel so terrible and am about to do show.

22nd June

I've reconnected to Great Spirit in a powerful way. When Steven Stone, the Oxford psychic said "more depths of despair."

He was right. Felt like I was dying on Saturday night. I had a Woody Allen moment where I thought perhaps I might have meningitis or SARS, after watching "The Sixth Sense," alone and crying my eyes out, I thought, "What if I'm already dead!

This morning as I ate an orange, drank hot water with lemon and spooned Greek bio Live yogurt with honey into my mouth, I listened to Outkaste's brilliant album. Each song made me think of a different man. The words, "I can't wait to get you home," and "I just love your sexy ass," made me think of Wayne. When I heard, "I think I'm in love again, you are the brightest one," I thought of Charlie Silver.

Hope I'm well enough to go to the England Portugal quarter final on Thursday. Yes we won against Croatia four goals to two!

12.45pm

So I'm on the psychic phone line and I feel I've been relegated. This is frustrating for me. Barry's sitting in the office and I feel very angry. I've let myself be disempowered. Why do I feel so shit? Because I set this show up and now I'm losing control, it's slipping away. I was offish with Tiffany and Petra when I arrived because I felt pushed out. Must rest later. Take time out for me. Re-evaluate what I want. Agh! Now I'm in the small box on the TV screen and I swore I'd never allow that to happen but it has! Oh I feel shit! Can't do this. Just can't, doesn't feel right. What mask am I wearing? "Wounded healer," I'm still healing others and I'm not healing myself!

23rd June
12.10pm: Home

I'm recovering from the flu, listening to Chilled Ibiza Gold. It's cold but refreshing outside, the wind rustling the trees is comforting to me, like a lullaby and the music is taking me to distant exotic lands with beaches where you can sunbathe topless and live in the coral filled blue sea. I had the gift of a blissful stone therapy treatment last night. It felt incredible to have a massage. What was divine is the guy Dirk, a Russian ex-athlete was so spot on with the pressure of his touch. I could feel the beauty of my body. I could sense all the curves, smoothness and definition of the hot stones as they glided over my skin. The cold stones invigorated my skin, making my body tingle inside and out. I felt a million dollars. Then had a shower in a shower gel called Stillness, it was blissful.

24ᵗʰ June

Wayne phoned yesterday. Fuck why am I obsessed by men right now? Is there something wrong with me? Why do I constantly need to talk about men? Am I sexually frustrated? No, maybe, well I think it's just the drove coming in after so many years of drought. Why do men want such a chase? Why can't they just be attracted and want me?

Wayne is a strange and dangerous man for me. He presses all my buttons. Of course he phoned when I least expected it. I was standing with Gary on the corner of Oxford Street, having just finished the show.

"So you're not talking with me," Wayne said.

"I answered the phone," I said.

"Yeah but that's reactive," he said.

"I'm just pissed off!" I said, but I don't think I can stay angry with him for long. I felt guilty when Wayne said, "Why you show my text to other people?"

He's right but everyone does it. Don't they?

I've worked Wayne into a whirlwind of fantasy and false intrigue. This morning I used my rabbit, then went back to sleep and dreamt of using my rabbit and being on this sexual plateau of pleasure and when I woke up, I used it again and gave myself a second orgasm and I hadn't even had breakfast. I must be getting better because my appetite and sex drive are returning with a vengeance.

25ᵗʰ June
3pm: Oxford Street Tube

I had a really good show, some challenging stuff came up also. Like a woman who lost her sister in a car accident and having to think on the spot and send her healing Live on Air. Pretty full on, painful and me having to then lift the tone of the show gently again. It is lovely and beautiful that we are helping people. Sometimes giving a "no," answer is hard. I'm keeping positive with the psychic Deidre Poole, even though I know she slagged me off. I think she may feel bad for the negative things she says about people and this is what keeps her weight on.

I've reconnected with Stefano. I'm disconnected from Matt. I haven't heard from Giorgio. I've got a strange dynamic going with Wayne. Charlie Silver hasn't called me back. If I ask anything of him, he can't cope. Yet, he wants to connect with me, every time I let go energetically. Why?

Last night Jason Briar hugged me, then kissed me good night on the lips. I contemplated that I could have snogged him but it probably isn't a good idea. I don't want to have sex with him because I know a relationship wouldn't work with him.

I have to have a rest before going out tonight. Crucial. Need to get balanced and chi gong would be a great idea, plus going to the gym. I'm about to meet Kate, will be good to see her!

27th June
6pm: Home

It's all been go! Gary, Jason and I drank Jack Daniels on the rocks and talked about life, listening to "The Doors," till the sun streamed in through the windows of Jason's basement flat. I walked back in Native American boots, black dress, white raincoat in broad daylight. I knew once my head hit the pillow, I'd collapse so I went home, instead changed into a bikini and shorts and went swimming at the gym. I must have been the only person there who hadn't gone to bed yet. Eventually slept at 11am.

28th June
10.50am: Beau Café

Pain au chocolat and latte for breakfast. I am not motivated right now.

After talking last night with Bill's mum, I discover he is still stuck in exactly the same patterns. His mum said he went to the Job Centre yet he's not accepting a job offer from Anna's café. Victoria's stocked up his groceries again. She said he now owes her

£800. He'd be homeless on the street if his brother didn't keep bailing him out. Oh and Victoria bought him £50 sandals for a holiday in France. She said Bill said he felt terrible. He's a pathetic little boy in a forty-year-old body.

I've been wishing time away so Wayne may want to see me again. Wayne what is it that attracts me to you so much? Is it that I can't have you? I know he's a tonic. He peps me up but then I come down, because I'm looking to be filled by his energy rather than creating my own fire. I must fill up with my own self-created life force. Give him the opportunity to come to me, if he so chooses.

A letter to Wayne's soul:

Dear Wayne,

It is Monday morning and I am on the train. I am sorry for my past behaviour. I have desperately been trying to control you, the outcome of us. Wanting you to want me and feeling devastated and rejected when you don't fill the holes in me. I have made demands of you at a time when you are going through your own challenges. I really want to have sex with you again. I desire you. I want you to want me. But I know I have to want myself. Love, Scarlet.

29th June
11.50am

Just realized there is a very superficial side to me. Wow, I'm judging this guy Bryan on his star sign. He's Aquarius. I hoped he wasn't, discovered he was. Because I fear as good looking as he is, my thought form is there may not be sexual chemistry with Aquarians. So why is it that even though Wayne is so naughty, I see him doing no wrong?

I dreamt I was making love with Jeremy, my sexy Scorpio boyfriend before Bill beneath a huge rainbow. So I decided to phone him. He answered the call. I told him the dream, of how we were making love and it was really nice. He said, "Yeah, it's surreal because it feels so real when having erotic dreams. You were in my dream the other night also. We were having sex."

I also dreamt I wanted Bill back in my life and Dad went ballistic with me for my decision. I was for the first time subconsciously considering taking Bill back because I wondered how I would ever meet anyone again who I would spend the rest of my life with. Would I? Will I?

Big black storm clouds on the horizon now. Please don't rain. I'm on the roof of the Circle Club. Today's show was incredible. Did a Live Akashic Records guided meditation. People got really powerful stuff through. I asked the viewers to visualize a book, see the page number they opened it on and to determine what was in the book. Words, symbols or a blank page? And then the type of writing instrument they were holding? Pen, pencil, paintbrush. Magical stuff. Going to do treasure chest meditation on Friday's show to clear people's heart pathways. Just bought my second copy of Soul Love by Sanaya Roman. Last time I read it, had so many miracles occur. Why did I dream of making love with Jeremy and not with Wayne or Charlie? It's triggering off my solar plexus with butterflies, so lifting the energy into my heart. It's my last night in Nancy's bed. So much old and new energy is erupting and I don't want to feel out of control.

1st July
11.40am: Ladbroke Grove Tube

I'm happy Nancy is home. Although I've moved to the basement, I feel really good things are going to happen. After having dinner with Jason, I confessed I wanted to snog him.

"Scarlet, it's crossed my mind to," Jason said.

"So why can't we just kiss," I said.

"Because then we'd end up having sex," he said.

"No we won't," I said.

"Yes we would," he said, putting emphasis on the word "would." Jason diagnosed that we needed to get this feeling out of our systems.

I think he's right and very switched on. Jason left at 12.45am, I returned Tom Spiegel's call.

"So, you want me to come over?" Tom said.

"Ok," I said rather than "yes."

We met at the end of the garden. A hedgehog was outside on the street. As I opened the gate for Tom, the hedgehog scuttled along with him into Eden, where my engagement ring was now buried amongst the herbs and roses in the earth, dancing with spider's power and dreaming the earth.

Tom snogged me, "hello". He tasted of cigarettes. I perceive him as a bad boy. We went into the inner garden and sat on the bench where I'd kissed Charlie so beautifully. The setting was romantic but Tom was not. It's all about sex with him. He's another Scorpio like me but the chemistry isn't there, like it wasn't with Bryan, the Aquarius. It's play for me, a distraction. A desire to be filled, my senses ignited by male passion merging with my female desire but no energy is matching mine, only Charlie and Wayne who are distant and I wonder why? I want more. I can't find it in these men. Where's Giorgio? He didn't call yet. Shame, perhaps he feels about me how I feel about Bryan and Tom.

The night before I had a lovely dinner with Bryan at The Circle Club and then we took the 23 bus home together. He texted me three times yesterday. He's very good looking but something feels clinical to me. Squeaky-clean. Perhaps that's why I snogged Tom, to bring back in the naughtiness. Tom's forty-one-years-old and Bryan's twenty-eight. I looked at Tom at one point and saw this very vulnerable hurt child needing love. This scared me because I know I can't give him what he wants and I don't want to imbue or imbibe his energy.

1.20pm

So I'm Live in the studio, sitting on the phone in the box on screen. I got the "Empowerment" card which feels positive. Did the treasure chest heart meditation, it was amazing. I love the shift of consciousness coming in. No callers online at present. I'm only doing three shows next week. I'm staying on at Nancy's and paying

£100 per week rent plus half the utilities. I feel an exciting energy of acting coming in, a new horizon. It will be interesting to see what flows in next.

2nd July
11.15am: Ladbroke Grove Tube

As I walked down Ladbroke Grove, I noticed these kids walking to school and I got a flash of Wayne as a twelve-year-old in the classroom. Cute, cheeky, unconfident with girls and again a flash of Tom Spiegel as the insecure and sensitive nine-year-old, totally misunderstood.

As a teenager Wayne was not a leader, he was in the pack but ranked number two. He didn't get the best girl, he got the second best girl because he felt he didn't deserve the best. Psychic insight: he not so much had an ugly ducking complex, more of a "I'm a butterfly but I don't have the mechanics of wings." So today at thirty-three-years-old, Wayne is quietly confident. He's scared. Wayne wants to be in control of every emotion within and the women around him. He also has a wild untamed streak, that is where I come in. Wayne intellectualizes passion. Scarlet you're angry with yourself so why do you want this man? What are his special qualities? Was it the one orgasm he gave you? When he took control, it turned you on. Why was that? My shadows arise with a vengeance, the unloved parts of myself cry, yearn for love. I stand still in the meadow, my eye is watching sideways on. I'm black and glistening with sweat from the sunlight above. Some flies move around me. I swish them away with my tail. I know I am a fine powerful specimen. I am free.

"See, look at my power, I'm a winner. I'm one of the players, back me, I'm your winning horse."

I feel like I'm a wild mare and Wayne is a beautiful pony. Funny, it doesn't look like that on the surface and in our physical actions but on a soul level it is my truth. I want to run freely in a beautiful meadow with a stallion like me. So we may dance and play and rest and work and travel together through time and space in pure love. Charlie Silver you have a key!

Moved into the basement at Nancy's. It's a really nice room but not the same as being in her beautiful bedroom. I still haven't put in my invoice for payment. Why am I not valuing my worth? I'm going to be betrayed. People are going to walk all over me. I feel out of control. My clothes have no storage now and my room is in chaos but I made a pretty altar with the pink sari Paula gave me, some white and pink flowers, a fig candle, a light bulb I found in the laundry room for the lamp and my abalone shell filled with jewellery and a quartz crystal. But I want to get my belongings back from Bill. Interesting that I feel I don't deserve to receive them, even though they're mine.

3.15pm

Great show and did brilliant readings. Doing the Soul Love sub-personality meditation was incredible. Same symbolism came through for two readings incorporating the willow tree representing a need for flexibility and grieving.

I no longer fear being needed, about my life changing, or being rejected for being different. I decided to speak with my angel within.

"Why are you sabotaging yourself?" the angel said.

"I don't know. Because I feel unworthy, that my ideas aren't that great," I said.

"How could you manifest your beautiful art?" the angel said.

"I don't know, I feel very vulnerable, alone and misunderstood, that my work will be shunned. I hate myself. I'm angry with and at the world," I said.

"How can you forgive yourself?" the angel said.

"I can't. I'm disempowered," I said.

"Who says so?" the angel said.

"Me," I said.

"Can you open to change?" the angel said.

"No!" I said.

"May I give you a gift?" the angel said.

"No…yes…maybe…I don't know, I don't deserve," I said.

"Well I'm giving it to you anyway. Open your hands," the angel said.

I reluctantly open my hands. "What is it?" I said.

"You know what it is," the angel said.

"I don't," I said.

"Look closer," the angel said.

"It's a smaller miniature version of me," I said.

"Exactly," the angel said, a broad smile upon her glowing features.

"What do I do with it?" I said.

"Know your greatness and talent to be shared and gifted into the world," the angel said.

So I thought the angel would be ok if I asked one more question, "I'd like to meet Wayne but what if he rejects me?"

"He won't. Only you may reject you. Keep your heart open, lift the energies and speak your heart's desires," the angel said.

So I sent Wayne a text at 3.35pm, "Hi beauty, tuning in 2 c how u r…also I'd like to give you your watch."

I know Nancy believes he's seeing someone but I want to keep being true to my feelings and in my power.

3rd July
10am: Nancy's Sofa

I had sex with Wayne out in the beautiful central garden last night. I sat on the bench in the cool night air where I'd kissed Charlie Silver and Wayne went down on me. The alcohol was swirling in my head as his tongue circled my clit. It felt so empowering to receive and be honoured like that and I allowed my throat charka to be open. Then he stood up and I took him in my mouth, it felt really good, very sexy, I so enjoyed kissing him there and then he sat on the bench and I straddled him, his glass of beer perched on the side. He put on a condom and then pulled my Myla panties to the side and plunged inside me. It felt the most natural thing in the world and the night air was crisp fresh and sobering enough to connect me to my body. Wayne didn't last too long. For the first time he came inside me. It was lovely and then he stayed in me for quite some time. I don't know how long but I massaged his head, felt the millions of thoughts of anxiety he's been storing and my fingers released them while his head leaned forward into my chest. It gave me a lot of pleasure seeing Wayne so relaxed. I asked the last time he had received a massage. He said "a long time ago."

I sent him an outrageous text at 4.30am once he'd left saying, "Thanx 4 garden experience…going 2 dream about u going down on me coz u do it so…"

Didn't hear back, probably because it's an overload for him. I need to honour his boundaries and give him the space.

3.50pm

Met with Bill for the first time in three months. It was really strange and good. Felt like I'd last seen him yesterday and I unexpectedly became rather emotional and vulnerable. I shed tears as I watched him look at me, the loss. I see Bill wants to do his best. We met at Café Gold on Goldborne Road and he paid for the coffees. We had a lovely conversation, very healing. We were dressed practically the same in tan army pants, brown t-shirts with hints of blue thrown in. We talked about anger, love and money. I feel sad at the loss of us. We then stopped into see Anna together, like the old days. She was glowing, all dressed in red with bright red lipstick, expecting her baby in six weeks around the time of Nancy's birthday. I cried in there as Bill and I held hands. I told him I buried the engagement ring amongst the herbs and roses of Nancy's garden. Bill said he felt that I shone so brightly, he couldn't see himself and now he was finding his feet again.

"We're like two magnets that rub off against each other but don't stick," Bill said.

Yes we had history. It felt strange sitting with him, knowing I had Wayne inside me the night before, out in the garden and no longer being physically intimate with Bill. Oh the pain, when we hugged goodbye. I sensed him protecting himself, scared to feel our connection, not wanting to get hurt. I love him still, a love like ours doesn't just die. It will take me, us time to heal.

Bill said we wouldn't have met if we both weren't strong. I don't know. I need quiet time, TLC, love and happiness. I need to get on my feet and organize my bedroom space. I'm getting my fleeces and Native American painting that Bill gave me as a Birthday gift. He's also giving me some money, that's positive. Big blocks are now receding. The breeze is rustling, speaking through the trees. It's calming in my time of disconcertion. I wonder what next? I'm going to take a little catnap now and recharge. Regroup. My solar plexus are muddled. Wayne, Charlie and Matt aren't the answers. I must grieve my loss and love for Bill and be gentle with myself because I feel ugly and fat today.

6th July
12.20am

Wayne texted me back on Saturday night, "Enjoyed the magic garden too. Didn't expect 2 find such a nice bush there. Crude I know!"

I like that he said, "magic garden," because it is so special and on some level he's acknowledging a spiritual connection even if it's unconscious.

Nancy and I went to the gym, swam and steamed and then ate lovely fish and salad for dinner followed by a Divine Will meditation. We talked till 2am and I got up on Sunday morning at 8am to meet Kate Tanworth at Paddington Station. While waiting for the 23 bus, bumped into Dick Jones and had a chat. It was good to see him settled in married life and I was very relieved I am not. I bought two pain au chocolat and a pain au raisin from Beau Café.

"You going to eat all of those?" the guy said, handing me the full brown paper bag.

"Obviously not," I said.

He'd hit a nerve in me but as he smiled, I then realized this was his way of flirting. I was the thinnest I'd been in years.

Kate and I had a great chat on the train while drinking our lattes. People eavesdropped as we talked drugs, sex, more sex, men and love. Her friend Frank picked us up from Slough and we zoomed off in his black Landrover to his house. He got out a block of hash which Kate eroded from 10am through till 11.30pm. I have never seen anyone smoke quite so many splifs. Denny, their friend said Kate and Stuart were like Cheech and Chong…oh yes! As we sat out in the glorious sunlight at 6.30pm just off the Isle of Wight, the boat wouldn't restart. Kate responded by rolling another joint and said she felt stoned. How could she not?

I ate a serious amount of food that day. Definitely the "munchies". I didn't smoke but was inhaling a fair amount of smoke passively from my time being in the car and on the boat. I had a chicken drumstick, salt and vinegar squares on the boat, followed by roast pork with crackling, apple and cinnamon sauce, potato puree and vegetables at the Jolly Sailor known for its appearance in the movie, "Howard's End." Oh and then a desert of gooseberry and ginger crumble with custard, bread and butter pudding with ice cream and red wine. On the boat got hungry again and had two Penguin chocolate biscuits, drank two Ribenas. When the boat wouldn't start and we had to wait for Sea Rescue ate another pack of salt and vinegar crisps. Thankfully the engine cooled down and Stuart got the boat started again, hero and then I got a text from Giorgio, the sexy Italian, "Ciao Scarlet, I am still away. Back on Sunday, love to catch up. Kiss."

On the way back in the car I finally decided to text, "Yes :)" at 8pm.

He then replied, "Who is there?" at 8.30pm. That confused me.

"Scarlet. Just been on boat in Isle of W…lovely + now on way 2 London…u back from Italy?" I texted at 8.33pm

"Just arrived from Paris…" he said at 8.40pm.

I said, "Wow…I'm in the car + just seen 3 rainbows… welcome back," at 8.48pm.

He said, "I'm going home to watch the last bit of the footie final…If you like we can have a drink when you get in…" at 8.58pm.

I took a while to reply because I think the passive joint smoking was affecting my clarity and we were at Stuart's film location office and I didn't know what was going on, as we did salutes to the sunset, arms outstretched.

I eventually replied, "Hey babe, let's make another day as still with friends…arriving late. Could meet Friday," at 9.25pm

He didn't reply. Did he feel blown out? Maybe he just thought he'd wait till later on in the week. Being psychic doesn't mean I know everything. I suppose some things I'm not meant to know in advance. Very relieved to get home in one piece as, Frank and Kate were so caned. We ended up on a very long shortcut. Spoke with Jason who's been pulling for England and Greece won the European Cup. Going past the pub in the car on the way home, saw it cordoned off. Think someone was murdered. Nancy came in and we drank tea. I got very defensive about the tumble dryer not working which we resolved over coffee on Monday morning.

Monday night at 10.05pm got an interesting mystery text, "If you're so psychic who am I, what am I thinking and what are the lottery numbers for next Saturday?"

That totally threw me and with my cousin Natalie's assistance I replied, "33, 12, 6, 44, 9, 7" at 11.13pm.

I wonder if it was Rick Jenkins coz I texted him at 8.48pm, "You in London?"

Definitely wouldn't be Matt or Wayne. Rather flirtatious. I've received no reply and am now intrigued. I think they may have used someone else's phone. I don't know, I'll ask one of the psychics on the show. I feel pretty good. Not attached to Wayne but love to see him soon as I haven't had a single orgasm for well over a week. It's time for sleep and maybe a date with my rabbit because I need release.

CHAPTER 9

THE LOTTERY STALKER

7th July
12.15am: Home

Feel quite vulnerable now. I revealed to Dad at dinner that I felt challenged by my living situation, I knocked over and broke the champagne glass that was full. Must keep my thoughts positive. Drank over half the bottle and some 1947 Armagnac that was lovely and listened to childhood tapes of how Chinese restaurants exist in heaven and have lots of tables. That everyone lives to 100 years old and children can't die. My birth was announced on Radio 2 after playing, "An Old Fashioned Love Song," and straight after the announcement, the theme to The Godfather was played which won lots of Oscars in 1972. It was the American elections and Edward Heath was Prime minister and Bobby Moore was cleared of pressed charges for stealing a gold bracelet in a hotel room in Bogota, Columbia. Dad sounded so proud as the plumy newsreader rejoiced in Dad's happiness at 1.15am on Air. Dad continued to play all the tapes of me. I talked so easily, never short of words or confidence, constantly doing impressions. From Margaret Thatcher to Tommy Cooper, Kenny Everett and Miss Piggy while Dad responded as Fussy Bear. I could talk at two years old but not very clearly and even at six years old, I missed out the number eleven when counting. It's like it didn't exist and yet it's such an important number to me now because when I see it, I feel new doorways are opening.

On the way home texted Wayne at 11.56pm, "Hi gorgeous…have a brilliant shoot – know your directing will shine…looking 4wd 2 the movies."

Felt ultra vulnerable after sending it because he's not directing till Thursday but wanted to connect on a positive friendship level without pressure or conditions.

He replied at 12.26am "Thanx babe."

I think it's best to leave it now and let him connect with me when he's ready.

Matt hasn't replied to me. Why? I may be psychic but what do I know? That I feel really fucking sensitive. Haven't heard from Charlie. It's like I'm regrouping. All the shards coming back together. I'm making myself whole again.

So the Mystery texter. Well he texts in exactly the same tone as Wayne and when I dowsed I got such a strong yes on Wayne, I guess because I wanted it to be him. So does dowsing work? No and yes. I got it so off but not so off because I did intuit Kate had given my number to someone.

Mystery texter said at 1.27pm "Will you go out for a drink with me if I don't win?"

I got the text after turning my phone on at the studio and became paranoid it was a mad stalker texting from the TV show. Serge, the technician checked the phone number but it didn't match.

I decided to reply at 4.33pm, "Will u give me half the money if you win?" I'm now feeling flustered and intrigued.

He said, "No," at 4.43pm.

I am shocked and disgusted and relieved. He has a bad attitude. I don't have to deal with this curiosity anymore.

At 4.44pm he texted, "Just kidding. Think I'd have to. Are these numbers for Wed or Sat or shall I do both?"

I texted at 4.54pm, "U asked for Saturday's numbers…by way I'm not into predictions…I believe in making own choices…but I do know u r v cheeky." I succumbed to a follow up text at 5.04pm "…and wondering why u don't want 2 reveal yourself?"

"Oops, probably think I'm some kind of lottery fixated stalker," he said at 5.32pm.

Aaggghh, he's driving me insane and then I get this weird feeling to phone Kate.

"Babe, did you give my number to anyone?" I said.

"Yes, Ken, did he call you?" Kate said.

Bingo, I've discovered the identity of the mystery texter.

9.50am: Beau Café

No TV show today except another opportunity to tidy my space that is truly chaotic. I'm also feeling worthless because no men are pursuing me who I'm into. I'm quite superficial thinking about men so much. This morning lying in bed, I reminisced about Max pushing me against the wardrobe and taking me from behind, then throwing me on the floor for more passionate steamy sex. But I don't want to go there with him. It's a part of me that's searching for deeper love and not knowing how to arrive there. How do I find the love?

3.15pm

Feel extremely vulnerable and unsettled. After having the flat to myself, I feel oh so fragmented and challenged. I want to spread my wings and fly. I feel limited. I don't have the bedroom space I desire. I'm inhabiting a space that is not mine, so transient. I'm unable to settle. How do I anchor? Am I meant to? I so want my own place. How do I manifest this? My heart is heavy. I don't like sleeping in a single bed and yet I sleep well in it. It's like the universe is saying, "Time out from men."

8th July
11.58am: Beau Café

Having dinner with Charlie Silver tonight and two of his mates. He's asked me to invite two of my gorgeous girlfriends. I hope Charlie wants me when he sees me. I feel so ugly right now. I want to go out tonight from a place of power, shining beautifully.

The "one-eyed," woman in the valley will be queen. I know I'm being fucked around at "The Psychic Show." I know there has been and there will continue to be a lack of integrity. I know I'm approaching a whole new phase of my life that I need to step into now. Dad's offered to buy me a plane ticket to LA for my birthday. That means I'll be able to go to my Native American ceremony. I've done my filing, tidied my bedroom and feel much better now that I've created a double bed, even though I'm sleeping in it alone. So my focus is share rather than commit.

I met Bill this afternoon. It was hard for me. I hit my head on the glass shelf in the bathroom that triggered me into tears. I found it incredibly difficult to take my belongings from Bill, including my Native American paining and stone Buddha.

We had a meditation group last night. There were five of us. Nancy, Gary, Hugh and Kurt. Eric, the porn-come-psychic producer didn't have the courtesy to let us know he wasn't turning up. We began with a heart meditation to lift the vibration because I was feeling pissed off with Eric. We each wrote ten things we'd secretly love to do, inspired by Julia Cameron's, "The Artist's Way." As we shared, thunder clapped and lightening flashed outside which felt rather auspicious to me. I believe something divine is occurring. Yes!

9th July
11.10am

I was quite nervous when I arrived at The District Club last night. Charlie was already there with his cute Aussie friend Trent and Shane Bentley who I'd recently snogged. Agh! How embarrassing. I felt much better after a mojito and then Tina and Gina arrived.

I'm pretty sure Charlie did a fair amount of cocaine because he kept disappearing off to the loo. We stayed at The District Club till it closed. We were last to leave. I felt like I was in a time warp with Charlie, picking up from where we left off with our romance from eight years ago. We headed off to Star Club in Golden Square where all the old clubbers were still partying, it's just everyone's older now. Tom Spiegel was there, wearing a funny red and white-stripped sailor's shirt. Champagne arrived. Charlie chinked his flute with mine and whispered in my ear, "I'll be quite frank, I think we're going to be having sex again and seeing more of each other. Maybe not tonight, but it will happen."

Charlie swigged down his champagne, put my glass down and whisked me out of the club and into a silver Mercedes. Our driver was called Godwin. Oh God-Win! And it was. Charlie took me back to his lovely flat in Chelsea and he said, "I just want to hold you. Be close with you."

We ended up making love and it felt incredible.

11th July
3.08pm: The Zen Gym

Feel unsettled about my living situation right now. Nancy says she wants me to live with her but her mood doesn't reflect this. Charlie didn't call me last night. I sensed he wouldn't when he said, "Bye," to me in the lobby of the Four Seasons hotel on Saturday. We got so close and intimate and then his panic set in with a vengeance. When I arrived at the hotel on Friday night, Charlie had been waiting there for me. He looked totally gorgeous. His dark chocolate hair flopped over his brow and his brown eyes mesmerised me. Charlie led me up to his room, "The Executive Suite." Not exactly a romantic interlude as ten people ended up hanging out with us, snorting large amounts of cocaine off of American Express Black Cards to the beats of The Beastie Boys and Zero 7. I simultaneously drank two glasses of champagne. Laurent Perrier and Moet Chandon. I couldn't decide which I preferred. By 6am I knew my body and mind required sleep. I told Charlie.

"Ok party's moving to another room," Charlie said.

I wish he'd just kick everyone out and come to bed with me. But he didn't.]This nasty girl called Courtney said in her bitchy East London twang, "Charlie why don't you say you want us to go so you can shag Scarlet."

The room went silent. I choked back tears as I felt her venom pierce my heart. I wasn't going to fight her. If she wanted Charlie, she could have him. I knew the alcohol and lack of sleep had tipped me into irrational pain. Why didn't he want to be with me? How much more time did he need with his friends?

The room was now empty. I sat listless on the bed alone as the drug fuelled frenzy continued in another room. I dragged myself into the bathroom for a long hot shower. I knew I needed to cleanse myself from the sleazy dirty energy vibration I'd allowed into my space. Wash away those daggers. The soap was fragrant and luxurious on my body. Fuck it. If Charlie wanted her, he just wouldn't have me again. I climbed beneath the crisp white sheets. I lit a small tea light candle to focus on positive thoughts, take my mind off the half filled champagne flutes with cigarette butts floating on the surface, the smell of stale tobacco seeping into the air. I switched off the mood light which was glowing golden peach to nothing. It was now 6.45am and no sign of Charlie. I closed my eyes and fell to sleep. I awoke to the sound of his clothes dropping to the floor. I think it was an hour later because the candle had burned out. I was grateful as his naked body pressed into my back. I felt protected as his arms enveloped me like the wings of an angel. We caressed each other in half sleep until he guided himself inside me. Except I couldn't fully let go as I felt Charlie's heart was emotionally unavailable. This made me sad. After Charlie came, he phoned downstairs and got a late check out time of 2pm. We curled up and went back to sleep and I had a powerful dream. It's still whirring in my head. I was given a small earthenware bowl of Thai curry. It was too hot to eat. It needed to cool down. I was offered an alternative of a plain white china dish but I knew it would take away the potency of the flavour. I decided to be patient and wait so I could eat the dish how it was meant to be eaten, no half measures. When I awoke, I knew considerable time would pass before I would see Charlie again. I wished it didn't have to be this way because my soul longs to be with his. As we dressed, Charlie felt increasingly distant towards me. I was frustrated. I wanted adoration for my insecurities.

"I'll call you later," Charlie said.

But I knew he wouldn't and he didn't. So I walked to the 23 bus stop on Regent's Street while he picked up his red Ferrari from the garage. I phoned Tina from the bus and she picked an angel card for me, and Charlie. It was, "New Love." Except, he still didn't call. I tried not to hurt inside. I dared not sleep to stop myself feeling the pain and headed over to Jason's flat. We went to Jack's Pub for lunch and ate eggs Florentine that wasn't appetising. I don't think it would have mattered what I ate. My body wanted to go to bed and sleep but my mind said, "No! Don't stop or you'll be in so much pain. Go meet Carla and get to The District Club."

My mind defeated my body. I got a text from him on Sunday that said, "Cool x."

What the fuck did that mean?

13th July
10.30pm: Notting Hill Tube

I feel so exhausted after Barry had his tantrum yesterday, just before we were about to go Live on Air. Today my eyes are watering. I feel fat but I know I'm not because my jeans fit, thankfully. I'm now thirty-two inches around the hips instead of thirty-six. I remember being so embarrassed the year before when I went to all these boutiques and not a single pair of jeans or trousers fitted me. It felt horrible. Men didn't look at me then but I didn't want them to, I was hoping that Bill and I would get married and that was only a year ago.

6.30pm

I know I need to manifest my next home. I also know Mum is concerned about me but it doesn't help when she stresses out. I need to take practical steps. Just spent £140 on Mac make-up but I feel entirely justified because I'll use it all, especially for when I'm on TV. I had a great show today because Tiffany wasn't there. I felt liberated without her.

14th July
12pm: Home

I feel run down. My energy keeps draining because beneath my cool happy exterior, I am paying the price of blowing all my money. Nancy is out working this morning and I have a day off to get my life together. I'm sitting on the white sofa, propped up on velvet cushions listening to the melodic and meditative tunes of Zero 7. I'm looking out at the vibrant greens of the communal garden and the rhythm of the song, "Home," flows through me. Black Cat sits on the arm of the sofa to my right. I want a home I can call my own. I'm going to do a collage with all the papers I've collected. It doesn't have to take me years to get back on the property ladder. I'm in a strange space. I feel secure, happy, vulnerable and unstable all at the same time.

On Monday after a lovely time with Dad, I had this desire grab me by the heart to speak with Wayne but I stopped myself. It's been over two weeks since I've seen him and ten days since we've had any contact. Yes I initiated the connection and he gave a lovely response but in reality, he's incapable of giving to me. So I'm not calling him, not because I want to play a game, to make him want me. I'm doing this because I want my connection with him to come into balance and maybe that won't happen. Perhaps I won't hear from him again.

I want heart with sex connection, not just sex. I feel it energetically when I'm having sex with someone, if their heart is open and connecting with mine. With Max it was a sex and solar plexus connection. With Wayne I felt the energy lift from solar plexus to the heart and Charlie has always been in my heart, he never left, I just didn't know it until right now.

Last night while doing Mermaid & Dolphin cards with Nancy, I had another epiphany. If I ever did get pregnant by Charlie, I'd love to have the baby. This surprised me because it's the first time

I've not been scared of having a child. But the beauty of this feeling was a comprehension that I truly feel such a depth to my soul connection with Charlie. Hypothetically, if I had a baby with Charlie, I know it would be totally magical and beautiful. I know he would be an incredible father. I know he would be very supportive. This is the first time ever in my life that I've felt having a child would be a strengthening experience, rather than debilitating. Thank you Charlie for that gift. I'm going to be very careful and conscientious about what I manifest because I got the Alchemy card and Nancy told me she got pregnant through a condom.

15th July
10am

I dreamt I was in LA. I stepped into an old white van and it started off down the road on it own. I kept putting my foot on the break but it kept going of its own accord. The message from spirit, "Let us guide you!" Then I heard the song, "One day my prince will come." A little girl appeared and she got on so well with this little boy, they were made for each other, two peas in a pod. She, the beautiful princess being courted and wooed by the handsome prince. He invited her up into his bedroom in the fairytale tower. There was a stone spiral staircase and the maid looked attentive and caring but she wasn't because I saw her face shape-shift into the evil wicked witch and she said, "Mirror, mirror on the wall, who is the fairest of them all?" She didn't know I knew that she had a poisonous apple for the princess. Witch's face was old and ugly. She had a wart on her chin, a crocked nose and a black cloth over her head. She was bitter and dangerous. I sensed I was in the tower and soon everything would be falling apart. Then the dream moved on and I was with Mum.

"I'm so happy I'm with Charlie, I feel so connected to him," I said.

"Yes but he's not for you. You're not going to end up with him," Mum said.

My heart sank because I knew she was right. This made me

feel sad and then disappointed because I thought, who is there for me to share my life?

A deep part of my soul said, "Demons and saboteurs within are being flushed out. you finally seen them and your fairy Godmother has arrived to protect you. Even if it doesn't feel like it."

"So mirror, mirror, what would you like to show me?"

"Scarlet, look for the fairness within. The outer shell is being revealed for it's true ugliness and the exposure of beauty is flowing now. It is an exciting time. Set your sights very high because the world is your oyster. Why settle for second best when you can go for gold. Do not feel bad that you are perceived as a witch because you are a seer and seers hold great wisdom."

8.30pm

Oh my God, I'm so excited, talk about manifestation. Jason just phoned to invite me to the "King Arthur" premier. I'm so positively blown away because of all the Hollywood actors, I chose only one photo for my manifestation collage and it was of Clive Owen playing King Arthur, this magic stuff really works! So let's see if my next manifestation wish occurs because it's a picture of me watching playback of my acting on set with Steven Spielberg.

16th July
5pm: The Gym

Wow! Just stopped in at the gym on spur of the moment and told someone at the reception I was looking for a flat to rent and they handed me a flyer of the most stunning flat with a roof terrace, communal gardens, set on three floors and it's on the same street! It's more than I want to spend but its perfect for me. I love the look of the bathroom. My fears are I won't be able to afford the bills, but it'd be my own space. Let's see. "Spirit, divine angels, please guide me to make the best decision for my highest good."

17th July
11.30am

What an amazing amount of synchronicities and miracles, I know not where to begin. I'm moving to 1 Ladbroke Gardens, yes, yes, yes! Henrietta who owns the flat is so lovely. If I hadn't gone to the gym yesterday to say hello to Tina, who wasn't there, I wouldn't have spoken with Joy and told her I was about to see a flat and she wouldn't have given me the flyer for Henrietta's flat and I wouldn't be moving in there and renting it for six months. Suddenly a weight has been lifted in my friendship with Nancy. I met Henrietta's friend Guy Ramsfield, whose Mum owns Beau Café where I drink my coffee every day! He makes jeans in LA. He asked if I'd like to do business with him and partner up. Sounds like another great opportunity.

Emily never called me back last night, I rang her twice but she never picked up. So I met up with Carla and Sally instead and we got a table on the top floor of The District Club. As I ate chicken Caesar salad with a mojito, feeling totally positive and relaxed, who should walk in? Wayne. Double whammy, I hadn't replied to his text he sent on Friday night, "Hey babe, how u doin? Shoot was amazing, very excited about it. Thanx 4 ur words of encouragement!"

I'd felt reserved and held back when I got his message. Wayne's friend Basil and Jason got talking with Carla and Sally and then Wayne asked if I wanted to go back to his hotel in Shepherds Bush, a step down from the Four Seasons hotel with Charlie the weekend before.

"Why you staying in a hotel?" I said.

"Builders are in my place, it's inhabitable right now and I needed a bed instead of sleeping sofa to sofa," Wayne said.

We took an elevator downstairs and walked a corridor that felt like an eternity and then the key to his room didn't work. We had to go all the way back again to reception to reprogram the key and I thought perhaps it was a sign I shouldn't stay but I ignored my intuition. As we walked back to the room once again, Wayne said, "I thought a lot about our time in the garden together."

I didn't reply. We entered the room. It was dingy and dark and looked out onto a car park. The room was clean and simple but a part of me felt dirty. What the hell was I doing here? Wayne pushed me back on the bed and tried to go down on me, I stopped him. It didn't feel right. He rebuffed my refusal and again put his head between my legs.

"No, let's relax. Anyway, it's my time of the month," I said.

"I'm all aroused," Wayne said.

I began to feel guilty. Wayne took my hand and placed it on his erect penis and it made me want him inside. Soon enough he was and I was feeling totally turned on and suddenly he stops.

"What's wrong?" I said.

"I can't carry on," Wayne said.

"Why?" I said.

He'd fought so hard to get in my knickers.

"The blood," he said, giving an embarrassed sideways glance.

"What?" I said.

"I'm squeamish," he said.

My mouth dropped open.

"But the blood represents female power, nothing's going to happen to you," I said.

"I don't feel comfortable, that's all," he said.

"Well that doesn't make me feel very good. I told you I had my period," I said.

I felt rejected, like absolute shit.

"I'm sorry babe. Why don't you have a shower, get cleaned up," Wayne said.

I did as he said because I was in shock. I'd never encountered a response like that before. I come back in from the bathroom and Wayne is lying on the bed watching TV. I lie down next to him. He takes my hand and places it on his prick. It's hard.

"I'm horny," he said.

"So?" I said.

"I want to come. I promise I'll make it up to you," Wayne said.

This was beginning to feel pretty one sided, and then like a total idiot, I ended up giving him a blowjob.

It was very hard for me to sleep, as energy was coursing through me. I felt blood rushing down Wayne' right arm and he'd jerk involuntarily. The only time I slept peacefully was in the morning when he held me. I then dreamt Wayne and I were inside a fenced area and a black bull charged for me. I slammed the gate shut to protect myself. I was more amused than scared and then the bull came at me again and then again from another angle forcing me to jump up on the fence. I realized I was exposed through the gaps in the wood to potential blows, so I backed off. I thought the bull's going to get me or jump over the fence and then a gift box arrived. I opened it. Inside was a pink toothbrush with a heart on it and three other gifts lay in the box and just as I was about to open them, Wayne woke me up. What gifts shall I receive from this experience?

19th July
10.25am: Ladbroke Tube

Off to do the show. Was lovely having lunch with dear Steven Kruger, the Academy award winner at The Oak. He's a real sweetie. He arrived on time and was sitting outside on a wooden park bench in front of a table reading a newspaper, wearing a brown t-shirt that said ASS on it in yellow letters. We talked about the last ten years in two hours. When I first met Steven, at twenty-one, I was heavily affected by the social scene.

"You're such an It Girl," Steven said.

I was slightly disgusted and flattered all at the same time. Yes I knew all the right people who wouldn't be there for me if I really needed them. I like Steven. I find him attractive. There is a reassuring and kind quality to him. He's a Virgo. So I've shifted away from magnetizing in all these Sagittarians and Scorpios. I always shunned Virgo's because my mum's one and she's so tidy. I think I threw the baby out with the bath water in that she's practical and grounded and I could do with some of that. Anyway I hope I'll see Steven again, I'm positive I will. I love the story he told of how he made a shit film, was so depressed, he went to watch a movie that had won an Oscar to get over his failure. Left the cinema so inspired, he went on to win an Oscar himself. I have the utmost respect for his achievement.

20th July
9.45am: Beau Cafe

Synchronicity. Just bumped into Nigel Hawker, the entertainment laywer whose number I couldn't find. It's another sign from the universe saying, "Move on Scarlet, move on from "The Psychic Show!"

Matt appeared in my dream for the first time since March. I release all fears, I release all lack of self worth, I release frustration, I release my anger, I release my friends who are not truly my friends, I release my expectations, I release my poverty consciousness, I release my need for love, I release my need for approval from others, I release all negative thought forms now.

21st July
12.20pm: Beau Cafe

I slept with Guy Ramsfield last night. He taught me a beautiful lesson, to receive. Oh and Max phoned again. This time he left a message. His voice sounded upbeat.

"Hello Scarlet, it's Max, my business is going really well. Maybe you'd like to meet up for a drink or not, just calling to say, 'hi,' hope all is well with you."

But my clairaudience heard his voicemail rather differently.

"Hey Scarlet, it's Max. You stupid bitch, I'm angry with you. No one fucking decides when it's over. I'm always in control because I'm too hurt and wounded to have another woman take control over me. I'm the one who calls the shots, so meet me for a drink so I can fuck you and fuck you up for dumping me."

Beneath his carefree lilt lies a quivering quavering volcanic eruption about to spew.

22nd July
11.20am: Ladbroke Grove Tube

I've successfully moved home. It's like living in a dolls house except I have terrible fears of how I will pay my rent and yet I know exciting opportunities are on the horizon. It is getting ballistic in the TV studio. Not on my show but in the basement of the building, I feel the energy of porn rising up and permeating ever cell of space. Surprisingly if money wasn't an issue, I still wouldn't leave the show right now. My intuition says I need to stay. Today I'll work with grounding violet and golden rays of light. Gary told me that on Sunday night, one of the girls from Pleasure Zone dropped a bouncy ball over the fire escape that smashed through the glass ceiling of the boardroom where Barry and Clive were snorting cocaine off the boardroom table. Then Barry threw up out the window and a fan sucked it through the ventilator that stunk out the entire room with vomit. Yuck! On a symbolic level, the boardroom is being filled with a lot of shit.

This morning I was doing Mermaid & Dolphin cards outside Beau Café and Guy pulled up in his Dad's car. He kissed me on the lips and I felt self conscious as I knew his mother was lingering inside the café. I offered Guy a divination card and he picked one. It was, "Simplify your Life." I got, "Accept Heaven's Help." Later on, Nancy said she thinks Guy's heart is very wounded.

3.50pm: Oxford St

Just had lunch with Veronica and then Barry phoned, rather synchronous.I had a strong intuition about the corporate politics and was reluctant to pass the message onto him. It was his mum coming through who had recently died. I felt like Barry was Julius Caesar, about to be stabbed in the back by his supposedly loyal friends and he needed to know but I didn't want to get involved. Eric and Clive both want Barry's job. Guy phoned while I was with

Veronica, he was friendly but cool. Didn't exactly ask me out on a date, just wanted to know what I was up to. So I said "What are you up to?"

"No concrete plans," Guy said.

My interpretation of that is, "I'd really like to see you but I'm scared you'll reject me, so I'm not going to ask you out. I'll go with the flow and see if you pursue me."

23rd July
11.40am: Beau Cafe

Woke up 11.10am. I felt strange. Didn't end up having sex with Guy last night. His sarcasm was dryer than the sherry my Grandmother used to drink. We talked a lot of crap. All I wanted was to know him a little better before he went down on me but I couldn't let myself because it all felt too shallow. Guy criticised my music collection, made me feel uncomfortable the minute he stepped inside my home.

"So am I the first guy to come back to your flat?" Guy said.

"Yes," I said, but I felt awkward. Was I a conquest?

Nancy later said, "That's not on."

I think she's right. I felt rigid when Guy edged down my panties and said, "So the gardener's been in."

Was he assuming I'd made an effort for him? I felt defensive. It was a hot balmy night and I wanted romance, not crudeness. I withdrew into myself and Guy sensed it.

"I need a cigarette," Guy said.

"It's a no smoking flat," I said.

"I'll smoke out the window," he said.

"No, it'll still smell. Let's go out to the garden," I said.

Guy looked pissed off and gave me a look of, "No one tells me what to do."

We went down to the garden but the damage was already done. Guy lit up a cigarette as we sat on the bench where Charlie had knelt down before me and said, "I love you Scarlet," almost like he was proposing a celestial marriage and I'd sat on top of Wayne, with him inside me under the stars. Now I sat here with Guy, his big muscular arm around my shoulder, while he smoked his cigarette. He kissed me but I felt weird, the energy was gone but in truth it was never there.

24th July
12.30pm: Carluccio's Restaurant

Wow it's a beautiful day and I have a glorious hangover, five mojitos later. I got rather emotional last night at about 3.30am. I burst into tears in front of Jason back at his flat. Bless him, he hugged me and reassured me. I felt so vulnerable, exposed and cheap seeing Guy Ramsfield, flirting by text with Giorgio and speaking with Larry in LA. I was juggling too many balls, way too many. I was royally drunk. Not a good thing. I phoned Charlie at 1am. Surprisingly he was asleep and I woke him. He was at a manor house in the countryside, preparing for his sister's wedding the following day. He said he'd call me tomorrow but somehow I didn't think he would.

Guy was a fucking asshole in The District Club. He said he was having dinner with a friend and would come back to find me but he didn't. I called him in my drunkenness from Jason's flat and invited him over but he never phoned back. Then I discovered he was in Narcotics Anonymous, which shocked me because I didn't pick up on it. All I know is he's a game player and it feels viscous and hurtful. He wants to break me down.

I took a taxi at 4am and turned up at Giorgio's house in Fulham like a prostitute, except I wasn't being paid.

"Nice surprise," Giorgio said as he opened the front door.

Why do this to myself? I walked inside.

"I promise to look after you. Drink?" he said, as he gestured for me to sit on the couch.

The TV was on.

"Water, please," I said.

He returned with a glass of fizzy water which didn't quench my thirst. It felt awkward between us and then he took the glass from my hand put it down and leaned into kiss me but I felt nothing. I was going through the motions.

"I'm a prostitute," I thought, as Giorgio led me into the bedroom, pulled my panties to the side and went down on me. He manoeuvred himself in front of my face and I remember thinking, "Oh, now I'm doing a sixty-nine and still not feeling anything."

He came quickly. The result, Giorgio had three orgasms, I had none. Am I abusing myself? Yes.

25th July
7.40pm: Home

Exhausted now, but delightfully. Beginning to feel rather vulnerable from how Aidan O'Leary opened me up to new experiences of myself. Yesterday I felt so bizarre, it was the come down from all the mojitos and my lack of connection to men. I met Oscar at the Country Club, which was fantastic. We swam in the pool and lay in the sun. I wore my rainbow bikini. Then we ate a lovely meal. I had roast pork with apple sauce, mashed potato, carrots and mange tout. Oscar had duck with rice. I felt vulnerable when he told me that this other psychic wanted to do our project. It was my idea and I felt betrayed but in truth, I hadn't stepped up to the plate. Oscar was giving me a royal kick up the ass to make this TV show happen. We went for a walk around the grounds and I admired the people dressed in black tie and ball gowns. We visited the river and watched the waves lap at the shore. After we sat on the crocket lawn and talked about life and love. Something extraordinary happened, as I could see the vibration lifting, dimensional doorways of opportunity were opening before my eyes, as I acknowledged myself and my desires. I received a clairvoyant vision. My soul said, "Scarlet, step up now. Yes, you're a pro on four foot waves but one day, you'll have to navigate twelve foot waves, so you may need to lie face down for a while until you feel ready to stand. There will always be bigger waves coming in as an integral part of your growth."

I prayed for a man to come into my life who understands, inspires and teaches me. Then Emma phones and asks if I want to go to The District Club. I make an excuse that I'm tired but the truth is, I feel so humiliated by my behaviour the night before. How can I face anyone?

Emma persuades me and I dress in tan army pants, my Hawaiian t-shirt and Gola trainers. I didn't even wash my hair. No effort for any men anymore. I led Emma up to The Chill Room on the top floor. It was pleasantly quiet. We took up residence in two large white rocking chairs. I initially refused alcohol but eventually succumbed as the evening progressed. Then this guy put his jacket on the back of my chair and that's how I met Aidan O'Leary.

"Would you like to go on a magical mystery tour?" he said in his Irish lilt.

"Yes," I said.

So Emma and I leave The District Club with four cute Irish guys. Aidan sits opposite me in the back of the people carrier as we head off to a club in Chelsea. Emma leans over and whispers in my ear, "I can't believe we're hanging out with Aidan O'Leary."

"Who?" I said.

"Who? Scarlet, he's a national TV star," Emma said.

I feel awkward. Before I was just sitting in a taxi with a guy having banter, now I don't want him to think I'm talking with him because he's well known. Aidan's not my usual type, pale skin, dyed blonde hair, brown eyes and Aquarius. We pull up outside the club, the red rope is lifted and a hostess leads us to the VIP table at the back of the club. Aidan invites me to sit down next to him and hands me a glass of champagne.

"So what do you do?" Aidan said.

"Produce and host a psychic TV show," I said.

I felt inadequate next to his achievements. I hid it well.

"What channel?" he said.

"Mega TV," I said, trying to be blasé.

"So can you read my palm?" he said.

If only Aidan knew how many times I'd been asked that and felt absolutely irritated. However, I was curious to discover more about Aidan and I'd never done palm reading. It couldn't be that difficult. I played along and decided to give it a go.

"Sure, give me your hand," I said.

He rested his hand in mine. I held it gently, ran my finger over his palm to connect and to my surprise, it worked. I began to channel information about his career. It was noisy in the club so I whispered the message into his ear, this was the sexiest psychic reading I'd ever done.

"Is any of what I'm saying making sense to you?" I said.

"Yes, all of it," Aidan said.

"What's your favourite colour?" I said.

"Usually sky blue but now I'm feeling hot red," he said.

The colour of passion I thought to myself and I could sense the energy building between us.

"What's your favourite colour?" Aidan said.

"Gold and pink," I said.

"You're content on the outside and lack self confidence inside. Whereas I feel no contentment on the outside and yet I have self confidence inside," Aidan said.

"So as opposites, we balance each other out," I said.

Aidan agreed and then I felt a shift.

"Why'd you just pull your energy back?" I said.

"Because we're on hot red now and either we leave together and sleep together or we don't," Aidan said.

I didn't reply and he took hold of my hand and led me out of the club. Emma and Aidan's friend Sean followed behind us and we got a cab back to his beautiful house off the King's Road.

Aidan whispered in my ear, "I'm going to go upstairs and then you're going to follow me."

He pushed me up against a shelf unit in the kitchen and kissed me passionately. It was delicious. Then Emma and Sean walked in and I pulled away. What turned me on is I felt Aidan got me on every level. He understood me better than I knew myself, and that made me want to know him better. Aidan led me into his bedroom. It was all white and serene with a seven-foot bed. We kissed and I was flowing with him, affirming, "I'm ready to receive," and I did. Four orgasms!

I lay on Aidan's hard wood floor, shagged on all levels. The green leaves rustled like emeralds outside. Aidan came over and lay his head on my lap. All I wanted to do was be with him all day. We smelt of sex, our scents mixed together. I wish he didn't have to go to this Cartier Polo event.

"I've got to go," Aidan said.

"I know," I said, trying to cover up the disappointment.

"Wish I could make love to you again," he said.

"Then why don't you?" I said, testing him.

"I can't, much as I want to, PR guy needs me for interviews with the press," he said.

"I understand," I said.

"Give me your number and I'll call you," he said.

"Phone me now and then I'll have yours to," I said. Damn, why did I say that! So desperate and needy, not trusting Scarlet, not trusting.

Aidan walked me to the door.

"I had fun. You know I'm going to call," he said.

So why did I have this niggling feeling he wouldn't?

Aidan kissed me passionately and closed the door gently behind me.

26th July
8.30am

My bed feels uncomfortable compared to Aidan's luxurious 7ft bed. Why hasn't he phoned me yet?

I feel vulnerable because I opened myself so much physically. I am laid bare, raw inside. I want him and I sense he doesn't want me.

27th July
9.50am: Home

I awoke forty-five minutes before my alarm. I've totally blown the whole Aidan situation out of proportion. How do I live just for today? I change my voice mail to a New Age greeting, "Just for today, please leave a magical message and remember how amazing you are."

Practise what you preach Scarlet!

30th July
11.50am: Beau Café

While having a lunch of rye bread, avocado and hummus with actress Hillary Crane, Eric Drag, man/boy who took my job phones on behalf of "The Psychic Show."

"Hi, it's Eric. Have you got time to talk now?" Eric said.

I did my best to hide my irritation in front of Hillary.

"Yes," I said, because I wanted to know what he was going to say next. I knew something was up.

"I'm not happy," he said.

"Why?" I said.

"Because I just spoke with Carina and she said you're getting paid double what everyone else gets," he said.

I was shocked. I'd already had my salary halved. I felt myself being pushed out, ego's at hand.

"Well it's my agreement with Mega TV," I said.

"I'm sorry Scarlet, that's going to change now," he said.

Yet I know he is so not sorry.

"But I've always been paid this rate," I said, watching myself become increasingly defensive.

"It has to be halved. Take it or leave it. I don't want to let you go but if you're not happy, I can get plenty of other psychics to replace you," Eric said.

"Thanks Eric," I said, knowing he understood the subtext.

"Can you come in this afternoon?" he said.

"I'd like to discuss this over the phone," I said.

"Just come in for five minutes so we can have a coffee and negotiate this. Sort it out," he said.

"Ok, I'll call you when I'm out of my meeting," I said, but my head was reeling and Hillary was looking at me curiously. I'm shaken. Even though I knew there would be backhanded tactics to get rid of me. I hate the philosophy, "Make more, pay everyone less." Where's the integrity gone?

I need to claim my power now. I rush off to meet Mum. She's on her way to my flat and as I sit in a cab, I sense her fears about me being able to make the rent.

We sit down with coffee and cake in the garden. A black Labrador keeps nudging Mum to play, "fetch," with a tattered ball. I notice her getting increasingly irritated.

"Scarlet, maybe you should think about getting a job as a secretary for a producer in a company," Mum said.

"Mum, I am a producer!" I said.

"Well, a PA or assistant producer," she said.

"No Mum, that doesn't work for me," I said.

"Well how are you going to earn money?" she said, concern washed across her face.

"From the shows I get commissioned," I said.

"What if they don't sell? Then you'll have to get a proper job, settle down," she said.

"They will sell Mum. I've already created a successful show which is on TV right now," I said.

She doesn't respond. I know Mum's genuinely concerned for me but it doesn't help. Her fears animate me to step it up. I have to. We walked out to her car.

"You look exhausted," Mum said.

I do my best to be resilient and smile, as I watch Mum drive away.

As I walked to Zen gym, I phoned Eric back.

"Hi darling," Eric said chirpily.

"Eric, I'm not coming in today. Let's discuss things when I'm next at the office. So, when am I scheduled?" I said.

I felt power surging into me, the quality of assertiveness building inside me.

"Tuesday," he said.

"Good, we can talk after the show. When else am I on?" I said.

"Thursday," he said.

"Is that it?" I said.

"Yes darling. Everyone's doing two days a week now," he said smarmily.

"And Tiffany?" I said.

"That's got nothing to do with you darling," he said.

Agh! I want to kill him. "Four shows as usual for Tif?" I said.

"We'll see you on Tuesday then?" Eric said, ignoring my question.

"Yes," I said, virtually spitting down the phone. Bastard. I have to get out of there before my ugly shadow takes over.

I meditated when I got back from the gym. I had to, as I couldn't escape myself. Jason called.

"I'm downstairs," Jason said.

I take a deep breath to compose myself best I can before opening the front door. Jason posed subtly in his racing green convertible.

"Scarlet, what's wrong? You look so low," he said.

"Doesn't matter," I said.

"Come on, tell me," he said.

And I do reluctantly because I wanted to remain positive, rather than spiral into rejection, fear and lack of self worth.

We parked up outside the District Club. Saw a few faces I knew inside. Tom Spiegel walked in soon after and said, "hi," to Jason but blanked me.

"Hey you, am I invisible?" I said.

"Oh hi Scarlet," he said so unconvincingly, pretending not to notice me. Obviously his ego was bruised because I never called when he wanted me to.

Jason and I sat on one of the large brown leather sofas. I checked out the room and noticed people checking me out in return including a tall dark handsome guy at the bar who I'd seen several times before but never spoken with. Jason headed off to the bar and returned with a mojito for me.

"There's a party. Let's go, it'll cheer you up," he said.

Only to discover as we were ready to leave that four people would be there.

"How about Star Club?" Jason said.

"It's shit there," I said, frustrated, wondering why I was even out.

"Everyone from the District Club is going," he said.

Same crowd, different locale. I must go home.

As we pull up outside, no one's there except the bouncer and Penelope who I remember from eons ago, still in charge of the guest list. We all made small talk, then pass beneath fluorescent lighting into an anti-climatic decorated basement.

"Oh my God, we might as well be at The District Club," I said.

"Let's stay five minutes, then check out Spice Club," Jason said.

Except I'm prepared to stay because the one guy I fancied from The District Club earlier is there. I have to meet him. I take courage.

"Hi, I always see you at the District Club," I said.

"Hi, I'm George, " he said, pulling me close into him for a rather seductive dance.

Jason swaggered over, he's drunk an excessive amount of vodka orange and it's now 2.45am.

"Let's head back to mine," Jason said.

"I can drive," I said.

"No Scarlet, I'm good, just get in the back with George. I need to catch up with Quinn about business up front," he said, chuckling.

I fastened my seatbelt and said a little prayer to the angels. Thankfully George was by my side. An exhilarating breeze swept through my hair as Jason charged along the empty London streets back to Notting Hill. I swear Jason's flat is on some disgruntled energy vortex because every time I'm there, some emotional drama occurs. Jason put music on, and vodka was poured. Jason, Quinn, George and I head out to the garden and Jason makes jabbing little comments indirectly to George.

"I've got something I want to show you," Jason said and disappeared inside.

Quinn leant into me and whispered, "I think Jason's trying to get some type of one up on George."

"Yes, I think you may be right," I said, hoping he wasn't.

Jason reappeared with a fencing sword in his right hand.

"Ok you, I want to show you something," he said, pointing the sword at George.

Quinn and I cracked up laughing.

"Come here," Jason said.

"I'd prefer not to," George said.

"I said, come here," Jason said, ignoring his protests.

"Give the sword to me," I said, stepping in between them.

It felt like a dual at dawn.

"I'm trained in fencing," George said.

"I'll go fetch my other sword," Jason said.

"Enough!" I said and outstretched my hand.

Jason reluctantly passed it to me.

"I'm going inside. I'm cold," I said and took the sword with me.

I heard George follow me inside but I didn't turn around.

"I can't get the CD to play," I said.

George bent down beside me and pressed one button and the CD began to play.

"Thanks," I said, standing up.

George pulled me close, took my hands, stretched out my arms and wrapped them behind my back. He lent forward and kissed my neck. He flirted and teased me and I closed my eyes and lifted my face, mouth slightly open. He brushed his lips half over mine and then pulled away.

"I'm going to be sordid and ask for your number," George said.

I didn't ask for his, like I did with Aidan. I'd learnt my lesson. It was now 4.45am.

"I need to sleep," George said.

"Me to," I said.

"I'll walk you home," he said.

We head outside to say, "Bye," to Jason.

"George's just walking me home," I said.

"I bet he is," Jason said, raising his eyebrow to Quinn.

I ignore his comment and kiss Jason goodnight on both cheeks and George and I walk hand in hand down the road. Daylight is increasing with every step and it is a little cold. We stood on the corner of Ladbroke Gardens and this time George kissed me gently on the lips. It was electric. He tried to put his hand up my dress but I extracted it. I wonder if he will call me? One thing for sure, I know I'll bump into his again at The District Club. I descended my white spiral staircase and fell into bed. I'm conflicted because I so want to have sex but really what I want more is love and I haven't had that in a long time.

31st July
2.40pm: Home, Balcony

Just got out of bed and it's really hot in London. A spider nests on a it's web, a butterfly fluttering above. I've just eaten a Sainsbury's chocolate sundae, which is past its sell by date but tastes fine. It's the first time I've come to sit outside since I moved in. I have a great view of Ladbroke Gardens. I can smell sausages cooking on a nearby barbeque and hear someone sprinkling water on their garden. I'm pretty spaced out right now. I wonder why I have a love hate relationship with The District Club? Is it because it makes me feel like an addict, always needing more?

Gary later on reminded me how I'd picked the fox medicine

card reversed representing camouflaging oneself to fit in and withdrawing inward. I definitely fell withdrawn. I don't want to be hurt myself anymore.

CHAPTER 10

LOVING THE DRAMA QUEEN

1st August
9.30am: Beau Café

Surprisingly I'm up out of bed. I woke up just before 9am. Lying naked in bed, a cool breeze floated in through the window. I began to feel angry. Angry at the men who had physically been inside me and their lack of honour, respect and integrity. Different thoughts ran through my head, like the following.

Scene One: I phone Aidan and say, "Hi, how are you?"

He says, "Yeah fine."

I'm angry that he's so blasé. I try and hold myself back but I can't.

"You know I don't give my body over easily and it hurts that you treated me like a shag. I have feelings, I'm hurting. Were you ever going to call me?"

"Yes of course," he says but my clairaudience screams, "No!"

Then I think of Oscar's attitude to women and how they're a conquest to him at times and he just fucks them. It's emotionless.

"Anyway I'll call you later in the week and we'll hook up," Aidan says.

"Yeah great," I say.

I know my resolve has weakened because it'll never happen.

"Bye," I say, put the phone down and feel like absolute shit. Wow I failed that self esteem and respect test.

Scene Two: I'm in The Chill Room on the top floor of The District Club with a group of my closest friends, Jason, Gary, Carla and Emma is there also who was with me when I first met Aidan. We're having a real laugh. I feel relaxed, in my power. No need for the love of men, thankfully I'm loving and caring for myself, focused on friendship. Aidan walks in with his friends and goes up to the bar. He doesn't see me till he turns around because I'm sitting in the corner. I wait and see if he'll come over and say, "hi". It's been two weeks since I had my night with him. He doesn't. He looks straight through me like I was a ghost and he isn't clairvoyant. My heart stops, it drops down into my stomach, it feels like lead weight. My feelings of, "You fucking bastard, how could you treat me like this?" have not yet exploded. "You've been inside me, you've kissed me on the most intimate sensitive part of my body and now you have no recognition, no memory of who I am? Yet you moaned in pleasure when experiencing me. That hurts."

"That's him, Aidan," I whispered to Carla.

"First class wanker," Carla said.

"Why don't you go say, hi," Emma says.

"Forget it," Jason says.

Aidan faces the bar and doesn't turn around, just continues talking to his mate. I'm waiting to see if he'll acknowledge me. He must. Mustn't he?

I can't contain myself any longer. I get up and stride coolly to the bar and tap him on the shoulder. He turns around instantly.

"Hi," I say.

I smile sweetly.

"Hey Scarlet, how are you?" Aidan says.

Absolute recognition. What was this, a game of power? I don't understand but it hurts me. I know I'm not a toy.

"I'm good," I lie, "What you been up to?" I say, really not giving a shit.

I want to know what's been so bloody important that you can't pick up the fucking phone to me?!

I watch Aidan's every move and monitor his internal thought process.

"Just been really busy, different events I don't want to be at, want to slow down, have some R and R, quality time," he says.

The words flow off his tongue in a singing Irish lilt.

I think how Charlie comes out with the same bullshit. It hurts. I know, I know the answers already, I'm just wishing my intuition was wrong and that I didn't care. Why can't the truth be told? Why?

"I was going to call you," Aidan says after a long pause. I know he has read my thoughts. He knows he is in unchartered territory and he wants to get to shore quickly.

"Really?" I say smiling. "When?"

"Soon," he says.

I notice a muscle twitching just below his right eye. I put my hands on my hips.

"Really?" I say, waiting to see where this is going and how he's going to extricate himself.

"Of course I had a great time with you and I'd like to do it again," he says.

Aidan's audacity sends me over the edge. I visualize myself slapping him hard on the cheek so it really burns, shocks him back to some sort of reality for his emotional abuse of me. I imagine throwing my mojito in his face but decide that would be wasted on him. I conclude he wouldn't be humiliated, it must have happened to him before. I take a deep breath in and on the release walk away.

The other response would be, "It's never going to happen

again, so cherish the memory," but that makes me feel like this cringy, self-obsessed, idiotic woman who's going to end up a spinster.

Friday night I had a beautiful dinner with Dad. I'm so grateful for all the love and support I have from him and Mum. We watched "The Three Kings," after drinking champagne and eating lobster. I love the abundance of good food and friendship I have been given. In the past I took it for granted. Now I understand that it has great worth and Dad and Mum truly are on amicable terms and have my best interests at heart. I am very very fortunate, I just couldn't see it before.

Although I was absolutely exhausted, I dragged myself to The District Club with Gary, and Jade met us there. As we walked in, me wearing my white long skirt, pink cardigan and Native American boots, I saw George, Mr District Club, electrifying kisser, self-absorbed advertising exec. I tapped him on the back and walked over to the bar. A couple of minutes later he came over, kissed me on the cheek and said, "Hi."

"So how was your day?" I said.

He had to think for a moment.

"Yes great, I went to the gym, had lunch at Q&A, got a massage in Soho," George said.

"And your presentation…how was it?" I said.

"Yes that was excellent," he said.

I wonder if he will ask how I am. It seems to be all about him. Then a woman with dark curly hair tied in a pigtail butts in and oozes ,"Hi". They kiss hello.

"You probably don't recognize me with my hair tied back," she said.

"Of course I do," he said.

"Why don't you join us? We're over there," she said, pointing toward the restaurant.

"Yeah," he said, turns to me at me and said, "See you," didn't quite finish his sentence and walked off.

I'm a little surprised and yet I'm not. His behaviour totally fits that of a media player. Gary and I go sit on a sofa. I decide not to wait for George to come back over because I sense he won't.

"Let's go upstairs," I say.

Gary and I enter The Chill Room. It's semi-full. I clock the room for someone I know. Henry is there chatting to a girl, very pretty. I say, "Hi," and then he introduces me to Marcus his flatmate who is seriously cute, 6ft 3, dark brown hair and beautiful blue eyes. He is charming and his friend Damian, a beautiful black guy, must be a model before. Gary goes and sits with Jade and I enter into a lovely flirtation with these two men.

"So do you prefer a guy to ask to kiss you?" Marcus says.

"Just kiss me," I say.

"I'm the one that has the animal instinct and just kisses," Damian says, "and Marcus's the one that holds back and asks."

"So do you have a boyfriend?" Marcus said.

"No," I said.

"How come you're single?" he said.

"I just came out of a seven year relationship," I said.

"When?" he said.

"A few months ago," I said, "I'm not used to this dating thing."

Although I haven't admitted that I've crammed a lot of learning and experience into the last four months. I notice the relief on their faces. That they're rationalizing why someone attractive like me, is now single and that, there isn't something seriously dysfunctional about me.

"So what do you do?" Marcus said.

"I'm a TV producer and presenter," I said.

"What you working on?" he said.

"A show called "The Psychic Show," I say, half embarrassed

and half proud of my achievement.

"What channel?" he said.

"Mega TV," I said.

"Damian, she's a TV presenter on Mega TV, does a psychic show," Marcus said.

I'm feeling shy now but loving the recognition.

"Can I kiss you?" Marcus said.

"No," I said.

I bite my lip and flick my hair coyly.

"I love when you do that with your hair," he said, "It's very sexy."

I look down again.

"Can you tell me what flavour this lollypop is?" Marcus said, holding it towards my lips.

I suck it and reply, "I think it's pear."

"Can you do that again and this time look into my eyes," he said.

"Okay," I said and he dips the lolly in my cranberry juice and I suck it again, looking straight at him. I notice how his eyes sparkle, they have a Superman quality. I read his mind. I don't need to be psychic to know he's evaluating the quality of the blow job I may give.

"So what's your passion?" I said.

"Writing about terrorism," he said.

"Wow, really?" I said.

"Yes, I'm fascinated by it," he said.

"I just saw The Three Kings with my Dad," I said.

"Yeah it's a great movie," he said.

Not only is he good looking, he's intelligent. He pushes my

hair behind my shoulder, leans forward and kisses my neck.

"Hasn't she got a beautiful neck?" Marcus said to Damian.

"Yes," Damian said.

Marcus then said accidentally on purpose, "I told Damian I fancy you."

Damian and Henry go downstairs and Marcus asks me to join him. I feel torn. I want to go with him but I don't. I also hope I don't bump into smarmy George.

"Back in a minute," I said to Gary and Jade who are deep in conversation on the sofa.

I stand in the hallway with Marcus and he pulls me close into his body and tries to kiss me.

"No," I said, my body aching with desire, "I'm not kissing you in The District Club."

Someone I know walks by and gives me a knowing look. It's like being eighteen and out on the club scene again. Then Damian and Henry and his friend Delilah, a beautiful black girl joins us in the hall. Marcus takes hold of my hand behind my back, while everyone discusses what to do next. Henry is gutted because some girl has played him for a fool and Damian had his bank card eaten and has no money to get home. Marcus has to look after both of them.

He whispers, "It's rather intimate holding your hand."

I'm surprised he finds that more so than kissing me.

"Really?" I said.

"Yes," he said and then Gary and Jade come out and we all go out onto Portobello Road. Marcus tries to kiss me again

"I'm setting my boundaries as I'm feeling sensitive tonight. I'm sorry," I said.

"I'll give you a lift home. I'm parked by The Swan," Marcus said.

I calculate that it'll take longer to walk there than home but decide to go for the entertainment. We say goodbye to everyone and Marcus, Henry and I walk together but Henry's negative mood seems to seep over us. I suggest getting the rest of the champagne I'd had for dinner and drinking it together. They both agree that's a good idea. We get in Marcus's Porsche and then Henry said, "I shouldn't have told her I like her."

I turn to face him.

"Yes, I think it's good you did. There's nothing wrong with saying how you feel. I see that as a strength, not a weakness," I said.

I feel Marcus watching me say every word as we sit at a red traffic light on Ladbroke Grove. A moment later we pull up outside my flat.

"You're home. Henry, you can get in the front," Marcus said. There's coldness in his voice.

I'm thrown by his sudden change in mood. What did I say?

"Fine," I said.

I hesitate, trying to assimilate the shift in energy. Henry gets out and we kiss goodbye on each cheek. I look at Marcus and feel his distance. I didn't say goodbye. I let myself into my flat, go upstairs, sit on the sofa and try to understand, but I don't. I stupidly phone him but he doesn't pick up. I leave a message, "Hey you, it's Scarlet, I feel awkward how we left it, give me a call, there's something I'd like to propose."

But he doesn't call. Was this a tactic on his part or a genuine feeling, a true response?

I went to sleep at 3am feeling pretty shit and rejected.

I woke up, went to the gym and reclaimed my power by doing a kick ass email to Eric, telling him, "I'm quitting "The Psychic Show," except the computer crashed as I finished it's forty minute creation. I am terrified how I'm ever going to get my next projects commissioned and yet I know I am destined for success, if only I stopped putting all my energy into men Fears keep arising. How am I going to pay my rent?

It triggers huge anger in me. Makes me feel out of control. I still haven't put away all my clothes and belonging at home. I know it would only take an hour but it physically represents some fundamental chaos inside me. I'm praying I'll bring the money in, especially after investing in a new laptop. Part of me wants to run away on holiday, except I want five star and haven't the money for it and another part of me says, "Scarlet, don't run, do deals, get an agent, do your TV treatments and get them commissioned now!"

Last night went for dinner with friends but felt very disconnected from the small talk. A friend of Carla's who seems well meaning but not, said, "So how do you find the dating scene in LA compared to London?"

She subtly flashed her rock of an engagement ring in my face, for the entire table to see.

"I don't know. I've just come out of a seven year relationship," I said dryly.

Yes, you could cut the atmosphere with a knife because that was a dagger I was not accepting in my back or heart.

"Bitch," I wanted to say, but I know she needs compassion. I think she's not a happy girl beneath. Rob, Jason's friend later on said, "She's like one of those reformed smokers."

I laughed knowingly. The dynamic between my male friends and Carla's female friends is painful. We all go to The District Club again. I decline the Star Club with Jason's posse and Spice Club with Carla's gang. I talk small with some old school north-west London connections and at 1.15am decide to resign to bed. I felt empty but centred. I know my strength will have to come from within.

2nd August
9.20am: Beau Café

Last night I went to sleep listening to the Divine Will tape, "The Will to Liberate," and it talked of the mist that stops one having clarity. It is a fog because of clouded emotions. Obviously I have a huge amount of emotions to cleanse right now.

Aidan O'Leary had been in my dream, I just can't remember in what capacity but it was the first time I felt his soul around me. I looked at my profile in the mirror. I felt helpless, absolutely powerless. At present there are no men in my life who want me. It's as if the tide has washed them away, off my shore back out into the depths of the ocean for purification, a deep cleansing. Some may make it into shore again. Some may be drowned. Nature will decide. She can be ruthless. Her wrath may unfold if she is not treated lovingly, respectfully. It makes me think of my connection with the moon and the release of blood. The utter shock that Wayne was disgusted and squeamish about a woman's blood. To me this says he fears female life-force. How can I receive a man who doesn't accept this fundamental part of woman, not just me for it is a denial of power and honouring women. He would probably think I'm being dramatic and ridiculous. I don't give a shit, he can go fuck himself in the nicest possible way.

I had an amazing day yesterday. I got up at 9am, had coffee here at Beau Café. I wrote a lot and then carried on writing in the communal gardens, sitting on a lovely wooden bench. Suddenly I had the energy to clear my space at home. I went back and began tidying and in the process made three collages out of magazine cuttings I had collected a few weeks ago when I was living at Nancy's. I made two collages of my desired home environment and one of my future TV work. I pinned all of my collages up on my bedroom wall. This triggered off some fear in me because I see a shift has taken place. The new collages are more simplified, bigger, more concrete images. They say to me, "Right here! Right now!" They say "If you want it, you can have it." They say, "Film production is upon you. No airy-fairy stuff. Very grounded, very powerful, no messing, I'm here, I'm ready for you. Let's make movies, we have the equipment and the tools to create the craft." The home situation says to me, "No matter what relationships come into your life. Embrace your own space, enjoy it."

I got the 23 bus and went to Piccadilly. Gary was sitting on the steps of Eros outside the Criterion Theatre. It was beautifully hot and tourists were milling around like bees to the mysterious energy of London. I'd just texted Charlie's friend Trent in New York to see how he was doing. He'd said he'd not had time to get out because of studying for exams.

I texted, "All work and no play makes Jack…"

He texted back, "Jack?" and then immediately after said, "I'm not dull honey."

I couldn't tell whether he was playing or offended although I felt it to be the latter and that wasn't my intention.

I'm pleased I was actually on time to meet Gary. I was so excited to go for Chinese Dim Sum. Nancy had just called to say she was still waiting for the train and running late. We made our way directly to a Chinese restaurant on Wardour Street. It reminded me of the tapes Dad had made where he said, "So what's your Heaven?" and I said, "There's Chinese restaurants in heaven with Chinese table and Chinese chairs."

So this outing with Gary, was me living heaven on earth. Gary had never had Dim Sum before, so I really enjoyed choosing all the dishes and eating exactly what I wanted. We ate barbequed duck, Chau Si Pau, Chinese broccoli and drank three pots of jasmine tea. I love hanging out with Gary because he gets me on all levels and helped me process all my anger towards Eric at work for being a two faced bastard.

Later on after the cinema, Nancy and I walked from Leicester Square to Manchester Street and got on a number seven bus. I was hungry again, so we got off at Edgware Road and went to Maroush for chicken kebab, tabouleh and fruit cocktail juice. I love the bustle and energy of it in there. We then got the 23 bus again, it was perfect timing because we didn't even have to wait and the same two seats were available at the front of the bus where we'd sat before. A girl behind us was being harassed. The same thing had happened to me earlier in the afternoon. We kept an eye on her. My intuition said, don't push it, this guy may have a knife. Nancy had intuited the same. We asked if she was ok and she said, "yes," giving her a cue to make it downstairs. I popped back to Nancy's for tea and then home to bed at 11.15pm. I feel like I'm really connecting with myself which is giving me power but also throwing up fears, because I'm wondering how I'll manifest all my dreams effortlessly if at all.

I wish I was truly happy. I wish I was free. I wish I had financial security. I wish I had clarity. I wish I had strength of purpose. I wish I had power within. I wish I wasn't surrounded by a bunch of bitches, including Eric. I wish I was positively free from "The Psychic Show." I wish for more spiritual growth. I wish men treated me lovingly with respect. I wish for courage. I wish for honesty. I wish for integrity. I wish for loyalty. I wish for love. I wish to release frustration. I wish to surrender. I wish for peace. I wish...

3rd August
10.15am: Beau Café

Woke up feeling exhausted but elated. My body is heavy, probably because so much tension is releasing. Screaming last night did me good because I'm so close to telling Eric to go fuck himself and Petra that, yes, she is the media whore she claims to be. I'm ready to go into Mega TV today and speak my truth. I feel this knot of energy in my belly from the injustice. Today, I will channel pure white blinding light of God, like Moses when he saw the Burning Bush. Love thy neighbour as thy self. Thou shall not commit adultery. It is crucial that I stand in the light and that light fuels me with power, love and wisdom. I call upon Christ Consciousness to be present with me and I ask for Lord Archangel Michael's sword of truth and healing. I pray that the shackles and cords may be cut away. Like fire melts ice, it shall be done.

I got to the office at 11.30am. I could smell the fag smoke from the reception area of Mega TV as I walked in the door. I climbed the stairs thinking, "I must put my invoice in. Why haven't I done that yet?"

Barry was in the office. He has been very calm and centred since his mum died. He's got a quality of kindness about him. He invited me into the space where I used to work every day while he was off doing coke, while I was putting The Psychic Show together.

"Everything alright darling?" Barry said.

"No," I said.

"Come in, shut the door," he said, gesturing for me to sit in a swivel chair with a broken back.

"Barry, if you want to get rid of me, just say it," I said.

"No darling. Where do you get that idea from?" Barry said.

"Eric phoned me on Thursday. Told me he wants to cut my pay by half and that just doesn't work for me," I said.

"Since when did Eric decide how much you get paid? I'm your boss," Barry said.

"I know. That's why I'm asking if you want to let me go?" I said.

"No. I want you to stay. Let me speak to Kevin tomorrow. You in then?" he said.

"No," I said.

"Well, don't worry about it," he said.

But I'm still not satisfied.

"So why did Eric say you want to get rid of me?" I said.

"I don't know," he said.

Eric appeared in the studio, outside the glass window.

"There he bloody is and he's late again. I haven't had a drink in three weeks," Barry said, leaning towards me.

"Wow," I said, trying to imagine Barry surviving without alcohol.

"Yeah, I've been good on it. I can actually think," he said.

Maybe I can trust him now. I have to protect myself. So I did something I didn't want to do.

"Barry, I think I need to make you aware that I'm working on other shows," I said.

"Of course darling, never expected you to stay here forever. Everyone moves on," he said.

"Eric asked me for the commissioning editor's details of Ultra

TV and I gave them to him. He wants to take "The Psychic Show" there. Just want you to be aware there's no loyalty and he wouldn't think twice about leaving here if they offered him a deal," I said.

"I know," Barry said and then Eric opened the door to the office.

"Hi there darling," Eric said.

He reached for both my hands to lift me out of the chair.

"Shall we go talk?" Eric said, smiling, his eyes were sparkling but full of pockets of mischief and he's not really asking, the subtext is, "I'm talking with you now, so get away from Barry before you do any damage but it's already nuclear fallout because he set the attack a long time before. I snatched my hands away from his.

"No! I don't want to talk with you now. I'm pissed off," I said, practically spitting blood from last week's knives that he'd put in my back.

"Ok, we're about to go Live on Air. Eric, I want to talk with you alone," Barry said.

That was my cue to leave. I got up shakily and prepared myself best I could for the show as adrenalin pumped around my body. Why am I learning to be a bitch? I hate myself for being all the things I don't want to be. I headed upstairs for some TLC from Veronica.

"You alright sweetheart?" Veronica said in her lovely broad Northern tone. She was dressed all in black.

"Yes, I just spoke with Barry," I said and led her by the hand into a toilet cubicle.

"And?" she said, her big blue eyes are expectant.

"Eric's in the office with Barry now. I told Barry how Eric's trying to get rid of me," I said.

"Don't worry, it'll all work out, but I've got to get back to work," Veronica said. She looked pre-occupied.

I felt unresolved as we headed back out into the smelly

hallway. I could feel the energy from "Pleasure Zone," the night before. I took a stifled breath as Veronica disappeared into her office. I glanced in vehemently at the Pleasure Zone beds in the studio. I cannot get my head around this surreal and crazy environment. I went back down to our studio and sat on the Psychic Sofa. It's now covered in a nasty violet synthetic fur. I'm giving a psychic reading on it by day. A topless girl is snogging another girl on it by night. She's titillating men, urging them to text and phone in and wank. And they do. An average of 4,000 phone minutes in a night, averaging three minutes per call. That's a lot of guys all having orgasms at the same time.

Tiffany walks into the studio. I'm trying to stay calm. She sits down next to me on the sofa.

"How are you Scarlet?" Tiffany said.

"Yeah, good," I said, lying.

I want to like her but I'm angry because she's sidled into my presenting slot and is steadily edging me out. I had dreamt this months before. Unfortunately my psychic intuition was correct. She told me how Dwight, one of our fans had emailed into the chat room, "Text to death for Tiffany."

I did my best to soften.

6th August
8pm

I'm sad and frustrated. I think it triggered me when Nancy snapped at me in our meditation group on Tuesday. Why am I allowing people to treat me like crap?

Steve Kruger called and left a nice message inviting me for dinner but I don't feel like calling him back now because he's blown me out twice.

I feel so fragile and raw inside, exposed and pained. If you abuse a child or an animal too much, there comes a point when it will not allow itself to be hit anymore and it bites back. Unfortunately it may then harm kind people also because it is so scared of being hurt. That is me right now. My heart is aching. It hurts so much it's actually numb. I cun't feel anything. I meant to say can't and wrote cunt by accident. Hmmm interesting. It's such an ugly unattractive word. Is that what I am? A cunt.

Is that how people see me? Am I allowing myself to be treated as a cunt? Yes I am.

Why? Because I don't love myself.

Classic FM plays in the background. Sounds like the theme from, "Inside the Actor's Studio." Soothes me. Dad's making dinner next door and I've just eaten asparagus with mayo. I'm in the TV room and I know guides are with me because the lights are flashing. Ah, a nice breeze just flowed in. Dad said I don't need to please everyone. He's right. I wonder if I can allow that to change. Tomorrow, I'm going to do an acting workshop. I'll be doing Ben Elton's, "Popcorn." That'll be fun. Hopefully clear this shit feeling inside me.

9th August
10.20am: Ladbroke Grove Tube

I didn't write yesterday or get down what I wanted to say the day before because it was too hot. I couldn't think. My head was whirring. I am on a rollercoaster. I went from sheer depression to an absolute high but not a loving high. A sexual high. The type of energy that brings me present in my body. I could feel my emotions being triggered from all these experiences. My cells popping and saying, "You don't know the truth."

Pins pricking my bubbles and shattering my illusions. Just got a text from my friend Beth reminding me her party is next Saturday not the one just gone which means that I've been a week ahead of myself. Why did I think it was the fourteenth on the seventh? That's bizarre. I guess I am meant to go to the Hollywood starlet party after all. Back to last Tuesday so I can get this energy clear and let it go. After the show, which was a good one. Eric comes up to me.

"Alright darling, shall we go for that chat?" he says.

Why does his high pitch twang annoy me so much? Is it the falseness oozing through a genuine façade? I cross my arms. Grant, his sidekick is right next to him, ever faithful like a lapdog.

"So I've spoken with Kevin and he's prepared to keep you on the same salary till the end of the month as a compromise and then it'll be lowered," Eric says.

"Hmm," I say, "I've never worked in a company that cuts people's pay as the revenue rises."

"Well that's what he's prepared to do," Eric says, as if he is doing me some sort of great favour.

"That doesn't work for me," I say.

I can feel my barriers of protection firming. Armour is etherically placed around and upon me, I am going to battle, "With all due respect, you're not my boss Eric. Barry and Kevin hired me so my salary has absolutely nothing to do with you."

"Of course, of course darling, it's just Alain said…" he says.

"I don't give a fuck Eric, didn't you hear what I said. You've stabbed me in the back and I don't like it," I say.

Eric looks very edgy now.

"Shall we go talk in the office," he says.

"Fine," I say, not giving a shit who hears. Fuck the lot of them.

I lead the way and Eric follows with Grant sidled behind. I lean up against the wall. It's like a stand off as Eric stands against the opposite wall. Grant shuts the door behind him and blocks it. I have no way out now but they know I'm happy about my position because now I can let rip. I place my hands on my hips. I can't help it. Anger and venom are building inside me. It's like rocket fuel is charging through my blood and cells and I can't stop or control its potency. Forgive me God for what I am about to say, for how I may behave. Steer me, guide me, I truly wish not to hurt a soul.

"So why didn't you just say to my face you want to get rid of me Eric?"

I'm glaring at him. I want to hit him. It's a rhetorical question so I get increasingly frustrated when he continues lying.

"Darling it was never me. It's been Barry from day one. I've always been your biggest fan," he says.

I notice his highly nervous disposition.

"Now why don't I believe that Eric?" I say, my natural emphasis upon his name.

"I don't know darling, it's the truth," he says.

I search his eyes and tune into his my heart and his soul.

"So why aren't I feeling it?" I say.

"I don't know," he says.

"I want to believe you, but I can't," I say.

I feel like a puppy that's been slapped so many times and I'm finally biting back as a grown dog, a Rotweiller.

"Scarlet, I really want you to stay. You're part of the team," he says.

"So why you trying to cut my salary in half and still pay Harry Morrison the same?" I say.

"I'm going to cut his salary too," he says.

"He'll leave, he won't do it for less," I say.

"Then we'll have to let him go," he says.

Grant is silent throughout this game.

"So if the figures are going up and up, why not raise everyone's salary to what Harry and I get instead of lowering us to theirs?" I say.

"Alain asked me to make cuts," he says.

"So don't you value me?" I say.

"I do Scarlet," he says.

"So you target me first," I say.

"Scarlet you get more than me, Grant, Tiffany and Petra," he says.

"That's because I'm bloody worth it and I'm good at what I do! If you've got an issue about how much you get paid, ask for a rise but don't take your shit out on me."

So the truth be told. Eric is jealous of the fact I get paid more and he wants to nail me.

"Scarlet please, I really want you to stay, the team wouldn't be the same without you," Eric says.

I know the only reason he says this is because he's scared. He'd rather have an enemy in his camp than outside. I'm silent now. My anger has subsided. I'm wounded and I don't know what I should be saying or feeling now.

"Ok," I say. My voice had softened.

Eric is reeling from the aftershock.

"So you coming to the production meeting?" he says.

"Yes," I say, wondering why I am going. Because then I can see what the devious fucker is up to.

We all head down to the Cock & Bull pub on Oxford Street. I'm walking with all the boys: Saul, Dwight, Jim, Grant and Eric. We arrive and Ron, Tiffany and Petra, the two faced psychic arrive a couple of minutes later. Ironically I find myself sitting next to Eric on the sofa. I stay quiet and listen. I have lost my voice. Eric has claimed my baby and I'm bitter, like a woman scorned and so the fury will unfold once again. You may have slain the dragon Eric, but I am the phoenix. It is in my nature to rise again from challenging circumstances.

"Alright everyone, as you all know, I'm off on holiday for two weeks," Eric says.

Everyone nods. I try and contain my frustration.

"If anyone, I mean anyone tries to make a single change to the schedule. Grant, you phone me right away.

Ok?" Grant says.

"We're going to have a Psychic Show party in October which Tiffany is organising and thanks to Petra we've got some great press."

Petra whips out a copy of News of the World and smiles proudly.

"What is it?" I say.

Laurent takes the paper from her who is sitting to my left and opens it to the centrefold. A spread of Petra's analysis of the housemates boobs from, "Big Brother." Petra psychically reading tits! Fan-fucking-tastic! I read down the page. Petra of Mega TV's, "The Psychic Show," celebrity psychic presenter. Oh God, I'm trying not to cringe and yet several psychics have warned me before that "The Psychic Show," would become a tabloid baby. A child of shame. Obviously I will have to move on. It's like Chinese whispers. My original vision has been battered.

On yesterday's show, it was so hot in the studio, I was wearing a pink strapless dress, and when Grant changed camera angle, you could only see my body on screen and none of the dress. It looked like I could have been topless!

After Eric's paranoid speech, I wonder how he will ever relax for a moment on his camping holiday. I wonder if he will learn from his mistakes and thoughtfulness by the time he is thirty-years-old. I fear not. Unless he gets whacked into humility.

Eric and I continue talking privately. I soften a little.

"Eric the only reason I'm being so hard on you is you stabbed me, multiple wounds in my back and I'm hurting a lot," I say.

I am a broken record. It's my victim emerging.

"I know. I'm sorry darling. It must be very hard for you," he says.

Yet we both know inside nothing is going to change unless I make a stand.

"Eric do you trust me?" I say.

I watch his face closely. I read his thoughts.

"Is this a trick question?" he's thinking.

"Seventy-five percent," he says.

I nod because he was wise not to say a hundred percent and if he said fifty percent or below, it would be "no," so it confirms to me that Eric is a clever and cunning young man. I interject.

"I trust you and I don't trust you. Right now looking in your eyes, I trust you. Three days from now, I know I may not trust you," I say.

Eric says nothing. I can see he's trying to work me out. My sharing is a cathartic release. I continue, "I also like you and I don't like you."

Eric nods with discomfort.

"So I guess we trust each other and we don't. We like each other and we don't but we've got to work together so we have to get on. Let's just be professional. If I'm going to stab you, I'll do it to your face. Can we agree on that?" I say.

Of course I'd love all peace and no knives but I know Eric will never go for a ceasefire. This is a lesson I'm not enjoying. Having to be a warrior and yet the universe seems to be throwing this lesson in my face. I probe deeper.

"Why do I still feel you want to get rid of me?" I say.

I'm like a dog with a bone that just can't give it up.

Eric looks highly shifty now.

"Maybe that's because you're picking up my back up plan," he says.

"What plan is that?" I say.

I want to scream at him but I am extraordinarily calm.

"In case you get angry one day and blow," he says.

Bull's eye.

"The only reason I'd get angry is if you treated me badly," I say.

A battle does come to a natural end. I look up on the train and see someone reading a copy of Heat. Nadia, "Big Brother," contestant is celebrity of the moment. Will we remember her a year from now? Are we all just little ants running around on a treadmill? Is there a bigger picture? "The Psychic Show," has been a big chapter for me.

12th August
10.30am: Beau Cafe

I woke up very unsettled by my dream. What does it mean? I was descending some stairs, I think an escalator. I walked past a man with his wife on my right. As they looked at me, they dropped their baby all the way down the stairs. It hurt me so much, as the child bashed, bounced and crashed like a rag doll on to concrete stairs. Why do I feel hardened stares? Who's scrutinizing me? The press? "Spineless bitch?" Is that what they're saying? How did such a tragedy occur?

I am triggered now with huge fears that my projects will be stolen rather than collapse.

13th August
9am: Beau Cafe

I woke naturally at 8.30am thinking about my connection with Marcus. I'd exposed myself leaving him that answer phone message the week before. Marcus had reeled me in and then backed off and that infuriates me. Last night when I walked into the District Club, low and behold, who should be there at the bar with Henry looking totally cute and sexy but Marcus with his naughty schoolboy look. He exudes mischievousness yet he looks like an angel. His eyes pierced me blue but I'm pissed off. "Hi," Marcus said.

I don't waste any time. "You never phoned back," I said.

"You didn't leave your number," he said.

"Missed call would have shown on your phone," I said, absolutely not believing him.

"Scarlet, I've got an ancient phone. It doesn't have that facility," he said.

I softened as I believed his genuine response having scrutinized his body language and listened to the tone of his voice. Yes it felt genuine. So we launched back into where we were a week ago. Flirtation. He leaned up against the white wall, all 6ft 3 inches of him and Jason began talking with a beautiful black woman called Ruby. It felt unimportant the words exchanged by Marcus and I at this point. It was the energetic connection. It was flowing like ping pong back and forth.

15th August
12.30pm: Ladbroke Grove Tube

Been so much activity the last couple of days, I have to catch up on my unfolding process. My connection with Marcus is unusual. I can't quite figure him out. Guess that's why I like him. Since my discovering he is a leading investigative journalist and was followed by the FBI and CIA for two years, I realize there is a lot hidden behind those innocent eyes. He played me brilliantly. Intentional or not. The more we talked, the more we flirted, we're both masters of this game and enjoy the quality of play. All I was thinking was "I want to kiss you," and I know he was thinking the same but we're both cool and composed. Then he said "I know if we kissed, it'd be really good."

"How do you know?" I said. I'm intrigued because I know his intuition is correct.

"Your lips, I know they'd fit with mine," he said.

I smiled. I didn't want to reveal too much but I knew he could see inside me. He stripped me down. "Let's go into the hall," Marcus said. He took me by the hand.

"No," I said. There's a beat between us. "I know where I want to kiss you and it's not here. Are you up for it?"

"Yes," he said.

The rest of the night, Ruby and I sat in big brown leather

armchairs while Marcus and Jason perched on a white glass covered coffee table. The conversation was a haze for me, a nicety. I'm absolutely ahead of myself, in the future. Marcus and I were playing out a dance. Ruby decided not to go back with Jason so there was an awkward moment between them outside. I wanted to extricate myself and leave with Marcus immediately. Then this girl Kirsten appeared and instead Jason went to party with her. We all said our goodbyes. I felt light and free as Marcus and I stepped onto Portobello Road. The air was warm and balmy. As we turned the corner onto Elgin Crescent, he clasped my hand. I was happy. "So are you up for an adventure?" I said.

"Yes," he said. Little did I know of his global adventures. Marcus is a living real life James Bond.

We arrived outside my front door. "Wait here," I said, as I let myself inside and ran up several flights of stairs. My destination, the fridge which held the chilled bottle of champagne that was meant to be finished with him a week before. I grabbed two champagne flutes and made my way back downstairs as fast as possible. Marcus looked positively intrigued as I stood before him. "Follow me," I said and he did. We walked up the street and I placed the key into the lock of the communal garden gate. We stepped over the threshold together. Although it was dark, I felt safe. I sensed the garden full of fairies and elves. The magic of the night was upon us. The soles of our feet crunched delightfully on the gravel beneath. As we arrived at my chosen destination, the centre of the garden, it was lit with an array of tea light candles. Someone had already claimed my intended magic spot. We carried on until we found a bench nestled amongst the trees. We could see out into the garden but we were hidden from view. I placed the champagne bottle and glasses on the ground and we sat down next to each other on the wooden bench. The night air felt slightly damp. Before I could think, Marcus leant over and kissed me. His lips were full and overpowering. The kiss was good but I was not entirely present. "Let me taste you," Marcus said.

I became coy. "No," I said. I was shocked he asked. He ignored my response, knelt down on the ground and pulled my legs apart. I was wearing a denim skirt and it was very short. "No," I said, this time more firmly and placed my hand in front of my crotch as his head hovered there expectantly. I yanked his head back up to the level of my face. Instead Marcus stood up, unzipped his jeans and pulled out his cock. "Marcus!" I gasped.

"Touch it," he said.

"No, put it away!"

Marcus hesitated a moment before fulfilling my wishes. He sat back down on the bench and I straddled him. Again we kissed. He took off my top and exposed my skin. He ran his hands down my spine and took my breast in his mouth. I gasped. I felt his hardness rise up and press against me. "You're wet. I can feel it," Marcus whispered.

"I know," I said and tried to pull myself off him but he held me still. Won't let me go. He slipped his fingers into my panties and I fought with myself to remove his hand. "No," I said but I'm screaming "yes," inside. Every part of my being desired him inside me. "I can't," I said.

"Can I stay?" he said.

I wanted to say yes but I knew it would be hard to stop him trying to have sex. "We can just snuggle up. I think we'd fit well together," he said.

I missed intimacy. Every night I went to sleep with Bill holding me and every morning I woke up with him close to me. I always felt so content, so grateful to have him by my side. "Yes, I'd like you to stay but we can't do anything. I feel too vulnerable right now," I said.

"Scarlet, I just want you to know I'm in quite a traumatic space right now. I can't get into a relationship," Marcus said.

"Me neither," I said as I put my top back on. I didn't have the courage to open my heart yet. We strolled through the garden. I wondered how Marcus at 6ft 3inches would fit in my tiny bed. He would be the first man to stay in my sacred space. Marcus descended my white spiral staircase and stripped naked before me. I hesitated before removing my clothes and slipping beneath the sheets with him. He wrapped his arm around my waist and pulled me close to him. I didn't remember falling asleep. Marcus walked with me in my dream. I can't remember what he did or said specifically. It was more a feeling of being led, guided to a destination. It was America. When I awoke, I remember two key issues. I would have a TV show out in the States and I was buying a home out there. I felt a powerful healing energy emanate from Marcus upon waking, violet light swirled in my third eye. Marcus tried to have sex with me. I refused because I liked him. The more I like someone, the less I want to have sex with them. I felt a special connection and wanted it to unfold for fear of being hurt. When I don't care, it's easier. I can open my body because I won't be hurt emotionally. This is a sad and fucked up psychology. Why am I doing this to myself?

It was very hot today. Almost thirty degrees Celsius. Marcus left via my bathroom. My flat has an amazingly unique layout. It's small but extends onto three floors. A narrow spiral staircase takes you from the lounge kitchenette down to the bedroom and below that is my gorgeous white and black tiled bathroom with divinely high ceilings and a window that opens out onto a roof terrace with a deckchair to watch the world go by. My stone Buddha sits alongside adorned in a turquoise Najavo necklace and a large tan spider's web stretches across my small green shrubs. I put on my blue shorts, a sleeveless T and Lacoste flip-flops and head off to Kentish Town where my acting workshop is taking place. We're doing Ben Elton's "Popcorn". I think I'm going to be late because I stayed in bed with Marcus. So I grabbed a latte and pain au chocolat from Beau Café and hop into a taxi. There were two other actors besides Steven, the teacher. A South African woman called Genevieve and a guy from Birmingham called Rob. I dived into the day excited, ready to embrace the roles but as the day continued, I felt exhausted energetically. Somehow I was failing to access the ditzy serial killer's character of Scout who worships her boyfriend Wayne and the famous porn star wannabe actress called Brook. I felt I could easily play the bitter, soon to be Jewish divorcee. This realization makes me feel rather uncomfortable.

16th August
Beau Café

This morning my neck feels extremely stiff, as does my whole body. My chi is stagnant. A chunk of my energy needs to shift but I'm not quite sure what it is. My dreams have been vivid of late. My Saturday night dream terrified me. I awoke very uneasy. I was in a tube station down on the platform. It was busy, a lot of tourists were around. The energy surrounding me was jagged. As I walked down the platform, I saw the red light of a flair shoot into the air. Fear erupted in me because I knew I was in a danger zone yet I couldn't escape fast enough. I tried to run through the throng of panicked people as a haze of smoke began to fill the platform. My intuition told me it would be safest to dive down onto the floor and cover my head. It would give me more time. I figured the smoke would take longest to get to the floor. In this moment, life felt extremely fragile as the smoke enveloped me. I wondered was I alive or dead. I had a deep sense of mortality and how I choose not to care for others because I am scared to open myself to pain. I wish I had because we only have each moment. I also had this urgent sense of the need to do so much in the world and for my soul to experience life. This dream reminded me of the energy of Iraq and The Tokyo train disaster with the deadly gas. Will there be an attack in London soon? Please please please God, I pray not.

The night after I dreamt of receiving extreme pleasure in water, connecting me to my creativity and potent sexuality and I danced with my eyes closed. I was led by an invisible energy and surrendered to it, albeit in fear. My personality wanted to control the dance. Know every move in advance. My soul wanted to be thrown, dipped, twirled, kissed, and it was. My personality trembled and baulked at the intensity of the dance. My soul stepped up a gear and dived in, embraced and challenged my mysterious dance partner. A man I do not know, to match me and he did because he didn't try and figure it out. He allowed his soul and spirit to be guided. We entered another realm together, new consciousness. His energy was that of a teacher, music in his veins, passion. He triggered the hidden point in my solar plexus. He was preparing me for my next steps of growth and interaction with men.

This man is beautiful. He doesn't strike me between the eyes. He is a steady flame that grows brighter and brighter until I can ignore my feelings for him no longer. I will meet him again in the dreamtime and next dance I will allow him into my heart and see what happens. Even if my heart breaks, it is meant to be, for that is part of my expansion, my evolvement. Who are you?

I have this deep trust in the universe and my soul path and a parallel of intense fear. Will everything be ok? "Yes, all is well. Trust like you've never trusted before," my soul says.

I'm booking a flight to Spain and then I'm going to LA. My mother's fears echo in my ears and mirror the part of me that doesn't have faith.

After the actor's workshop I felt complete but unsatisfied. I had opened another area that lacked depth within me. I believe the more acting I do, the more I'm allowing it to manifest. I completed my application form for Equity which I sent off on Friday so hopefully membership will come through very soon. All-important for launching my career in the States.

My dear old friend Emma came over on Saturday night and we went for dinner at La Chiave with Sedrick who I'd met several months before in the steam room. We had a lovely table outside. The evening was truly summer. I felt very relaxed. An English actor was sitting on the table to my left, someone old school. At the end of our meal a Brazilian woman who was a friend of Sedrick's joined us. She sat down with a guy who had sandy blonde brown hair and very blue eyes that reflected light. He was dressed in jeans and a t-shirt. "I love exotic dark women," he said to Emma. I caught myself register that I was neither dark or exotic, so he definitely wouldn't fancy me. And then something strange happened. I felt my attention drawn to his hands. In that moment I had never seen such beauty. Then I realized I was having a clairvoyant experience. His hands were revealing his spirit and soul. I felt I could be open with him because I felt he wouldn't be attracted to me. "You have beautiful hands," I said.

"What do you see?" he said looking into my eyes.

Suddenly I felt a spark ignite between us and I can't remember his name, even though we were introduced. I tune in before responding. "You have a lot of earth and fire in you. You're very grounded, connected to the earth but you're also an extremely passionate person, inspired by life," I said. As I study his hands, I feel myself reading his soul. Images are flashing within my psychic vision and I see an open book to his soul. The synchronicities unfold. He lives in Hampstead, the next road from my Dad and then he mentions the hospice where my grandmother died. I was having psychic experiences that I didn't understand.

I knew when my grandma was going to die. My family had stood with the doctor. They were deciding how to prolong her existence on the earth plane with drugs. Grandma had told me she was tired and wanted to die. Such a beautiful, elegant, larger than life woman. I'm literally in tears writing about this. I miss you Grandma Doris. I love you. You were always so kind to me. Your biggest gift to me was your unconditional love for me. Thank you. "Why give her more drugs?" I said.

"Scarlet, how can you say that," my Mum said.

"She's going to die anyway. She told me she doesn't want to live anymore. She's in too much pain," I said.

Mum and Aunt Louise agreed to a new medicine intake with the hope of Grandma gently getting better even though she had sever cancer of the liver and colon. We left the hospice. The next night I was meant to go out clubbing with my best friend Mandy and a guy called Stuart. I was twenty-one years old and remember feeling Grandma with me but I didn't understand how I felt her presence so strongly. It was a Saturday afternoon in summer. I had laid down for a nap at 5pm. I closed my eyes but my body felt full of energy. At 5.20pm I sat bolt upright. I got out of bed, put on a t-shirt and a pair of denim shorts. I plaited my hair Native American style. "Mum, is it ok if I go see Grandma?"

"Of course, I going in a couple of hours," Mum said.

A sense of urgency filled me as I left my house and trod the cobbled mews. Within a few minutes I have reached the end of the tree lined street. As I walked into the building, it smelt of sickness and death. I calmly approached Grandma's bed. Her breathing was so shallow. I took her hand. I sensed she was close to the end. I quickly let her hand go and ran down the hallway to the nurse. "I know this may sound crazy but I think my Grandma is about to die. Could you come take a look?" I said.

The nurse smiled sympathetically and followed me. She tended to my Grandma, looked up at me and said "Yes, she has about ten minutes left."

Panic filled me. "My Mum, she needs to know," I said.

"Don't worry, I'll call her now. Your grandmother can't respond but she can hear you," the nurse said.

I sat down next to Grandma and took her left hand. I clasped it and did my best to connect with her. "Hang on Grandma Doris. Please don't go. Mum and Auntie Louise are on their way. They want to say goodbye before you go," I said. The other cancer patients in the open ward looked over at me sympathetically. They know they will soon follow. As I held Grandma's hand, I felt the life force drain out of her. It made me feel weak. I wanted to let go of her hand because I felt physically sick but I didn't. I sensed I was a bridge for her to cross over to the other side. Grandma's breathing became increasingly shallow but I could feel Grandma's love. The ten minutes I had with her felt timeless. I was so relieved when Mum arrived. I stepped back and let Mum speak with Grandma. I can't remember what she said but I saw the love exchange between them. My aunt and cousin arrived soon after. As soon as they said their farewells, Grandma stopped breathing. She was gone. I knew something magical had occurred. That night Grandpa stayed in my bed so Mum could look after him and I stayed with my best friend Todd. We kissed for the first time. Life, love and passion along with death. I chose to sleep alone on a mattress on the floor. Sunday morning I awoke to the stroke of a hand on my arm. I sat up suddenly but no one was there. I know it was Grandma Doris. As I write about her now, I realize she was a major catalyst for my spiritual growth.

I think I met this stranger Brett to connect me to my matriarchal lineage and power. That is a beautiful gift. It surprises me that I am grieving now. I love you Grandma Doris, so much. I miss you with all my heart.

I had a good psychic session with a stripper called Stacey. I picked up on her offer from Playboy and about the movie roles she'd been given in LA.

Charlie just phoned me. He was lovely and told me all about his weekend with ex-fiancé. How they talked and nothing sexual occurred. "I'm looking forward to seeing you Scarlet. Have you thought about what you'd like to do," Charlie said. I don't know," I said, feeling bashful and wanting him to take the lead.

"Maybe we'll end up in your magical garden," he said.

"Yes," I said and giggled.

"Why do you always laugh when I'm on the phone with you?" he said.

"You make me happy," I said.

"I'm sorry I've been selfish Scarlet. I really didn't mean to hurt you," he said.

"Babe, there's nothing to be sorry for. Anyway, I booked my flight to LA today and I'm going to Spain first," I said.

"Getting a tan in Spain for LA?" Charlie said.

"Yes," I said and laughed, he knew me well.

I think Charlie feels safe knowing I'm going away, it allows him to be more open and intimate with me. It's the same for me to. "I think you hurt me because my connection with you is special Charlie, it's not just a shag. For me, it's making love and the only way I can do that is by opening myself and it hurt me because I felt so vulnerable and yet I have expectations of you," I said. And so, I revelled in that Charlie and I will always be connected, whatever happens.

17th August
10am: Beau Café

Wow, that is the most beautiful thing anyone has done for me. I am positively blown away. I came down the stairs after a chat on the phone with Gary, ready for my morning latte and pain au chocolat and saw a big brown puffed out envelope on the doormat with my name on it. As I picked it up, I noticed how light it felt. Then I remembered Brett had asked for my address yesterday. I carefully opened the package and peeked inside. The beautiful smell of sweet sage wafted into my nostrils, as I inhaled the divine scent. I unfolded a piece of white paper inside and read "Hi sweetheart, happy smudging – sage from the heart of California. Lots of love, Brett xxx."

I was so excited that Brett had such sensitivity and awareness. So why am I scared to see you? The connection is so powerful between us that it overwhelms me and I end up feeling safe by reaching out to people like Wayne instead. Brett I honour you so much, but I'm not quite ready to see you. I don't fully understand why. I don't want to hurt you or me.

On Sunday evening, Jason walked me home after watching "Along Came Polly." I'm positive I saw Matt sitting in his car with a girl. He looked at me, more like straight through me and then downwards as he carried on talking. I couldn't see properly but am ninety percent certain it was him. I sense he will be getting ready for marriage soon. That's why I never heard back from him. So in the space of a few months, I've pulled in Brett who at the age of thirty, is the most spiritually and soul aware man I have ever met. He is a true shaman. He gives me insights to me like when I first knew Bill. So why do I still back away?

After acting class last night, I did my own version of the Meisner technique in front of my gold leaf mirror. I sat on a white fluffy fleece, wearing a thong, my hair loosely pulled together atop my head and faced myself. I put on Sanaya Roman's "Awakening your Heart Center" CD and lit my fig scented candles. Then I placed colour essences on top of my new archangel cards which lay on top of my journal. I felt a balanced and inspired love that could be communicated effortlessly, needed to flow. As I repeated said "I love you" to my reflection, my face began to shape-shift. The ugly unloved parts of myself revealed themselves and I received glimpses of the beautiful radiant parts also. I let the meditation unfold without direction. "You're bitter," I said.

"I'm bitter?" I said.

"You're bitter," I said, almost spitting venom at the mirror.

"I am bitter," I said, a hurt look upon my face.

"You're sad," I said.

"I am sad," I said, absolute recognition and acceptance flowing through every cell of my being. I moved through intense fear, anger, happiness, power, sexiness, love and beauty. Ugly images arose on my face that I knew if I didn't confront and accept these parts of myself, I would remain blocked. As I embraced my shadow, I saw shards of light cracking through the shades of darkness and an extreme beauty revealed itself like I'd never seen before. "You're beautiful?" I said.

"I am beautiful," I said amazed.

"You're beautiful!" I said, the realization washing over me. "I am beautiful," I said proudly. Yes, I am the ugly ducking who has transformed into a swan. Yes, I am a swan.

Last night, Grandpa Stanley visited me in my dream. "Will you go for a walk with me?" he said.

"Yes," I said, but I sense I'm keeping him waiting. I can't remember the walk but I know I spoke with him. I met him at Maitland Road. He was pleased to see me. I still have no contact with Grandma Penny, my one living grandparent. What an irony.

11.30am

I'm feeling a little overwhelmed right now. The archangel cards keep showing me I require a healthier lifestyle so Spain will be perfect for me. I feel it important to have time on my own with Mum and Stuart rather than take a friend.

After I met Brett last Saturday, Emma and I went to The District Club. Jason and Robbie were already there with Jason's new girlfriend Kirsten. As I walked in, I saw Marcus. I felt angry but only marginally. "You never asked for my number," I said.

"I know, I thought that when I left," Marcus said.

"You don't exactly seem like you want to ask for it," I said feeling rather confused.

"Let's go outside and I'll take it right now," he said and I laugh nervously. I suppose because I don't entirely believe he wants to. I told him about my acting workshop. Some seats come free, the armchairs I'd sat in the night before with Ruby. I sit down next to Kirsten and Marcus moves away towards the bar. I feel his eyes half on me. After a few moments, I decide to empower myself. I get up and ask Emma if she'll come up to the Playroom with me. However, I have been slightly calculating. This is a very painful confession for me because I noticed Connor Huntley, a TV host has already checked me out several times. I decide to test this out. The moment Emma and I enter the Playroom, he makes a beeline for me. I'm thinking "stuff Marcus, screw him!" Wow, my shadow is revealing herself beautifully. "Hi, I'm Connor," Connor said and he extended his hand. I shake it.

"Scarlet, pleased to meet you," I said.

Emma leans over and whispers to me "I went up to him earlier and said "you don't look as good in person as you do on TV," and he just looked at me slightly taken aback. I think I may have offended him." I laughed as Emma scoffed. She is a good luck charm male magnet for me. Connor reached his arm around my waist. He's tall, I judged 6ft 3 inches. His friend Mark came over and handed me, then Emma, a cocktail each. It looked quite a lethal concoction, glowing orange and pink. I accepted it dubiously. Emma went downstairs and I was left in the Chill Room with Connor. He swayed from side to side. He was drunk. I felt uncomfortable, especially because I knew Marcus could walk upstairs at any moment. Connor took my hand and then I noticed his friend slip some pills into his other hand. Connor then tried to drag me into the toilet with him. Thank God it was occupied. Instead I led him upstairs. As we walked into the conference room, we were confronted by a group of Aussies baring their naked chests. Sweat filled the room and hard dance tunes banged out of the speakers. Connor directed me to the far corner of the room. He tried to kiss me but I turned my head away. "Connor, I think you look out of place, why don't you take your top off?" I said, teasing him. To my amazement, he did. He swished from side to side as he struggled to pull his stripped rugby t-shirt over the back of his neck but lost his balance in the process and fell backwards onto the floor. Several Aussies broke his crashing fall. "You alright mate?" said one of the Aussies, as he pulled Connor upright. Connor reached for my hand and gave a goofy smile. This would have made interesting headlines for the well known Children's BBC TV presenter. Life was full of surprises. But beneath the surface, there was a more urgent issue at hand. I sensed the energy of a man in turmoil, desperately unhappy. I wanted to tell him everything would be ok but I sensed he was heading towards some type of breakdown and it was just a matter of when his collapse would occur. "Can we leave?" he said, as he struggled to put his t-shirt back on. On his first attempt, he put the t-shirt on back to front and on the second attempt he put it on inside out. I gave up trying to help him and we descend the District Club stairs, Connor wearing his t-shirt inside out and slipped into a mini-cab. I prayed no one would see me. I knew I was about to do something bad. I didn't know why. I guess a part of me still needed to abuse myself but I am going in eyes wide open. We pulled up outside Connor's apartment off of Ladbroke Grove. As we entered his space, I felt such similar energies to Aidan's home except they were darker, more sinister. I was genuinely concerned that he would be ok. "Have you done drugs?" I said.

"No," he said. I wanted to believe him. I actually tricked myself that this was so but I knew when I searched my heart that indeed he had. Connor led me to his bedroom. A large poster of Michael Cane with a gun in "Get Carter" loomed on his wall. I noticed how the gun pointed towards the bed. Connor stripped in front of me. I froze. I knew I didn't have to stay. He stepped toward me and pulled my clothes off me. I protested but it fell on deaf ears. Suddenly, I was naked in Connor's bed. He kissed me. I was surprised by the sensitivity of his lips and how there was a flow between us. He pulled me on top of him and then lifted me up. I found my crotch hovering above his face. I tried to back down but he held me there firmly, wrapped his arms around my hips and pulled my body down on to his face. I decided to let go and enjoy the experience. I let his tongue move in circles over my clitoris. I moaned in pleasure and arched my back. I looked down and his eyes were open, taking me in. He kept going and for a long time. I'm having a déjà vu moment. It's like my experience with Aidan except that I opened my heart and soul to Aidan and so wanted to see him again but with Connor I knew this would be a one night stand and my lesson was to receive pleasure and I did. Connor kissed and licked me so much, his tongue probing inside me, eventually I came. I felt the orgasm move right through me. It was like my body was being cleansed. He then wrapped his arms around me and whispered "I love you," which I knew he did not and we fell asleep.

A couple of hours later, I awoke suddenly to Connor grabbing hold of me in tears. I could feel his pain and anguish. I pulled his head onto my chest, put my arms around him, my hand over his heart and the other upon his head and prayed for the angels to bring in healing. He then kneeled forward in child's pose and fell asleep once again. I found this experience quite unsettling because I felt helpless. I wanted to support him, one human being, one soul to another.

In the morning, he entered inside me. He didn't last long. "Oh that's terrible," he said.

"Thanks," I said.

"I'm sorry, I didn't mean that," he said and held me as we lay in silence for a while. "How did you end up in my bed?" Connor said.

Wow, what a fucking idiot, I thought. Talk about major denial. I don't know why I said it but I did. "The District Club, we met at The District Club." Now I was playing his game.

"I can't believe this happened," he said.

"Now you're making me feel really good," I said.

"I think I better take you home," he said and left the room.

I sat on the edge of his bed, lifeless. How could he suddenly claim such ignorance? So he could feel the pleasure and suppress the guilt. But he had to live with it, he had to live with himself. Then Connor walked back in the room. I was angry at his lack of sensitivity. "I've just come out of a seven year relationship. I was getting married," I said. Fuck, I sounded like a broken record. Who was I kidding? I was in as much denial as he was. But as I later on discover, he was going out with someone and had been unfaithful and I was a free agent. "Well you seem to be taking this rather well," Connor said and that pressed all my buttons, made me want to cry. But I didn't. He wasn't worth it.

"Where do you live?" he said.

"Ladbroke Gardens," I said.

"I'll drive you home," he said.

I'm surprised he has any decency. I guess it's because he wants to get me out of his home as fast as possible. We get into his black jeep. The air conditioning cools the psychic tension in the car. "So how long have you lived in Ladbroke Gardens?" Connor said.

"Only a few months. I was in LA before," I said.

"What were you doing in LA," he said.

"Film," I said.

"So you going to tell anyone?" he said.

"Connor, let's put it down to experience. It was just one of those things," I said.

He looked relieved as we sat outside my home. "Take care," I said, as I got out of his car. It is a beautiful day. I decided to go for coffee at Beau Café. It's only 10am and I'm likely to be in with a chance of getting a pain au chocolat.

18th August
11.55pm

I'm doing the show tomorrow. I've tidied my space. Some sort of clarity is finally setting in. I'm pleased because I did chi gung today properly for the first time in a couple of weeks. My body so needs it. The stagnancy is shifting. I ate healthier today and drank no alcohol although, I did have two lattes and a pain au chocolat. Gosh, I feel like a muffin tomorrow.

19th August
10.30am: Tube

I dreamt I was in these beautiful gardens in Chelsea. Charlie was holding my left hand. "Let's run," Charlie said. So I ran alongside him and then he began to run faster and the terrain remained beautiful but became rocky. I was scared I would fall and then I lost my vision. "Charlie, I can't run because I can't see where I'm going," I said.

"Trust me," he said and I did, I kept running, all the while he held my hand and then he let go and ran out in front of me and I remember the ground travelling faster and faster beneath me and then I saw an emerald hue and resonance of the grass, so lush and the most incredible daffodils everywhere. I saw a black cat in the garden, she was mysterious and very agile. I copied and followed her footsteps as she moved close to the ground. So gentle in pace and yet focused and aware. She knew what she wanted. Her energy was powerful. Her beauty radiated with each movement. I shape-shifted into her and experienced her connection to nature. It took me to a place of peace and sensuality. Suddenly the soul connection felt so deep with Charlie. I could feel his spirit reaching out to me. So what is it I'm not seeing?

6.05pm

Oh shit, this situation with Brett is triggering me. I feel so fucking torn up about it. Brett still wants to see me for dinner. I can't handle it. I told him about Charlie. "I just want to be friends," Brett said. But I know he doesn't.

"I don't want a relationship, just an interaction," he said. But all the signs said he does. Now I'm feeling guilty. In my heart, I don't want to have dinner with him. In my head, I think I should. I don't want to hurt him but I will if I see him. Am I pushing away the connection?

"I need a quiet night alone," I said. Brett shouted down the phone at me. I know I made the right choice.

20th August
10.50am: Beau Café

Gary just phoned. I sipped my latte and then launched into relaying my episode with Brett. "Brett tried to blame me for smoking again. It went like this," I said to Gary.

"Cough, cough. I started smoking again," Brett said.

"Why?" I said, not playing into his blame game.

"You know why?" he said. Yeah, like I'm holding a gun to his head and making him smoke. I'm putting him under such stress and duress because I won't go on a second date with him. I predicted that if I was in a relationship with Brett, we'd eventually have a big row and he'd begin smoking again with a vengeance but if I was truly "spiritual" and "in love" I'd except his imperfection of needing to smoke. "But you were never going to give up," I said.

"I did. For three days and then when I woke up this morning I knew you'd cancel dinner tonight so I started again," Brett said.

Bingo, the jackpot of golden blame. Take responsibility for your life. Something huge I've learnt is spiritual people can be very unspiritual and that includes myself. The difference is, I'm not in denial about it.

"Why can't people be on my spiritual level?

People push me away because I'm a fallen angel. I don't even want to be here. I'm just here to help the world" Brett said.

"What about helping you?" I said, because this is a scary echo of Dr Clive Gray, the wannabe psychic guru saying "Scarlet, I did it all for you, to help you. What other person would do that?"

I call this "God complex". Just because someone looks after themselves doesn't make them a selfish asshole or bitch. "Fallen angel?" I said, Lucifer springing into my mind.

"Yes, I'm an angel who has fallen to earth," Brett said.

My gut felt uneasy and then Brett launched into a personal attack.

"We went on one date. I had dinner with you. We didn't do anything!" I said.

"You should have told me about this other guy," he said.

"No, that's private to me. It's got nothing to do with you," I said.

"So why you telling me now?" he said.

"Because if I went for dinner with you tonight, you'd expect more and I'm not prepared to give that because you'd eventually want a commitment and I'm not letting go of my connection with Charlie because I love him," I said.

"I don't want a relationship. I just want to interface once or twice a week," he said.

Wow, intense and I haven't even gone on a second date. "I'm seeing Charlie on Wednesday, which was planned two weeks before I even met you. I'm not prepared to give that up," I said.

"Are you sleeping with him?" Brett said.

I'm quite shocked he asked. "Yes, because I want you to know the truth," I said.

"God, Scarlet!" he said, like I'd betrayed him, been unfaithful.

"Brett, I'm not going out with you. You can't compare my connection with you to Charlie. I've known him for ten years," I said.

"It's wrong. Why don't we have dinner anyway, as friends. I need to process this. You can get a taxi home, I've still got a table booked for dinner," he said.

Fuck, he still isn't getting it. "Yes, I know I can get a taxi home," I said, knowing he'll do everything in his power to strip naked and get me to stay.

"I honour your decision, Scarlet," he said.

"No you don't," I said.

"Well no, but I can't change how you feel," he said.

"So why say you honour me?" I said.

"Because I have to," he said.

"You don't," I said. When Dad said "Scarlet, you have a neon sign on your head attracting idiots," he was right. I was vulnerable and raw and now honouring my process. I didn't need any man to honour me.

Later on that night Brett sent me a text "Hi sweetheart, may the spirit of your ancestors always be with you as you walk the sacred pathway. Good dreams. Brett X". His text felt needy. I texted back "Bless you angel, may the path continue 2 unfold beautifully for u X."

My path led me to phone Trudy in LA. She invited me to stay at her new home, everything was unfolding perfectly. I also spoke with Kelly and I accepted the duty of helping in kitchen lodge at the Native American ceremony called Long Dance. Bring it on.

21st August

I think Steven Freeman was an asshole last night, first class. We met in the District Club. He brought Troy and I came with Ruby. "Why you so edgy?" I said.

"I'm not," Steven said.

"Come on, tell me," I said.

"Domestic," he said.

"Domestic?" I said.

As he launched into an elaboration, I saw this would be cathartic for him. "Yeah, I've been seeing this girl, but there's no connection. And I've said I don't want to see here but she won't leave me alone," he said.

Bull fucking shit. He was in a major co-dependency situation.

"So, just say it's over," I said.

"I have, but she won't listen," he said.

I read his energy. He was hooked, line and sinker because as I returned from the loo, he already had his jacket on and was leaving.

"Steven's ex-girlfriend is here," Troy said.

"What?!" I said.

"That's why he left," Troy said.

"I don't understand," I said.

"She's at the bar," Troy said.

"Where?" I said, looking around.

"Over there," he said, half pointing.

I saw her charge out of the Chill Room on Steven's heels.

"She's stalking him," Troy said.

"Yes," I said, quite horrified when I discovered she'd turned up on her own at the bar and had been hiding, spying on us talking. How can a forty year old man who is brilliantly talented and won an Oscar put himself in this most ridiculous situation?

That affirms to me that I mustn't call back Max. It would open the door for chaos to unfold. Max had sounded so cheerful when we spoke but I know he doesn't just want a drink, he's got an agenda.

That felt so good! I have mud on my writing hand and in my fingernails. I scattered the earth over my released fears. I went to the spot near where Marcus and I had kissed on the bench, beneath the trees. The ground was cool and damp. Like woodlands in the heart of London, a little piece of magic. Last night I wrote a list of all the things I chose to release and surrender. I folded it up and placed it under my special red stone from a beach in California. Today I have a hangover. I only had two mojitos but I think it was the kamikaze that made my head pound. I bought a Parma ham, olive oil and mild cheddar ciabatta sandwich and sipped latte. After, I set alight my paper with matches from the District Club. To my delight, it burned effortlessly. A beautiful green plant sheltered the flames as I watched the paper turn to ash then dust. I had let the unwanted parts of me die for they no longer served any purpose. It was a great feeling as I let my body sigh and releases occurred in waves and prisms of light.

22nd August

I'm knackered. It was light outside when I went to sleep at 6am. Ended up having a full on "Sex and the City" chat, spiritual style back at my apartment with the girls. I had dinner with gorgeous model Carla beforehand and told her about Steven and what had happened on Friday night. "Ah! I knew it," Carla said as we drank Earl Grey tea and ate chocolate profiteroles. Verity texted from a party in Notting Hill and said it was busy so Carla, Ruby and I hopped in a cab and then Carla bailed out and went home because she had to be up for a photo shoot in the morning.. The party was heaving. Very "I'm trendy and beautiful but too cool to show it," basically, pretentious as fuck. One of the girl's was freaking out that her carpet would be ruined. Yes, it was cream and she had over a hundred people partying in her flat. Then the noise patrol from Westminster Council arrived and we all had to leave.

23rd August

It's wet out today and Notting Hill Carnival is fast approaching. Clouds are looming, it's not a beautiful summer's day. Jade phoned to tell me that she overheard Brett tell Lenny "I've finally come to terms with the fact that I'm too good looking." Yuck.

After I got off the phone, I put on Capital Radio and they were playing my favourite track by Shape shifters. I leapt out of bed and started dancing wildly. I was ecstatic, naked and jumped around my cave of a bedroom.

4.05pm: Oxford Street Tube

Just had a good show but Eric's energy irritated me. I've felt so positive the last two weeks and now that he's back, I find him so controlling. I feel his fear. Eric asked me for a psychic reading in the office, which I gave reluctantly despite my intuition being correct, he didn't want to listen. He's still threatened by me, doesn't want me there although he said "I miss you."

Eric it's not true. You are see-thru! We are a couple of rams locking horns and neither one of us wants to back down. How is this going to work out?

My guides suggested gentleness. I'm taking their advice. This doesn't mean weakness or low self esteem. It's an inner strength radiating outwards. Eric reaffirmed my need to move on to greener pastures. The land is fallow for me at Mega TV. There is a surface smattering of fresh snow but the white cloaked landscape will all too quickly reveal the mud beneath.

Earlier today, someone whispered to me online in the Chatroom "Scarlet, is this a porn website?"

"Gertrude, I don't understand?" I typed back.

She whispered again "I saw girls with their tits out, talking on the phone."

"So sorry Valerie, I still don't understand," I typed.

"Eric, what's happened? I'm getting all these questions about porn," I said.

"Just say we've been having technical difficulties," Eric said.

You fucking idiot, you don't understand that the integrity and energy of the show is being lowered by your being irresponsible and leaving the Pleasure Zone video stream Live and playing all weekend. So anyone visiting our Psychic Chatroom for readings and healings would have seen topless girls instead. Sexual healing, yeah right! Word is out you can check out tits on our psychic website. Soon the viewers will discover that we share the same sofa with Pleasure Zone, not good. It's not my responsibility but if I'd been in charge, it wouldn't have happened. Eric is a megalomaniac. Eric I know you are trying to get me into a place of submission by being all pally with me but my eyes are wide open. Very open!

CHAPTER 11

KARMIC CLOSURE

24th August

Brett phoned last night while I was cooking dinner for Jason. I answered it only because it showed "withheld" number and I thought it was Dad. Brett drove me nuts. "Hello," I said. I was curt in my response because I was starving and my blood sugar level was low.

"Hey Scarlet, it's Brett. How are you?" he said, his voice all sing song like but I can psychically hear his aggression.

"Cooking," I said.

"Oh. I really wanted to have a chat with you," he said.

"Well I can't, I'm catching up with a friend," I said.

"Can you phone me when they're gone?" he said.

"I'm at their house, actually," I said.

"Ok, so when you leave?" he said.

Fuck, he was so persistent. What part of "no" was he not understanding. "I'm going to be here late," I said.

"You can call me tomorrow," he said.

"Brett, I'm trying to cook," I said.

"Ok, speak tomorrow," he said.

"Bye," I said, without the affirmation.

2pm: Hairdressers

About to have my hair highlighted and cut, just in time for tomorrow's show and because I'm meeting with Charlie. I'm sitting with a whole load of foils in my hair and I've just eaten a Ploughman's sandwich wedge with prawn cocktail chips from Tesco's supermarket. I felt satisfied and then I got the text from Aidan. It was an essay. I'm going to delete it. It said "Hey I'm truly sorry about not replyin to you but I'm also getting over a complicated relationship and am very confused about what I'm doing at the moment…I honesty feel crap coz I'm a good person too and did not plan what happened or set out to hurt you in any way. I don't expect this will help but wanted you to know I'm not that type of asshole even if my behaviour suggests otherwise…I genuinely apologize but can't help where my head is at…X"

Wow Aidan that was a long text! I felt sick to my stomach but replied a couple of days later "Bless u angel, yes you have integrity, your text has made a difference. I'm positive you'll receive clarity. Remember time is a great healer. Love & light, Scarlet x." I never heard from him again.

I was frustrated with Wayne and wanted closure so I sent him a text "I feel like this is a one-sided friendship. I give up, take care."

He texted straight back "Look, I'm sorry but I've got a load of shit 2 deal with at the mo, I'm not round much. Sorry u feel like that."

He'd treated me like shit yet on a deeper soul level my heart said "stay open" so I texted him again "I'm positive everything will work out. Sending you lots of love."

It cleared the air and he texted "thanx." We spoke a few days later.

"How's your apartment?" Wayne said.

"Yes good. I'm really happy because I'm off to Spain and Los

Angeles. How's your love life?" I said.

"Yeah, good," he said.

"Bastard," I thought to myself. It's the wheel of life. He rejected me and I rejected Brett and Aidan rejected me and I rejected Max. Souls connecting and disconnecting. So why do I feel like such a bitch about Brett? I'm not! I also discovered that Mr James Bond had a threesome with Jade. There is no escape for me from the incestuous nature of the London media scene. I'm exhausted right now. I'm meant to meet Carla after my haircut. I need to slow down but I can't.

25th August
10.15am: Ladbroke Grove Tube

It's warm today. I think it's going to get really hot. I love my new haircut. This morning when I'd done my make up and was dressed and ready to go, I couldn't believe the image starring back at me. I felt like I was an entirely new person. I did an hour of chi gung before going to bed last night and six meditations. When I switched on my phone I saw I had a new text message. Charlie had sent it at 6.45am "On way to UK from Italy and straight to office! See u later x"

We haven't spoken since I had the dream because I feel the bond. It's timeless. I'm frightened of the depth because I sense there is no end to it.

10.45am

I'm in Baguette's now drinking O.J. I must do that email to Eric when I get into the studio and remember to copy in Barry and Kevin. I must also text Charlie.

4.55pm

Yes! I'm meeting Charlie in Chelsea at 7pm. The psychic sofa felt so yuck and oppressive today. Turns out I was picking up on the Pussy War they had on it the night before. I fear that Charlie was with his ex-fiancé in Italy because he sounded distracted on the phone earlier. Think I'll do a meditation now to balance out. I'd love to wear my new dress but jeans would be better, more appropriate and relaxed.

11pm

I felt so depressed tonight when I arrived home from seeing Charlie. I could barely move. I wanted to stop myself feeling any pain so I thought what better way to anesthetize than not be present with my feelings. I phoned Gary but his phone was switched off so I called Jason and he pressed all my buttons, didn't help me feel better because the truth hurt. "He gave me a candle," I said to Jason.

"So what, Scarlet, I'm a Virgo, I'm practical," Jason said.

"That hurt," I thought to myself, but Jason had a good point. I went to the fridge and extracted a chocolate mousse to dull the feeling of rejection. I lit the candle anyway. I tried to focus on the nuggets of gold instead of the barbed words and thorns. I imagined the scent of roses and jasmine wafting through the breeze and touching long grasses. I knew I had to appreciate the gifts I was receiving right now. I prayed for a Divine kick up the ass so I could stop re-creating shit for myself. Next week I would be in Spain, away from the buzz of London.

26th August
9.20am: Beau Café

I received a text from Charlie when I turned my phone on this morning. "Good to see you last night. Sorry I am being so work focused! So pleased to be aligned again."

As I lay in bed, I tried to get my head around his words, instead of letting my heart open. After speaking with Gary, I realize I am trying to control Charlie and his love for me rather than accept the existence and timeless connection of our souls. His soul is saying to mine "Expand Scarlet, open to new miracles, the joy of life, the sun rising every morning and the moon bathing the earth in luminescence at night."

I'm resisting. I'm a child stomping her foot and saying "Where are my toys?"

"Scarlet, you have an array of toys," he says.

"No, it's not enough, I want more," I say and then I heard a story on the radio of a woman who loved a man. They were in a car accident together. As they lay by each others side she sang "Love me, love me. Say that you love me." He died later that night yet she focused on how the last moments she shared with him were this song, this love and not the sadness of his death.

Oh, Great Spirit I'll do my best to surrender to love and I'll do my best to stop needing.

29th August

I feel strange tonight. My forehead is lined. I'm confused. It's the night before Carnival. I feel exhausted from two late nights. Thursday, I had dinner at The District Club with Brett's friend Lenny, a gorgeous black guy. He told me the story behind his ten tattoos on his body and I told him about how I met Matt and the vision I received from his tattoo. Then we went to a Star club with Jade and Jason. I finally got to bed at 7.15am and Friday I slept at 5am. I can hardly lift my pen now...

30th August

I'm sitting on a beautiful silk sofa with divine puff cushions at my place of birth, which is now a luxury hotel in the heart of London. Melodies from the forties are wafting through from the library. The last time I came here was three years ago with Bill for Valentines Day. We had dinner and danced and yes, I paid for him. I'm tired from Carnival and smoking a lot of grass. Something I don't do anymore, except yesterday. I ate a ridiculous amount of BBQ chicken, plantains and chocolate. The pot definitely gave me the munchies. It also calmed me in the chaos of the Carnival crowd or I think I would have been fraught. I'm ultra sensitive to energy in big crowds.

31st August

It's a little chilly this morning. They said on the radio it would be 72 degrees. Well I'm not feeling it yet. As I walked up Ladbroke Grove to catch the tube, the street cleaners swept away the aftermath of Carnival. The stench of rubbish mixed with beer and chewed chicken bones was quite vile. I'd set my alarm for 8.30am this morning, woke up at 7.40am and got up at 9am. I wanted to dream more so I could receive insights but none came.

1st September

It's going to be a very hot day. I'm on the train and we're about to depart from Tottenham Hale train station. Oscar is moving into my flat for a few days while I'm away in Spain. He gave me a £60 as a contribution which I accepted. I need the money to pay my rent. I felt Bill thinking about me this morning. Him asking "why did we break up?"

Bill, if you truly loved me, didn't want to loose me, you would have done any job to provide half the rent. You're kidding yourself. Bill, you just let me go, dropped me. At least Max wanted to make an effort to get me back and I pushed him away but that's because he smoked sixty cigarettes a day and drank a quarter of a bottle of Jack. Are there any normal men out there?

Sunlight is streaming onto this page. Green trees rush past me. Two horses prance around a paddock. The train is slowing down, I think we're about to arrive at Standstead airport. Today was the first day I saw a poster of "Terminal" the movie. It's on one of my manifestation boards, a picture of me sitting in a chair checking the monitor with director Steven Spielberg, now that would be a dream come true.

4th September
8.05pm: Spanish Home

So much to catch up on. I was feeling angry when I got out the shower thinking of Charlie. Then I went into the bedroom and found a text from Trent "Mate Ibiza baby." I know Charlie's there to. Interesting timing.

5th September
1.55am: Bed, Spain

I am wired. I have fear in me. I haven't written the last few days. Instead I've been staying up late and watching TV movies Bill wouldn't let me or rather wouldn't approve of me watching. That's partly why I'm doing it. Yes it's brainless shit but it's my way of switching off. I'm carrying fear in my belly. She says "help!" She's frightened of sleeping, letting go and missing something. As mum said tonight at dinner "You may go through an arid patch."

"Yes, I'm definitely going through that," I said.

"Well it's not a bad thing," she said.

I consider this, except it feels like a lifetime ago that I was last held. All the men in my life seem to have evaporated and I feel lonely. I just got undressed, removed my eye makeup and moisturized my face. Then I let down my hair, which was ultra sun-kissed. My skin radiated the day's rays, glistening in my pores. I was and am in the best physical shape I've been in for years and yet I'm alone. I crave attention and kindness, tenderness and kisses. To have a man I adore wrap his arms around my body and hold me tight. A mutual respect, dance and flow between us. I felt that with Marcus. I liked him holding me in his arms. I felt so safe. I also felt that same feeling with Charlie except I'm angry with Charlie now. I don't know why but my intuition tells me he is deceiving me. He says he hasn't had sex with anyone since me but I know he has, I can feel it. Mum said she thought he definitely had. So why doesn't he admit it? We're not committed in a relationship. I would have respected his honesty. Mum said it's because he wants to keep me on the backburner. Except I'm not prepared to over cook. I feel like Christ in the desert, having to resist temptation. How ridiculous Scarlet! Get over it. Why is this deep fear and longing arising in me? I hold the beautiful stone Angelica gave me at Rainbow ranch. It represents my connection to The Sisters of the Dance. So much has happened since last year's ceremony. Trudy will not be there with me this year. She's shooting an indie movie in New Mexico. So ten days to go and I'll be in LA. Today there was an explosion at Los Angeles airport. Yes it will be ok. It is safe.

10.55am

This morning Mum asked why I stay up so late. I don't usually, it's only been out here in Spain. A part of me is scared to sleep because of the realm I may enter and yet my sixth sense says "Scarlet, when the veil grows thin between your waking hour and the world of sleep, it is the dimension of truth that becomes crystal clear and other worlds and people and beings are accessible. We hover around you, ready and waiting.

I've watched some pretty dark films the last couple of days, not in their entirety but enough to create a knot of unease in my belly. A young beautiful woman being out of balance. Her shadow aspect craving love and without reciprocation, killing kind handsome men who have become victims, through succumbing to women's sexuality, prowess. Then he wants to back away because a part of that potency, the orgasm, the thrill is her shadow intermeshed, wild and carefree. As this part of her is unleashed, as the shadow receives the light and love, it wants more light and if the light will not embrace the shadow, it decides that it must be destroyed. I feel a story of Original Sin is being told here. Adam has partaken of the forbidden fruit, Eve. He wants things to go back to how they were before. But how can they?

6th September
10.30am: The Terrace, Spanish Home

As I stepped outside, I could feel the heat searing. I'm relieved we are going to the beach. There is barely a breeze in the hills. I've just eaten some toast with jam and butter and drinking green tea. My belly is in knots. The mosquitoes seem to keep me on edge. Last night lying in bed doing a meditation I thought I heard that vile buzz that makes all my hairs stand on end. No, it's just the tape machine whirring but then the sound got louder. It was upon me and I leapt in the air, scrapping with the headphones and flicked the light switch on. My eyes surveyed the room, searching for the bloodsucker, nothing. So I lay on the bed and waited. Suddenly it appeared on the ceiling. Again I sprung from my bed, got a book, stomped on it and killed it. The mosquito now gone, I returned to bed but as weary as I felt, I couldn't sleep. I've been feeling rather wired at night. I think the mossies are just a metaphor for a deeper irritation in my life. Eric, the mother fucker. He is an absolute two faced bastard. My suspicions are confirmed that he's trying to get rid of me and I so badly want to jump ship, except there's not even a gang plank and if I dive into the ocean, how long will I be able to swim?

Why can't the QE2 just pull up alongside me and say "All aboard".

I returned from a lovely day on the beach. I lounged and walked and then for old times sake, strolled casually into the luxurious Beach Club as if I belonged. It's just I wasn't a guest there this time. I wondered if someone would stop me but they didn't. My Gucci shades hid my self consciousness. I made my way to the toilet, checked myself in the mirror, let down my hair and then headed out to the beautiful pool. I took off my sunglasses and dived beneath the waterfall and from the other side watched the sunlight glisten in the drops of water. I miss my social life with my friends, the buzz and bustle of London. I'm surprised I feel this way. I'm so enjoying being looked after by Mum but I'm struggling to be present with myself. I'm aware I desire distractions. Men in particular, except there are no sexy men out here and I think any man will look desirable soon because I'm uncomfortable with me.

I texted Eric and asked him to confirm Thursday and Friday's shows and he replied back saying "Yes for Thursday. Have to check the schedule for Friday as a lot of new people coming in."

Bastard, but then he is the monkey, not the organ grinder, that's Kevin. So I asked "Does that mean everyone else is doing just one day?" Let's see what he says. My left shoulder just clicked, it never does that, actually I think it just realigned. Yes I have been out of sorts and yet all is sugar coated on the surface. You know when you look at a picture from a distance and it looks great but the closer you get, the more apparent the flaws.

Meeting with Liberty for coffee at Aporto on Goldborne Road at 10am on Wednesday for a good catch up and girly gossip. Then

Thursday morning breakfast at The District Club with Oscar and Nigel to talk about the new TV show 'Psychic Visions'. I can't believe I'll be in LA one week from now. I guess when I get back from LA, I'll no longer be doing The Psychic Show. As I said to Mum "One door closes, another door opens." I'm scared. I know I shouldn't be but I am and yet I know I deserve more. I have so much to give. Will people judge me terribly for my confessions? I hope they have some compassion but that's the risk I'm prepared to take because my friends are truly my friends and they accept me lovingly. I'm very grateful for that. I'm excited to go home and see everyone in London. So I'm out on the gang plank, let's see what happens next…

8.15pm

Just had a shower, got dressed. Oscar texted again confirming Thursday's meeting but no text from Eric. The ocean looks so peaceful and inviting as I sit on the terrace. I'm furious. Except the anger is so deeply embedded. I wonder how there may be a safe outlet for it. Today on the beach as I watched the waves, I thought of how I shared them with Bill boogie boarding, riding the wake together, walking hand in hand along the beach, engaged, I was engaged to Bill. Now it feels like a lifetime ago. A part of me feels free, another part deeply alone, but not lonely, because I know I made this choice and it's for my best. Swallows fly in the evening sky and jasmine wafts up from the lawn. I'm angry with Charlie, I don't know why I feel so aggrieved. It's like history repeating. He doesn't honour me, he's full of shit. He's great at entertainment PR and saying the right thing yet, his actions do not align. More than anything Eric, Bill, Charlie, they all highlight the anger I have towards myself. Because I allowed it. What if I'd said "no", how would things be different?

But I was too scared to say "no".

7th September
9.40am: The Terrace, Spanish Home

Major dream, I felt so frustrated but when I awoke. I found Veronica.

"I need to talk," I said.

"Alright sweetheart, let's go outside," she said.

I could tell she though I just wanted to gossip, talk boys.

"Let's chat in my car," she said and we got into a silver Peugeot 306 and she reversed the car backwards into a space. Killed the engine and turned to me, her big blue eyes open wide. "What is it?" she said. Concern now filled her voice.

"They're trying to get rid of me," I said. I knew I didn't have to say anymore.

"Who?" she said. Then she piped up "It's Eric isn't it, that bastard."

"Yes and no," I said.

"What do you mean?" she said.

"I've got to talk to Kevin, this situation is not good," I said. I could feel time slipping away through my hour glass.

"Scarlet, it's alright," Veronica said except she didn't understand the urgency. "There's Kevin now," she said, pointing to Kevin leaving the building.

Already throughout the dream my wallet had kept disappearing and then reappearing like a holograph from my red handbag. My bag had been left unzipped, even though I thought I closed it. The realization is occurring that Eric is going back to Kevin and telling him everything and Kevin telling Eric what to do.

I leapt out of Veronica's car and cornered Kevin. He had a cardboard box filled with two coffees and a couple of greasy fry up sandwiches from the café.

"Hi Kevin, I need to talk," I said.

"Oh hi," he said, but I could see he looked like a frightened animal that was about to be caged and wanted to escape.

"It'll only take a moment," I said and led him over to Veronica's car. I wanted a witness and support. Kevin felt shifty, hard to pin down and suddenly we were back inside the building but it was slightly bigger, different. We were upstairs at the top of the building where Pleasure Play Zone is aired.

"Kevin, Eric's trying to get rid of me," I said and I felt sick as I watched his reaction or rather non-reaction because I could see his eyes dart side to side, couldn't look into mine and I knew he had given Eric the instruction. Yes Kevin is the organ grinder and Eric his pet monkey. He stayed silent so I decided to think quickly on my feet and negotiate.

"Kevin I've seen you've got all these new people in and giving them psychic tests. There's so many of them," I said.

It was really turning into a battery psy-chic farm. Kevin pretended to look like he didn't know what I was talking about.

"Does that mean you're putting me down to one day a week presenting?" I said.

Kevin didn't reply. He hated being put on the spot.

"Why won't you let me produce again?" I said.

Kevin shook his head and began walking into another room. I must have looked truly desperate now because I was. Everything I built was slipping away and I wouldn't see a penny of the profits. I saw the signs early on when he wanted me to cut everyone's salary, now I was on the receiving end. I knew it was just a matter of time before it happened.

Suddenly we were standing in the main studio with Veronica and all these female presenters from Play Zone. The turnover of girls was fast on Pleasure Zone as well.

"What's going on?" Veronica said. She stared at Kevin, hands on her hips.

Kevin didn't reply. Everyone was looking at him.

"Am I getting the sack?" Veronica said.

Again Kevin didn't answer.

"Kevin I've worked hard, looking after these girls, hiring them, running things," she said, accusation in her tone. Kevin suddenly exploded.

"Fuck all of you!" he said, arms flailing in the air. "You're all a bunch of whores from Bosnia, go on go!" Now he looked each one of us in the eye, daring us to challenge him. Not the sweet Northern boy next door. The veneer was now gone and the devil revealed. His look frightened me. This was an evil, greedy man who wouldn't let the sweet kind person sink deeper than beneath the surface. "You're fired!" he shouted at Veronica and I remember her jaw dropping open, as if to say "after all I've done for you."

As I walked through the Mega TV building, I felt like a stranger. Everyone exuded self-importance but I knew they were only pawns on a chessboard. I felt uneasy because a part of me was not trusting that a mysterious force moved and guided these pieces on the chessboard and I had to trust that it would guide me also.

11pm: Aeroplane In The Sky

I'm on the aeroplane sitting at the back, going through turbulence, consumed by fear. My heart is pounding. I take a deep sigh. My legs tingle. The cabin crew looks so relaxed. One sings gaily. I'm fucking terrified. I'm sitting alone, fear rises from the pit of my stomach. I'm not in control. There's nothing I can do to change this moment except surrender to it. I put my hands up to my face and wonder if my fear is visible. It's passing a little, as I write I'm praying the plane doesn't jolt anymore. I think I'll meditate, see if I can calm down. Every time the plane sways from side to side, my heart moves with it. Today I felt physically sick after I picked two divination cards for where I am at now. The first card I got was Career Transition, it brings tears to my eyes.

The message from Archangel Chamuel "Your life purpose is triggering a blessed career change." And I'm crying now and I don't know why. I feel like I'm letting go of a baby I've nurtured. As much hate as there has been, I have a love and appreciation for my last six months at The Psychic Show. What next? What lies ahead of me?

I've been in denial. As I witnessed Pleasure Zone, girls in skimpy underwear on the sofa, the sofa that I sit on in the daytime and give psychic readings from. The extent of it is only hitting me now. I've been detached and numb because I've been working in that building but seeing it on TV and the texts the men send in. I can feel the energy of some of them. "I want you lovely girls to feel each other's tits and kiss." Another text: "Hey girls touch your bums together and give me a cry of pleasure." And another: "Lovelies show me your soles and touch your nips" and so the texts go on. I change channels again as my head hurts, can't quite fathom it and it's Play Zone 2. More girls gyrating their hips saying "fuck me" to the camera as they hold the phone to their ear. I can see their souls dance somewhere outside of their bodies, they're switched off, it's a job and it pays. The contrast to the texts on our show: "Love you guys. Can you pick a card for me?" and "I had a dream, can you interpret what a golden swan is? Love the show." So much positive feedback. And yes the stuck people who don't want to take responsibility for their lives: "I want an affair with a married man. He says he loves me? Can you pick a card." And "He hasn't proposed yet, I'm Scorpio and he's Gemini, should I leave him?"

These questions make my heart sink. These people only want to hear what they want to hear. I'm like the hobo, I've done my work at The Psychic Show but I'm clinging on. When I watched Tiffany present "Speed Date" and a gambling show called "Cash Cow Winner". She looks lifeless, like she's going through the motions of presenting, it's all about the money. She vaguely comes to life on The Psychic Show, it's the only time I see her remotely happy. As I watched the shows, I tried to ignore my soul's cry to move on from tabloid TV. Do I leave The Psychic Show before I go to the USA next week?

It is time to leave and leave with grace. I'm compromising myself too strongly now. It is causing me low self-esteem and great pain. I need to hand in my notice and move to green pastures. Yes it is greener on the other side in this instance. When Cinderella goes to the ball, she needs to be well groomed and that takes preparation. Yes my unseen helpers are here to support me. Step into your power Scarlet, claim it back!

As I sit on the plane and look at the picture of Archangel Chamuel, a feeling of peace and serenity temporarily wash over me. What will people think when they read my most intimate secrets, as I share a part of my tainted heart and vulnerable soul?

I'm fragmented, like humpty dumpty. Maybe I'm not meant to be super glued back together. I heard spirit screaming at me "Move on Scarlet! Time for a dramatic life change!"

"No!" my personality cried back "I'm not ready!"

"When are you ever going to be?" the wise loving part of myself said to the saboteur within.

I grieved. Tears rolled down my cheeks, as I felt chunks of myself falling away. I was finally exposed, another layer shining in the stark light of day. But the pain was a cathartic release for me. I could feel myself being propelled forward. I thanked God and the angels silently as the plane's wheels hit the runway and I was home again on British soil. I had missed England, albeit had only been six days. Customs was effortless and my bag arrived quickly on the carousel. It was only 1.15am and I felt excitement mixed with stress. I made my way down to the train platform at Stanstead airport. I could feel a chill from the steely stone structure, emanating off the walls and floor. It was peaceful on the platform. I made my way over to a metal bench and sat down. Now I could feel the chill in my bones as the cool night air crept in around me. I got out my book by Candace Bushnell, "Trading Up" and began reading. Within a couple of minutes my flow was interrupted. A young guy in his twenties approached me.

"Hi," he said "do you know when the next train is?"

I'd already checked the leaflet. "Every 30 minutes," I said.

"Thanks," he said.

I noticed he was quite cute. He had spiky brown hair and rich chocolate eyes. I carried on reading.

"Where you going?" he said.

"Notting Hill," I said "and you?"

"Stanmore," he said. He sat down on the bench, two seats were empty between us. "I was meant to catch a flight but I'm not going," he said.

"Why?" I said.

"A girl I like," he said. His face began to glow. "Do you think I should go back for her or take my flight?"

"Doesn't matter what I think. What do you want?" I said.

"To see her," he said.

"Well there's your answer, trust it," I said. I was enjoying the synchronicity of this moment. It definitely felt like we were meant to meet. Then he got up and left his large rucksack on the floor next to me and walked away. He didn't ask me to watch his bag. For a moment I wondered if he had a bomb in his luggage and then thought how ridiculous I was being. Like he was really going to blow up an empty platform at 1.30 in the morning. I continued reading and then moments later he came back.

"Maybe I should go?" he said.

"Where?" I said.

"Spain," he said.

"I've just come from there," I said "Where in Spain?"

"Barcelona," he said.

"I've never been there," I said, "So what time's your flight?"

"10am," he said, "I've been here all night, haven't slept or washed for three days and I've got nowhere to stay."

Alarm bells went off in my head. Why did I always attract the crazy people?

"So where are you going?" he said.

Why was he asking me again?

"Notting Hill," I said. I looked up at the clock. I could hear it ticking, it was now 1.50am and no train. I could see one person sitting at the other end of the platform, apart from that it was empty. "Maybe the train's not coming?" I said.

"Don't know," he said. He looked preoccupied.

"So how did you meet this girl?" I said.

"In the institution," he said.

"What do you mean?" I said, wondering if I heard him correctly.

"I was seriously depressed in care and she's still in there. I met her on the ward, except she's a manic depressive," he said.

I'd remembered dating a couple of those, one was on lithium, he was highly intelligent and sexy but extremely complicated and the other one who was totally gorgeous he committed suicide at 21 years old, a devastatingly sad situation.

"Have you ever tried to commit suicide?" I said.

"No," he said but I felt he was lying. "I miss her."

He got up and sat right beside me and put his arm around me, resting it on the bench. I didn't sit back. It was now 2am and I was sitting alone on a train platform with someone rather unbalanced.

"Maybe the train isn't coming," I said.

He remained silent. I began reading again but none of the words registered. I knew I needed to check the timetable but if I took my luggage a few feet across the way and then back to the bench, he'd feel I didn't trust him. I hinted for him to find out but he didn't move.

"Maybe I should go to Spain," he said.

"Yes," I said.

"But am I trying to run away?" he said.

"I don't know, are you?" I said.

"Yes and no," he said.

"I'm going to check the train times," I said and got up steadily. My bag had everything in it; my wallet, phone, passport, laptop, my life basically and knew I had to look totally carefree. Please don't take my bag, I prayed. I quickly extracted a leaflet and strided back to my belongings. As I read the timetable, I saw a small asterisk which said *2-4am night coach. I'd sat for 45 minutes on the platform putting myself through a bizarre interaction. I picked up my luggage and he followed suit. We made our way to the escalators together and out to the coach stop, except we'd just missed one. It was even colder outside. Tourists and late night travellers littered the area. They looked tired and weary. A small group of guys were smoking grass and drinking whisky from a brown paper bag. I went into the coach station.

"When's the next coach?" I said.

"4am," the man said.

This journey was turning into a nightmare. My new travel companion sidled over to me.

"It's an hour till the next coach," I said.

"I think I'm going to catch that flight after all," he said.

Relief swept over me. I could do the last leg of my journey in peace. I knew if I'd invited him to come home with me, he would have jumped at the opportunity.

"What you going to do there?" I said.

"Maybe write a book, contemplate life," he said.

"I'm writing a book," I said, "it's almost finished."

"Really what's it about?" he said.

"My journey, life, you'll be in it," I said.

"What's it called?" he said.

"Confessions of a Psychic," I said.

"Wow, sounds great. I'll look out for it." He held out his hand to shake mine and leant forward to kiss me on each cheek and he was gone.

8th September
10.35am: Home

I awoke with a heavy feeling. I still hadn't heard from Eric with the schedule. I felt near to explosion point. My blood was seething and spitting and I still hadn't got my period, my body felt nauseated.

The day went by in a blur. I didn't really get anything done and then I had a run in with Charlie. I felt angry and deceived and in the process, worked myself into a frenzy. Charlie wasn't giving me the sympathy I wanted. I found him thoughtless and arrogant. His texts left me reeling.

I'd previously sent him two texts and had no response. Not that I expected one but I felt a strange energy between us and I wanted to disconnect from it so I texted "Shame..don't know what happened but feel so disconnected from u x."

He texted straight back "I went on holiday and got back a day ago! How are u?"

Was it my imagination or was there a hint of sarcasm in his text? So I said "Going through a big shift yet again. Got back from Spain last night. Decided 2 leave my tv show b4 LA. Feel some truths missing btw us. Please note it's just a sense that I have. Not a judgement. It came through when I meditated w candle b4 went away. Then disconnected. Did u have a great time?"

I knew Charlie had been partying hard and I felt the energy of cocaine strongly around him. His reply totally took me by surprise.

"I think u worry too much. If u look for problems u will find them. I feel fairly light of spirit in spite of a huge issue facing me. Take it easier Scarlet otherwise you won't enjoy life or your friends. Xx"

"Fucking asshole," I wanted to text but didn't. So much for empathy and instead I replied "Thanx. I'm not worrying and love my friends and life. Just going through huge transition! Yes I know u r 2. I think u misunderstood my text + don't appreciate what u said. You're just not getting it/me. Sorry x x x."

I thought maybe now Charlie would back down, soften but he didn't. He said "It's all ok Scarlet!x"

I wanted to scream "Whatever!" or "You selfish fucker" or "It isn't!" but again I decided to be diplomatic, yet truthful. I said "Really?! That's not true. We're not seeing eye 2 eye right now" and then I took the candle he gave me off the altar and another response came through that made my disconnection final "..but I know we will in the future. Take care babe x"

I knew I had to clear my head so I dragged myself to the gym to steam away the fears and hurts.

That morning I'd had coffee with Liberty and not worn my watch because I remembered thinking I might be mugged. As I left the gym, an overwhelming fatigue hit me. I'd only swum a couple of lengths in the pool and the steam room had been too hot for me. I bought some salad and Bouillon soup to drink. I just wanted to collapse. As I walked down Westbourne Grove, shopping bag in one hand, phone in the other talking to Wanda in LA, the universe gave me a right whack. It all happened so fast, the three boys on bikes made a formation in front of me.

"Oh no," I said into the phone as they sped towards me. I froze praying the boys would go straight past, but they didn't. One of the teenagers punched me in the face and the gift I received was adrenalin and gut instinct. I let my body relax as I took the blow and then the second smack, this time on the side of my head and suddenly his hand was clenched over mine and he was trying to extract my phone. I'd been praying for all the anger in me to be released and now I had the golden opportunity.

"Get away from me!" I screamed. I felt the words explode from deep inside my belly. The noise pierced the space around me, shattering the darkness and then somehow, I felt Dad with me, protecting me. I remembered instinctively all the karate moves he'd taught me and I twisted my wrist and yanked back my arm. I screamed at full pitch now, louder than an opera singer "help me, somebody help me!" I ran blindly across the road, shaking like a leaf. Miraculously no cars hit me. Several witnesses saw the event but they quickly disappeared. I stood alone on the pavement. Call 999, I thought but how ridiculous. They didn't steal anything, they'd failed and then I realized I'd been punched in the face. I felt my nose for blood but none flowed. The side of my head and ear were burning. I panicked as I thought I'd lost one of my diamond earrings from my great grandmother but as I felt my ear, it was still there. What if this gang attacked someone else? I called Emergency services.

"I've just been assaulted," I said.

"Police, ambulance or fire department?" the operator said.

It took me a moment to register. "Police," I said. I knew I was in shock. I struggled to tell them the exact location of the gang, it frustrated me.

"Do you need an ambulance?" she said.

"No," I said.

"Ok three units are out looking for them now. Another's on its way to you. Can you stay where you are?" she said.

"Yes," I said, except I was terrified the gang would come back for me. I stood in shorts, flip flops and my denim jacket on the corner where I'd been attacked, my hair was still wet. Had I drawn this event to me because I'd been feeling negative and angry or was it meant to happen? Was this a blow I'd receive from the TV show?

It felt like an endless wait for the police. I was so relieved when they finally arrived. I had to give a full statement when all I wanted to do was go home. "I don't understand why no one helped?" I said.

"They don't," the policeman said.

"That's terrible," I said.

"People don't want to get involved," he said.

"So they keep getting away with it?" I said.

"Afraid so," he said.

"Come and wait in the car while we get you an ambulance," another officer said, as a couple of shifty looking guys hovered by the phone box opposite watching me.

I felt weird stepping into the ambulance. I saw a trolley bed laid out, a chair and a lot of different equipment. The space felt alien and frightening. I noticed how pristine, stark and organized it was. I held my breath. What might they do to me? A female paramedic dressed in green overalls smiled sympathetically.

"So I just need to take some details from you and your blood pressure," she said.

So long as no needles are involved, I thought. I relayed the events while the band around my arm grew tighter. I could feel the blood pumping through my hand. It makes me feel faint just writing about it. She then placed a contraption on my finger. She was aware of my anxiety. "Not much longer," she said.

I gritted my teeth. Breathe, Scarlet, breathe.

"Well the good news is your blood pressure is a 137 over 47 and you've got 100% oxygen circulation which is excellent. You're obviously very fit and healthy, considering what just happened," she said.

"I'm very grateful for the work you do and looking after me," I said.

She looked taken aback. "In all the years, no one has ever said that to me before. Thank you," the female paramedic said.

I felt emotion wash over me as I caught the happiness of being recognized. A policeman stepped into the van.

"You up to looking at some mug shots down at the station?" the policeman said.

I could feel the aftershock of adrenalin pumping through my body. "I don't know," I said.

"You can always come down the station tomorrow," he said.

"But I've got to the show," I said, "I'll come now."

"Well you got off lightly," the female paramedic said, "Good luck."

"Thanks," I said and followed the policeman out to a car and got in the backseat. The two kids were still there. I felt scared they might remember me for a future attack.

"So someone said you do a TV show," a different policeman said, as he started the engine.

Although I was in shock, I couldn't help noticing how good looking he was, seriously fit. "Yes," I said.

"So what's it about?" he said.

"A psychic TV show," I said. I was interested to see his reaction and that of the female officer next to him.

"Psychic?" he said, mulling over the word, "So is that all that star sign stuff?"

"Some of it," I said "and yes if I was so psychic why didn't I know I was going to be mugged tonight?" I said and couldn't help but laugh.

"That's what I was going to ask next," he said.

"I know," I said.

"So what star sign are you?" he said.

"Scorpio," I said.

"Oh they're dangerous, I went out with one of those," he said.

Yes I'd definitely like to go out on a date with you, I thought. The prospect of him handcuffing me and seducing me flashed through my mind. I quickly changed topic.

"I really admire what you guys do. Thank you for looking after me. I think you're really brave," I said.

The car pulled up outside the station.

"Wow thanks. No one's ever said that to us before, they're always complaining, giving us dirty looks," the female officer said.

"Really?" I said, remembering as a teenager how my friends would call them 'pigs'. "This is the first time someone's said thank you," she said.

I felt my heart expanding. It was worth being punched in the face just to have that connection with the female paramedic and policewoman. I knew I could never do what they do. I followed her in through the back of the station and into an interview room. Mirrors were on every wall. I knew from all the movies I'd seen the police could watch from behind the glass. The policewoman spoke into her walkie talkie "I have the victim here with me now."

The word "victim" pierced me, that word made me feel

powerless, like I had no control over my life. Another policeman came in "Sorry to inconvenience you, it'll be just a few more minutes," he said. He left me on my own.

My right arm was hurting, it kept clicking from when the guy had grabbed at my phone, the side of my head stung and my cheek felt tender. I sat quietly, I wasn't ready to phone Jason back. He'd left a message to call and that he was at The Swan pub. Shock is a strange thing, everything feels fragmented and upside down. And then the sexy copper came in.

"Can I get you anything to drink?" he said.

"Some water would be great," I said, and some consolation I thought. He left the room and again I was alone. I wondered if anyone was watching me. Obviously my circumstances were nowhere as dramatic as the character of Sophie Neveau in 'The Da Vinci Code' but a part of me wished they were. The cute guy came back in with my water, then left as another two cops came in and sat down before me with a blue book. He opened it. Rows of faces stared back at me from the page.

"Him," I said, pointing at the photo, "he looks a lot like one of them."

"You have to give a definite "yes", a maybe can't be accepted," he said.

"Well it's a maybe," I said, my heart sinking, knowing these bastards would stay out on the street and hurt someone else. And then the strangest thing happened as I looked at all the suspects, their faces came alive, I could see their features moving, eyes sparking and glazing over, facial expressions smirking. I thought they might jump out from their photos and come to life, knives in hand, palms outstretched, offering crack and syringes to shoot up. Nausea shot through me. This one page in particular was the epitomy of dark. I was given a stark reminder that these people were out on the street. Have I been walking around in a bubble? Have I been so unaware?

"Did you know you can read from photos psychically?" I said to the policeman.

He didn't say "yes" or "no", just laughed and it made me think of the movie "Hearts in Atlantis" where they use psychic ability to track down criminals.

So why wouldn't my intuition tell me who and where this guy was? I felt angry and sorry for the kids who assaulted me.

"So what time are you on TV tomorrow?" the cop asked.

"Between 12 and 2pm," I said.

"Oh, I'll be sleeping then. I finish my shift 7am, maybe the wife can record it," he said. "Well thanks for coming in. Can we give you a lift home?"

As I sat in the back of the police van, fascinated by it's navigational system, I wondered if I would have the courage to resign Live on air? I knew it best to leave that decision till morning. I locked the door to my flat once inside and made myself a cup of vegetable broth. I hadn't slept for hours and knew I was still in shock. Jason phoned. "Come on Scarlet, I think you need to get out for a drink. I'm with Ruby and Greg," he said.

"I don't know," I said. I couldn't make a decision as conflicting thoughts crashed in my head.

"It'll do you good," he said.

"Ok," I said, realizing I didn't want to be alone.

"We're on our way," he said.

I phoned Karen in LA. She'd just received devastating news that she had breast cancer and her dad had a cancerous tumour removed but wouldn't stop drinking alcohol. Life felt so fragile to me. I then phoned Wanda back and explained what happened.

"Sounds like they're telling you to shut up," she said.

"They," meaning my angels and guides. In my heart this didn't feel like my truth. I believe I was attacked to help me know my own strength. That I am more powerful than I realized. Also I was given an outlet to scream at the top of my lungs and release the excess anger I was carrying inside me towards Bill and the bosses at Mega TV. I felt so wired and exhausted all at the same time. I changed out of my turquoise shorts and put on my white skirt, cream cardigan and slip on sandals. I felt scared to be alone, so I kept chatting with Wanda until Jason arrived with Ruby and Greg. I walked her downstairs with me on the cell phone. "Wanda I've gotta go, Jason's here," I said.

"So have you shagged him?" Wanda said, not realizing I had my phone on loudspeaker and Jason could hear every word. I watched one of Jason's eyebrows raise exceedingly high.

"I did that a long time ago, we're just friends now," I said.

"But a good rogering would do you good," she said.

"No," I said.

Everyone started laughing.

"I think you should have sex with him anyway, get you over the shock," she said.

"Wanda, you're on loudspeaker," I said.

"Why didn't you tell me?" she said.

"I didn't know you were going to say that. Here, speak to Jason," I said, passing him the phone. Jason looked helpless. He is also extremely handsome and intelligent and that's why I want to keep him as my best friend. Sex would definitely ruin the friendship.

"Scarlet's my best friend," Jason said.

"Well friends can still have sex. What star sign are you?" Wanda said.

"Virgo," Jason said.

"Oohhh," she said, "maybe not then."

Jason's mouth dropped open wide. "Where d'you find her?" he said, placing his hand over the receiver.

"Just give me the phone," I said, taking it without waiting for a response. "Wanda, I'll see you next week. I arrive in LA on Wednesday but I'll call you before then, to triple confirm."

"Ok dear," she said in her mock plumy accent.

Home at The District Club, Jason walked over from the bar with a large whisky on the rocks and handed it to me. I drank it fast and checked out the room for cute guys simultaneously. There weren't any. I had another Jack Daniels and then I notice this guy smile at me from across the room, he's tanned and good looking except as he comes closer, I feel repelled. It's Giorgio. I haven't seen him since I slept with him a couple of months ago. I flash back to the mediocrity of the sex. I thought that an Italian lover would be good in bed but I just felt like I was going through the motions with him and the ocean so wasn't moving. The morning after when he said "I'll call you later." I knew he wouldn't and I was relieved, this was not someone worth pursuing. Not that he's a bad person. He's an asshole, selfish, conceited, that's all. "Hi," I said and gave a curt wave and unfriendly smile in return but as he walked past Ruby and I, he turned left, draped himself over to kiss me.

"How are you?" Giorgio said, "You look great."

Perhaps he'd forgotten what I looked like and was pleasantly surprised. I was still in shock and couldn't think straight. "I was just attacked by a gang in Notting Hill," I said.

"My God, that's terrible," he said, "did they take anything?"

"No," I said, "I managed to defend myself." Now wishing I hadn't given him my body. He didn't deserve me. My self esteem had been very low that night. I was so vulnerable. He promised he'd look after me. I believed him. Like a hooker, I went to his house in a cab at 4am and he didn't even pay me.

"Listen, I have to go, it's good to see you. I'll call you," he said.

"Ok," I said. Why did I say that?! I should have told him to "fuck off", but instead he kissed me on each cheek and was gone. Bastard.

"Who was that?" Ruby said, her perfect features quizzing.

"Someone I wish I hadn't shagged, a mistake," I said.

"What did he say?" she said.

"That he'd call," I said.

"Do you want him to?" she said.

"No," I said.

"Why didn't you blank him?" she said.

"I was too in shock, I don't think I'll hear from him anyway and I've already deleted him from my phone," I said.

"So if he texts, you can say "Who is this?" she said.

Ruby had this brilliant knack of making me laugh. Anyway a lesson well learnt. I certainly won't make that mistake again. Meanwhile some girls had been chatting up Jason at the bar.

I'm going, you coming back to mine?" Jason said, two hefty blondes in tow; gagging for it.

"I don't know," I said, unable to decide.

"Don't let me go on my own, save me," the Aussie girl said in a mock whisper.

Ruby and I decided to stay put. A guy with thick horn-rimmed glasses and grey hair asked if we wanted to go party with his friend in the West End.

"Thanks but got to get up early in the morning," I said.

"Can I take your number," he said.

"No, but thanks for asking," I said.

"But I thought we had a connection across the room. We made eye contact," he said.

"I'm sorry," I said, not wanting to hurt his feelings.

"I'll be embarrassed next time I see you," he said.

I smiled, shook his hand and gently walked away but I wasn't ready to go home and neither was Ruby. We were only round the corner from Jason and decided to stop by. As the Aussie girl answered the door, her face dropped. I couldn't help laughing internally. Ruby rolled a joint, while Jason DJ'd and the other girl desperately shoved her tits and ass in his face. I indulged myself and had a few drags to calm my nerves. Tomorrow would be a big day for me. "I should be in bed," I said to Ruby, who was flicking through a hardback book of amazing photos of supermodels.

"You'll be fine," she said.

I knew she was right but everything felt so up in the air. Why am I abusing my body with alcohol and grass? I just wanted some balance, it all feels too spiritual at times. I need some naughtiness. At 3.15am Ruby and I left Jason behind with the gagging girls. Ruby ordered a taxi from mine and I locked the door behind me when she was gone, lay some colour bottles on me to undo the harm I had self-inflicted and drifted off to sleep listening to a Divine Will meditation.

9th September

Oscar texted me at 8am "Good morning, are we still meeting?"

"Yes," I said, although my body resisted. It wanted peace, recovery time. I dragged myself back to The District Club to meet with Oscar and Nigel, my lawyer who was already there. Sunlight streamed in through the chinks of metal adorning the large open faced window. I guess I was still in shock because I couldn't focus properly, felt edgy and insecure. Would I actually follow through with my plan to resign Live on air?

Once again I relayed the story of my attack by the gang to Nigel and Oscar, who responded with the expected sympathy. I didn't tell them that this would be the last morning I would go to Mega TV to present The Psychic Show. Instead we talked about Oscar's and my new TV project "Illusions." Nigel said he loved the idea. I was pleased I had something new to focus on. We split the bill three ways and I got a text from Gary as I was walking to the station so I quickly replied suggesting we meet for coffee. I arrived at 10.45am. Gary was sitting on a banquette. He got up and gave me a big hug. I ordered my second breakfast of a latte and pain au chocolat. I wasn't hungry. I don't know why I even ordered it because I felt sick to my stomach. "I think I'm going to resign Live on air," I said. In my heart, I already knew it was a done deal. I searched Gary's face for some reassurance and as always he gave it to me a thousand-fold.

"I couldn't do it," he said. "It's just so brave what you're doing."

"Is it?" I said.

"You know it is. You're claiming your power," he said.

"I hope you're right," I said. I was being treated like shit and had to put an end to it.

"I fully support you," Gary said. "I want to leave to, I'll be following behind you soon after."

Gary had just started moderating on Pleasure Zone at night to pay the bills so he could do his creative writing degree. "I hate it in there. It brings up all my shit doing the night time stuff," he said.

"I'm not surprised," I said, remembering how Barry had told me to zoom in on a girl's crotch to encourage callers. My one night in the studio was enough. It felt like living inside a porn movie.

"I know this may sound crazy but one of The Council of Nine is in the corner of the room holding a book and quill. They're confirming I need to resign Live on air but stressing I do it with absolute grace."

"Well that makes sense," Gary said.

I remembered how the Council of Nine deals with karma and I knew I didn't want to create any negativity at all costs. I felt like I was being severely tested and mustn't fail. "Come on, let's go," I said. I just wanted to get in the building and be done with the anticipation.

Gary paid the bill and we strolled down Great Portland Street. As we climbed the stinky stairs to the studio, I felt like Gary was a guardian angel to me, giving me support and protection and keeping me in check. Tiffany was already there on the Psychic Sofa smoking a cigarette with Eric. I felt disgust rise up in me when I saw Eric's smarmy face. I wanted to tell him to "fuck off".

"Alright darling," Eric said.

As I turned away, I noticed a pink piece of paper stuck on the door to my old office. It had the week's schedule and everyone was down for three days except me who was down for one. Confirmation that Eric had know the dates all along and decided to conceal them from me, mother fucker. I hate you Eric. You're an asshole. Scarlet stay calm, you can't make a scene, remember grace Scarlet, grace.

"How was Spain?" Tiffany chirped.

"Lovely," I said. I wasn't listening. I was pre-occupied, anger seething in my blood and veins. "Shall we do a circle?" I said. I knew I had to bring in the light and keep positive. I knew I could sabotage myself in one foul swoop. Eric conveniently disappeared downstairs.

"I'd love to," Tiffany said and Gary appeared by my side and we all joined hands for the last time; left palm up and right palm down. We visualized golden light coming in through the top of the head and circulated love and peace in a double ring of light around us.

"Five minutes," Wayne said, "Who wants to present first?"

"I do," I said. I disliked the coldness in my voice. And before I could think.

"Three, two, one and we're Live," Wayne said.

"Hello and welcome to The Psychic Show," Tiffany said, except I wasn't listening, I was calculating when to deliver my news. I put my hand on Tiffany's arm.

"I'll be sharing some news later on in the show," I said.

"Oh great," Tiffany said and then she churned out the psychic pin numbers for the phone lines and I knew I couldn't wait any longer.

I had been taken advantage of and used enough. "Tiffany, I need to make an announcement," I said. I could see her trying to figure what I wanted to share. I paused for effect. "Today is my last show," I said.

"Scarlet, no!" Tiffany said, "I can't believe it."

It amazed me this could be such a shock to Tiffany. I thought she'd be jumping for joy, however I feel Tiffany and I had reached a place of respect for each other. We'd never be friends but we had definitely transcended some major shit unlike Petra, the media whore who had stabbed me in the back. I knew I had to let go of my anger and invest it on the page. Stupid bitch.

"The chat room's going nuts," Gary said from across the studio, "they don't want you to leave."

"I'm off to LA, shooting a new pilot," I said, "I'm really excited, of course I'll miss you all." In truth, I was shit scared to make the leap out of my shitty comfort zone. And then the frenzy of texts flooded in. "Love you Scarlet…we'll miss you so much!"

Eric had texted in the chat room "Yes, Scarlet will be greatly missed."

I wanted to scream "You lying bastard!" But I restrained myself. Then one of the chat room regulars asked what leaving song I'd like as a Live Caller Comment and I chose "All You Need is Love," by the Beatles coz that's what popped in my head and as much as I wanted to be furious back on set; as I received one well wishing text after another, Tiffany walked in with a big bouquet of beautiful flowers, red roses and green and orange. "All Need is Love, love is all you need" was played in the studio and Gary and Tiffany hugged me and then I burst into tears. I felt like this is a fraction of what it's like to win an Oscar as I sniffled, "I can't believe I'm crying Live on air. I said I wouldn't," I said wiping my nose and Gary said "That's what Jerry Maguire said." And I laughed and cried "Mum, Dad, I love you so much and I wouldn't be where I am now without you." Yes rather dramatic for satellite TV but I knew it would make great viewing for that moment and then would be forgotten, sure enough.

"Thirty seconds till we're off," Eric said.

"I love you all very much, thanks for supporting the show," I said waving to camera.

"And we're gone," Eric said and that was the end of my

journey on The Psychic Show. What with the attack and resignation I felt numb. Eric took us for lunch at the pub on the company credit card.

"What you like to drink?" Eric said.

"Jack Daniels on the rocks," I said.

"Me to," Gary said.

"That's a great idea," Tiffany said.

"And me," Chris said.

So we all drank Jack and I bit my lip to be polite to Eric. We both knew the score. Thankfully I had a meeting at the Circle Club with Melanie at 5.30pm, which I felt like cancelling and I had a dinner set with Dad for 7pm.

Eric popped out on the phone and was gone for a while and I made a quick exit. No love lost in not saying "goodbye".

As I walked past St Paul's Cathedral, I knew I should text George, his question was "How are you fixed this weekend?" rang like sweet bells in my head. I texted that I'd been attacked by a gang but had a lucky escape and Sunday was good. As I stepped into the restaurant and hugged Dad, the phone went and it was George. I quickly rushed outside to speak with him. "Hi," I said, and noticed how much I was holding my breath. George and I hadn't spoken for a while and although my intuition screamed at me "Scarlet, he's a player!" My pheromones drifted over to his and wrapped around him and I wanted to be in his arms, kissing him, even though I knew he was bad for me.

"Oh my God, are you ok?" George said.

"Yes," I said, grateful for his concern. This was a good sign he had a conscience, so maybe he wasn't such a player after all. Once again I relayed the story of how the gang attacked me and as I'm writing this, my hand is trying to stop the pain in my spleen because fear and low self worth is trapped there and then George said "That's terrible, and in the good part of Notting Hill?"

"On Westbourne Grove," I said.

"Oh, I'm sorry," he said.

I could sense Dad getting agitated inside. "I have to go and have dinner, can you make Sunday?" I said.

"Yes, Sunday's good, I'll call on the weekend," he said.

I wished I'd had more time to talk with him. I think I'm attracted to his elusiveness. He's a mirage. Unlike me because it bothered me when Charlie said "Scarlet, you're the most complicated person I know." Well you might be if you felt everyone's feelings and thoughts in and around you and when it's not nice, it fucking hurts.

I went back into the restaurant and hurried into my seat. "Sorry Dad," I said.

"So what's going on? Dad said.

I didn't know where to start. "I got attacked by a gang and left The Psychic Show," I said.

Dad's faced dropped. "But I felt like you were there with me, protecting me like a guardian angel," I said.

"Well, that's very kind," he said modestly. "But it doesn't surprise me about the TV show."

"I know," I said, as I saw a thousand thoughts rush through his mind.

"I'll be ok," I said.

"What next?" he said.

A good question for which, I didn't have a complete answer. I mustered my confidence. "I'm shooting a pilot in LA," I said.

Dad was quick to respond. "I thought you were going on holiday?" he said in a clipped tone.

"I am going on holiday and working also," I said.

"You never said that before," he said.

"Yes, I did," I said.

"Who's paying for it?" he said.

"Oscar said he'll put some money in and Trudy has camera equipment and we'll only take a day to shoot at Chateau Marmont and then we'll take it to the networks," I said.

"What's your timescale?" Dad said.

"Two weeks," I said.

"What type of dumb cunt answer is that?" he said.

"What I just said."

"Well you're out of your fucking mind," he said.

Dad's words hurt. I did my best not to take it on because I knew he cared, Dad loved me. "Why?" I said.

"Scarlet, I'm not questioning your talent but it'll take nine months," he said.

"Maybe," I said. Why couldn't I get a show commissioned quickly? Why nine months?

"I remember when you came up with that bullshit financing structure.

He was right. Bill and I calculated a thousand pound investment would generate a five million pound profit. How ridiculous because we all ended up losing money and eventually I lost my home, everything. "Dad, I've made a successful TV show this year," I said.

"Yeah and they screwed you financially," he said.

"I knew that would happened when I went in there because I had to prove myself in the interactive market," I said. On second thought, I had to prove myself, period. My ego was suffering in luxury, drinking chilled Muscadet and eating langoustine, calves liver and roasted figs with ice cream.

"Did you read the Evening Standard today?" Dad said.

"No, why?" I said.

Dad unfolded his newspaper and turned the page. "I thought of you when I read this. A thirty-two year old actress, living in Notting Hill committed suicide, just as her career was taking off.

To everyone else, she seemed perfectly happy." Dad's face became emotional. "You'd tell me if you were feeling depressed. Wouldn't you?" he said. Dad searched my face for an answer.

"I'd never commit suicide. I love living too much," I said.

"Because I couldn't fly first class around the world and stay in five star hotels knowing you're dead," he said.

"Dad, it's not going to happen, but it freaked me out, the similarities between me and this girl and then I remembered Gary telling me about the same story this morning in the studio before we went on air.

"So, how you going to survive financially?" Dad said.

"I haven't asked you for anything," I said.

"I want to help you but it's too soon since you split from Bill," he said.

"I know, but I can tell you categorically, we won't be getting back together, it's over. Dad, I'm my own worst energy. I sabotage myself," I said.

"If you get in trouble, we'll sit down with Mum and work out a plan to help you," he said.

"Thank you," I said. I felt like I was six years old.

Dad stood up and stretched out his arms, tears filled his eyes. "I love you kid, you're all I've got," he said and hugged me tight.

"I love you Dad," I said, hugging him back.

CHAPTER 12

CALIFORNIA DREAMIN'

10th September
5.30pm

I read the end of Julia Cameron's "Vein of Gold" and then embarked upon making a God Jar out of a shoebox. I made a slot in the top to post my prayers, wishes, dreams and goals. I sat on the floor of my living room and cut out pictures from Premiere magazine which contained The Hollywood Power 100 List. I stuck Tom and Steven and Jerry Bruckheimer and many more onto my God jar along with pictures of beautiful beaches and landscapes. Then Ruby texted "Still want to go to The District Club?"

I felt tired but restless to get out. I wanted to meet some sexy guy so I put on my Helen of Troy olive dress and Native American boots and headed down to The District Club. Ruby was waiting outside with her friend Willard Jones from New York. Ruby was wearing a beautiful white dress with high heels. The District Club was buzzing inside. People were back from their holidays. "The new season's begun," Ruby said.

We both surveyed the room for cute guys but there weren't any. I was beginning to feel like a predator. Ruby went off to the restroom and left me with Willard. He was handsome, but I didn't fancy him. And then Guy Ramsfield appeared before me and smiled. At first I didn't recognize him, it had been almost three months since I'd last seen him. His brown hair flopped over his forehead and he had a slight stubble. I was excited to see him.

"Hi," Guy said, kissing me on both cheeks.

"Hi," I said, pleased he'd got to see me in my dress.

"How are you?" he said.

"Much better. You?" I said.

"Good, but I've just arrived so I've got to get upstairs and meet some friends," he said.

"Oh, ok," I said, trying to hide my disappointment. Perhaps he thought I was here on a date with Willard. Damn, and then he was gone and Willard carried on talking but my mind was with Guy, wondering what he was doing upstairs. I couldn't help feeling he was meeting with another woman.

Ruby arrived back and we chatted to one guy we knew, after the other and Guy still hadn't come back downstairs. My curiosity engulfed me and I made an excuse to go up to the toilet. I actually didn't need to go except, there'd be no harm poking my head around the Chill Room doorway. And when I did, Guy was too embroiled in conversation and intimacy to notice me see him. Yes, my intuition that he was a player was correct and somehow I felt he wouldn't call on Sunday to meet and he didn't. As much as I was disappointed, I knew it was for the best. I just wanted intimacy so I didn't have to acknowledge how lonely I was.

Then Jason turned up with his new girlfriend, Kirsten and a few other old timers, meaning a few of my old school shags from before I went out with Bill. One of them, Terry had gone bald and fat. He was till cute but had let himself go. I thought he looked unhappy.

"I'll get in so much trouble for being out this late," Terry said. I watched his brow furrow.

"Why?" I said.

"The wife, she'll be up waiting, she's two months pregnant," he said.

"Wow, that's great news, a younger version of you on the way," I said, and then I wondered if it really was great. Terry had been quite a terror on the club scene. I remember him dangling me over the roof of his apartment, high on coke and threatening to drop me.

"Thanks for being nice to me, even though I was a complete asshole," he said.

I smiled. Yes he had been an absolute bastard, but I'd allowed him to treat me like shit.

"Hey, do you want to do a line of coke in the toilet?" Terry said.

"No thanks," I said.

"No?" he said, his eyebrows arching.

"I don't do coke," I said.

"Really?" he said.

"Never have," I said, relieved that I didn't have any need for this expensive habit. I'd much rather spend the money on a pair of shoes or a massage.

"Why don't you try it? You'll like it, come on," he said.

"Terry, why do I want to start at thirty-one years old?" I said.

"Wow, that's amazing that you're not like those coke whores," he said.

"Thanks," I said but thought to myself, yeah but you just tried to turn me into one. "Excuse me, I need the loo," I said and made a quick escape. I felt like I was in a time warp. All these years later and still the same shit. I'd finally exhausted my nights at The District Club and felt incredibly grateful that in five days I'd be in California, a needed change of setting for me.

When I came back from the toilet, another ex-boyfriend was there. He was friendly and so was I, enough water had passed under the bridge. Closing time arrived and Ruby headed off home, she had a photo shoot the next morning and an 8am call.

I agreed to go to a late night drinking spot below the supermarket on Portobello Road with the entourage of exe-s which I found highly amusing. As we entered the club, the stench of cigarettes hit me hard that mixed with the heat, I began perspiring immediately. A talk guy approached and offered me a drink. I asked for a JD on the rocks when I knew I should have gone home. Why was I still there? And then Tom Spiegel sidled up to me. "You still haven't called me," Tom said. He smiled knowing this was one of his assets to charm.

"I know. I've been busy taking a break from men," I said.

"So why don't you take me home with you, then we can finish off what we started," he said.

For a moment, I was tempted but decided I wasn't desperate. Actually it was time for me to be alone. I'd gone this long without a guy, what was another day, possibly week, hopefully not a year. "Thanks for the offer but I'm going home alone," I said.

"Well, if you change your mind," he said and disappeared off into the smoke.

Henry, an ex-snog, who lives with Marcus appeared at my side. "Come on, let's go. We could all hang at mine," Henry said.

I wondered who "all" was? Perhaps he was just being friendly and he knew I'd already snogged Marcus?

Suddenly the JD guy came bounding over like an expectant puppy and launched into conversation. I could see Henry willing me to extract myself and as soon as JD guy paused to refill with breath, I made my departure.

The cigarette smoke clung to me as we hit the night air at 3am. "Henry, could you walk me home? I'm a little scared after the attack" I said.

"Sure," Henry said, and then Tom Spiegel was behind us and I know he assumed I was taking Henry back with me instead of him and I watched Tom walk ahead of us, trying to look busy on his phone.

"Don't worry, you're safe with me," Henry said, and I knew

this to be true.

The streets were beautifully quiet and we soon arrived outside my flat. "Well, here it is. I feel so lucky, I love my space, can you see the spiral staircase?" I said, pointing upwards.

"I'd see it much better if you invited me in," Henry said.

"I'm sorry, I can't do that, but thanks for walking me home," I said.

"Sorry, I'm drunk, I didn't mean it like that," he said, but we both knew the truth. We hugged goodbye. I liked Henry but felt good about honouring my boundaries. When I got inside, I wasn't tired. I decided to finish creating my God Jar. As I completed it, a text message came through from Larry in LA, "I AM."

I knew what he meant but I felt cocky. "You are what?" I said.

"I AM!" he said.

"Sounds good to me," I said.

"Yes. Thank you," he said.

This is ridiculous, I thought and phoned Lenny. He picked up right away.

"Hey, what you still doing up? It's late over there," Lenny said.

"I know, it's 4am. Just got back from The District Club and I was putting a wish in my newly created God Jar and then you called!" I said.

"That's cool," he said.

"Yes, it is, because I just finished reading Julia Cameron's "Vein of Gold" and the last words in her book were "I am, I am!" I said. Lenny had been an instrument of divine synchronicity in my life ever since the day I met him. I was happy we'd remained friends.

"So, you coming to LA?" he said.

"Of course, I'm not bailing out like you did on coming to London," I said.

"Well, call me when you get in," he said.

"I will," I said. Bring on LA, five days to go!

11th September
Home

Now I realize why I slept all day. Because it is 9/11. My dream said "Look to the House of Babel…"

I got up at 5.30pm. The exhaustion of resigning from the show and going to bed at 5am had caught up with me. Every time I tried to get up, I fell straight back to sleep. My body and soul needed to heal. Ruby texted me "I've made sweet potato salad for Jason's BBQ," and Carla was coming over to my place at 6.45pm so I dragged myself out of bed and went for a swim and steam at the gym. We arrived at Jason's at 8.15pm. His barbeque yet to be constructed sat in the middle of his living room. "It's taken two hours to build so far and I'm nowhere near finished," Jason said, scratching his head.

"I'm so hungry," Carla whispered. Me to, I thought. Kirsten his girlfriend, busily prepared meat and salad in the kitchen while Jason's brother drank a beer in the corner of the room. An hour passed and still the barbeque wasn't constructed, so Kirsten stuck the meat in the oven. At this point I was starving. Then the fat from the sausages in the oven created a huge amount of smoke and within minutes, everyone's eyes were soar. A perfect English barbeque. However, it worked out perfectly in the end as Ruby arrived and the six of us sat down at Jason's dining table and tucked into a glorious meal. The highlight of dinner was when we were talking movies and Jason with glass of wine in hand said "I really want to see that film starring Scarlet Johansson, "The Girl with the Pearl Necklace."

"I think you mean Pearl Earring," Ruby and I said simultaneously and we all cracked up laughing. I felt blessed to have such great friends, life was good.

After dinner, we all headed off to The District Club. Soon after arriving, Marcus aka James Bond entered. He looked pretty gorgeous but he was dressed all in black and I sensed he was stressed. He walked straight past Ruby and I, as we perched on our regular chairs. I felt quite regal but defensiveness took over. "He didn't say hi," I said to Ruby.

"He didn't see you because he probably isn't wearing his contacts," Ruby said.

"Maybe," I said distracted, as I watched him head towards the restaurant area.

"Henry said Marcus just got back from Moldova. Apparently, he was captured by the KGB and detained with the BBC crew for over twelve hours. It used to happen to Dave, my ex-boyfriend all the time," Ruby said, as she took a sip of her champagne.

Yes, any expectation I had of more romance with Marcus seemed quite ridiculous, but that made me want him more.

"Let me introduce you to Fred and Lloyd. They're part of his hard core posse, they're lovely," Ruby said and within moments we were all speaking and laughing and a mojito was placed in my hand and then my friend Trent who I know through Charlie handed me a glass of champagne and Ruby fancied him except, he was moving to New York. "I'm going to the toilet and I'll say 'hi' to Marcus on the way," Ruby said and before I could respond, she was gone and I saw them chatting and I had to admit, I felt slightly jealous. I couldn't focus until I'd spoken with him. Then Ruby and Marcus walked towards me. Relief washed over me as he leaned forward to kiss me on both cheeks. Marcus smiled but he was quiet and introverted. "Hello James Bond. What's going on, you look stressed?" I said.

Marcus sat down on the arm of a sofa next to me. "I got arrested by the KGB and I'm off to Somalia on Friday. I still don't know the location of the warlords," Marcus said.

For the first time, I saw Marcus's brow pinched on both sides. He looked weary. "So don't go," I said.

"I've already signed a contract," he said.

"Yes, like that's worth your life," I said.

"So how are you?" he said, intentionally avoiding my question.

"Got attacked by a gang and resigned Live on Air from the show. Except that's not quite as dramatic as being arrested by the KGB," I said.

Marcus laughed and his face grew lighter momentarily. "I'm not going to LA," he said.

"Huh?" I said.

"I texted you back saying I might be there the same time as you," he said.

"I never got it," I said and then his friend Lloyd joined our conversation and I listened to them as Marcus pressed his thigh against my leg, put his hand up my skirt and stroked my leg, while no one else could see. I wanted him to come home with me, stay the night and just hold me. I nodded my head in agreement, but I wasn't listening to the conversation and then Marcus stood up and said "I've got to go home."

"No, why?" I said. I didn't care if I exposed my vulnerability. I was hoping that maybe, he would change his mind.

"I have to be up at 8am. I've got a lot of prep for Somalia," he said.

"On Sunday?" I said, knowing he probably did but wishing he didn't.

"Yes," he said, as he leant forward and kissed me on both my cheeks. My heart sunk and depression washed over me, as I watched him leave. I hid my feelings by turning towards Lloyd, forcing a smile and talking about property and how the prices had gone through the roof.

12th September

Veronica had stayed the night. We'd been back at Jason's till 4am and then her and I drank tea, ate chocolate and chatted till 6am. In the morning we got lattes and pain au chocolat from Beau Café. Veronica was feeling the shit from the politics at Mega TV and I was relieved that I was out of there. Then she went home and Ruby and I met at The Westbourne, immediately got chatted up by a group of Italians and a table of Aussies. Henry soon arrived to our rescue. I knew he fancied Ruby because he told me and Ruby had said "If only he was a little bit taller," and then I flashed back to last night in my mind and remembered Marcus saying "So I hear Henry walked you home." I hoped he hadn't got the wrong impression. As we left The Westbourne, I noticed a gang of ten boys on bikes, cycling down Westbourne Park Road. I was relieved I was in Ruby's friend's car, safe from harm. Ruby lent me a great suitcase and holdall for my trip to Los Angeles. Only a couple of days to go!

13th September

I did lots of paperwork and felt really good, organized. Verity phoned and I agreed to meet her for a late lunch at 3.30pm. She gave me a lift to the laundrette so I could get all my washing done. We found a parking meter with some time left on it and a picture of Christ, beaming light in rainbow colours from his hands. The same picture as Paula had given me as a gift for holding the workshop back in February that she had attended. I was positively blown away by the synchronicity. My laundry was soon ready and Verity kindly offered to help me make business cards for my trip to LA. I didn't realize it would take till 2am but Verity gave me some great clothes as a gift including a pair of Brazilian sandals, which fit me perfectly. We were moving into a new moon so I created a ceremony for Verity and her flatmate Jane. It was amazingly powerful. I ended up staying the night and sleeping on the sofa. I felt totally nurtured.

14th September
Ladbroke Gardens, Notting Hill

One day to go! All my washing is clean but not packed. The day flew by and before I knew it, I was walking up Portobello Road to make my way to the Circle Club. I had all the colour essences in my bag and over my shoulder and then I saw Nancy coming towards me. I hadn't seen her since our meditation night. She seemed in her own world and then she noticed me.

"Hi Nancy," I said. I felt my voice sounded quite curt.

"Hi Scarlet," Nancy said and sounded incredibly fake. "Love your coat."

We both kept on walking. To me it was interesting timing as it was the first time I was publicly going to work with the colours since our meditation group. I was only a few minutes late when I arrived at the Circle Club. Gary was already there and so were the two other psychics. I got everyone together in a meditation circle and we picked cards to create a focus for the event. I anticipated we'd do a talk and a small amount of tarot readings but we ended up doing psychic readings solidly for four hours, instead of the original time scale of two hours. As different people sat down, I felt them presenting life long baggage at my feet and saying on a clairaudient level, invisible to the untrained ear "I've been carrying this shit for a long time; some of it my whole life, please can you take it away so I can heal?"

And there it was already dumped in front of me and I worked bloody hard. I had one quick break to rush to the loo and then I hit a burn out. This was much more challenging than doing the TV show because the bar got so noisy at one point and people were smoking and drinking but my soul said "Come on Scarlet, you can do this, you wanted your next test and here it is."

Finally I stopped. I knew if I didn't, I'd get a nose bleed and then this woman plonked herself down in front of me and said "I want a reading." No 'please' word in there and I said "I'm sorry, I'm absolutely exhausted, I've been non-stop all night." I smiled at her.

"But I've waited all night for the crowds to die down," she said.

"I'm sorry, I just wouldn't give you a good reading and I have to respect my boundaries," I said.

She huffed and said "Well, better not waste my time talking to you any longer."

And I thought, love and light, as she got up to stop myself telling her what a selfish bitch she was because my soul knew her soul didn't know any better. Later on I discovered the other psychics and Gary had all read for her, given the same information and she'd become cross with all of them. I was delighted I'd said "no".

Gary offered me a drink and I opted for a mojito and ate a lobster BLT. I was leaving in the morning and hadn't packed and it was now 1.30am. Ruby, Gary and I shared a cab. I was pleased because Doreen, one of the psychics offered her agent to me for Psychic TV work. Good synchronicity. I had the phone number safely in my bag and thankfully people positively raved about the accuracy of all our readings. We definitely were the A-team. I collapsed into bed just after 2am and hoped I'd have enough time to pack in the morning.

I grabbed a takeaway latte in between eliminating the clothes I needed to leave behind so I wouldn't over pack and smoothed my legs with my epilator between sips of coffee. The taxi was ten minutes early and, I ended up being ten minutes late. It all felt so surreal. I'm going to LA, I thought. On my own and at 12.10pm I was being driven to Heathrow airport. I spoke with Mum and Dad and texted some friends. It felt like I'd be going for more than three weeks the way everyone was saying farewell to me. Excitement washed over me as I arrived at the Virgin check in desk. I'd been upgraded to business class. Yes! I sat in the executive lounge and booked a car from Hertz, ready for my arrival in LA. It felt good to be leaving London behind, especially the weight and wound of The Psychic Show. I knew the Long Dance ceremony would cleanse me. A miracle of no turbulence on the flight. I sipped champagne and ate English cream tea while watching "Harry Potter" followed by "The Day After Tomorrow". The further we flew, the lighter I felt. I decided to finish off reading Candace Bushnell's book "Trading Up". What was totally surreal was that as we were forty-five minutes from landing, I read the part where Janey leaves New York to start a new life in LA. She's been invited to The Oscars and she's on the plane and I thought, "Wow, I'll be doing that at some point, it's got to be confirmation, hasn't it?" Except I wasn't going to the Oscars with a limo waiting for me at LAX airport and I wasn't flying first class…yet…

When I landed at LAX. I felt so good, my head clear and my eyes bright. I was engrossed in the book as I headed towards Immigration control. As I waited in line, British passport in one hand and book in the other. I was next in line to officially cross the threshold onto US soil for the next stage of my adventure. As I reached the last page I read the lines about how Janey stood out on the terrace up in the Hollywood Hills and looked out at the sparkly lights of LA below and thought she'd "arrived", and as I read that I knew I had.

The End.

Scarlet's Confession to be continued…

ABOUT THE AUTHOR

Joanna Garzilli does private psychic readings that have included notable names: Monica Lewinsky, Goldie Hawn and Jenna Dewan which led to her first book, "Unleash The Psychic In You". Joanna is author of, "Big Miracles," published by Harper Collins, praised by Publisher's Weekly to, "Help readers remember the love, power, and strength of the soul". Joanna is talk show host of, "Life Stories," on Focus TV Network. She's been a guest on: BBC, Fox News, Daily Mail, NPR, Coast To Coast, Well+Good and Hay House Radio. Joanna lives with her husband, Nick and their son, Dominick in Los Angeles, CA.

PRIVATE PSYCHIC READINGS and PUBLIC ENGAGEMENTS

DM @joannagarzilli on Instagram or email:
joanna@joannagarzilli.com to schedule:
- Private psychic reading
- Tarot + Tea
- For you next special event
- TV + Radio Shows